# OPERATION: JERICHO

### A Novel

## Jonathan Ball

MIKE!
You BIG STUD.
THANK You FOR ALL
THE LOVE AND SUPPORT.

(M·J)

NEW YORK

NASHVILLE • MELBOURNE • VANCOUVER

# OPERATION: JERICO
© 2017 Jonathan Ball

Published in New York, New York, by Morgan James Publishing. Morgan James is a trademark of Morgan James, LLC.
www.MorganJamesPublishing.com

The Morgan James Speakers Group can bring authors to your live event. For more information or to book an event visit The Morgan James Speakers Group at www.TheMorganJamesSpeakersGroup.com.

ISBN 978-1-68350-353-8 paperback
ISBN 978-1-68350-356-9 eBook
Library of Congress Control Number: 2016920331

**Cover Design by:**
Rachel Lopez

**Interior Design by:**
Megan Whitney
Creative Ninja Designs
megan@creativeninjadesigns.com

In an effort to support local communities, raise awareness and funds, Morgan James Publishing donates a percentage of all book sales for the life of each book to Habitat for Humanity Peninsula and Greater Williamsburg.

Get involved today! Visit
www.MorganJamesBuilds.com

# CONTENTS

To the men and women who have given everything in the service of their nation, in the name of liberty, and for the love of their brothers and sisters in arms

*"And the LORD said to Joshua, 'See, I have given Jericho into your hand, with its king and the valiant warriors.'"*

—JOSHUA 6:2

# FLASH FORWARD: DOWN

I man wrapped his fists around the buttstock of his standard-issued M-4 assault rifle. He stared distantly into the iron and plastic of the gun. The weapon's muzzle rested between the heels of his desert-tan combat boots. His gun barrel rattled lightly against the equally hard floor as the transport helicopter vibrated in the air. He sat, shoulder-to-shoulder, with men he knew as friends despite a strange distance between them. He was with like-minded warriors, called to carry out the same mission, but he was alone. He was not of their tightly run, hardened, and ready brethren. He shared their toughness to the harsh desert, but he was softer in heart to what they must do. He worried, not for himself, but for her. Iman held his weapon in hope. He held onto his thoughts in faith. He held his fear with resolve.

Iman broke his distant stare for a moment to look upon his brother, Hasim. They glanced, one at the other, wanting to say something. They exchanged their silent pleas of hope, but they knew any words spoken would be drowned out by the blasting sounds of the helicopter's propellers. Even if they could hear each other, their condoling utterances would have come to no value. There was nothing they could say to each other that would repair the damages done in blind faith, in love, and in war. There was nothing to be done that might reverse the mechanisms of warfare amassing to destroy their target. One person, friend or foe, would yield little difference for the sake of defying the machine put into motion.

Hasim nudged his left shoulder into Iman's right. That was the last of what could be said on the matter at hand. Iman returned his absent gaze to the rear portion of his rifle. Hasim was worried for his brother's heart as he looked the weary warrior over. *Uniform.* Hasim considered the irony of his immediate situation. He was on the back of a military helicopter, dressed identically to the other men aboard, carrying the same issued equipment, moving with the same purpose, and wielding the same sword. The only thing that separated Hasim and Iman from the rest was the Koran tucked neatly into the tops of their packs. They were, without a doubt, part of the small Marine unit selected to seek out and destroy a high value target. He grinned at the irony. He was not cynical. He was simply amused in spite of his fear.

Iman continued to look away, unable to mask his feelings of remorse. Hasim knew his brother well. He knew that Iman was questioning their purpose. He knew that Allah had set a path for Iman, but no man among them could explain the complex call to serve. Hasim knew that Iman was questioning many things, but the one thing that would not be questioned was Iman's undying faith. Hasim knew his brother was steadfast and strong. In that strength, Hasim found the courage to do what he must. He leaned on Iman well beyond a brotherly nudge of reassurance.

A faint voice could be heard from the front of the troop compartment on the Super Stallion helicopter. "Two minutes!" was a whispered scream as the onboard crew chief held up his index and little fingers. Every man aboard bumped his fist against the knee of the next man and repeated the call with the same hand signal. Everyone was informed.

Iman became lost within his inner monologue. *Two minutes. Two minutes until touchdown. That means we will be on target by tomorrow morning. This is going to be a very long night.* His mind raced in the timeline of the events to come. The well-orchestrated, over-briefed plan was to set the team down in the open desert on the south side of a steep and rocky hill. It was the only place the team knew their enemy to be weak. The armed opposition, arrogant in their homeland advantage, assumed that no army could ascend the loose rocks. No infringing force of tanks and equipment could climb through the unforgiving land so deep in Afghanistan. The Russians tried and failed. The British were met with the same results. The assumption was then made that the Americans would realize a similar fate. Iman laughed to himself. *The enemy never fully understands Americans. If we can't send an army to win with civility, we will send twenty-six Marines to win by any means.*

Iman was right to grin. The militants imbedded in the mountains of Afghanistan became complacent to their weak side. They took for granted their false sense of protection in the hillsides. Slope-dwelling terrorists were correct in their knowledge that America could not send tanks or equipment against broken mountain trails and loose desert stones set on steep pitches. The rocky cliffside provided too strong of a natural defense to be defeated by machine. The United States also knew it to be true, so Command opted to send a unit of hardened war-fighters to do what tanks could not.

Once on the ground, the Marines would move in from the south. Yet their approach from the open desert into the broken mountains would not be completely unabated if they moved during the day. Sporadic defensive positions were set at the peaks of the hills surrounding the wide valley. Hasim knew where each of the positions was placed, each set into new holes beneath ancient stones. Every man on the helicopter knew where the light machine guns and rocket-propelled grenades were staged. The Marines had undergone so many intelligence briefs before the mission was authorized that they could find their target blindfolded.

However, Hasim knew the defenses intimately. He knew who among the guards was a heroin-addicted gangster with nowhere else to go. He knew who was a true *believer*. Hasim knew the depths of the fighting holes, what amenities could be found for comfort in the immediate areas, how the soil felt beneath him, how the rocks impeded the view, and how the call to prayer went ignored. He knew because only days prior he was among them.

Shouts, previously unheard through the mind-consuming depths of thought and the resounding chop of the helicopter, overcame the inside of the metal bird. Iman and Hasim looked to the caged red light flashing its panicked call into the darkness of the troop area. The universal sign of a red flashing light came with reasonable despair.

"Alfonso! We're hit!" the pilot screamed into his headset microphone. He jerked and retched with the helicopter controls in his fight to stay in the air. The young captain broke Marine protocol and yelled his copilot's first name into the radio. The copilot, Lieutenant Sanchez, looked back to the crew chief through the open area between seats separating the cockpit from the troop compartment.

"We're going down!" Alfonso screamed rearward to the crew chief. He yelled to be heard rather than out of fright. Then he turned back to the controls and did what he could to assist. Alfonso flicked a switch and spoke plainly into his microphone. "One Alpha, One Alpha," he called to Command and continued. "One Juliet is hit. We are going down," Alfonso broadcast to anyone listening fåor the radio call. He had no time to wait for recognition or reply. No one would be able to talk the helicopter gently down from a tailspin out of the sky.

The foot pedals rattled uncontrollably at the captain's feet. He tried to remember his training. He tried to fight physics. He tried to keep the helicopter in the air even without the use of the tail rotor. Then, hope was lost.

The tail rotor crashed into the helicopter's hull, leaving a large dent in the metal body before falling free into the depths of the desert sand. The Super Stallion, unstable without a tail control, spun freely to the power of the main propeller. The captain repeated over and over, "We're going down. We're going down." He repeated the call until the cockpit dug into the desert floor. Dirt, blood, and chaos erupted into the front of the aircraft as pieces of metal and windshield ripped through the captain and Alfonso. The pilot's valiant effort to remain in the air was thwarted by gravity and fate. His fight ended with his life, half-buried and mangled, in the floor of Afghanistan. Alfonso, calm and strong to his last breath, died instantly with the crew chief and his friend.

What remained of the helicopter, the hull full of Marines, was twisted and broken. However, the aircraft's fuselage remained intact. Remnant pieces of metal, plastic, and copper wire were scattered about on the ground. Stumps that once served as propellers continued to rotate before choking to a halt. The Marines inside were alive, coughing in clouds of dust and groaning against the pain; but they were alive.

Iman gasped for breath. His chest fought for shallow sips of air. Hasim and several others were thrown forward from the force of the crash landing. The helicopter's near-vertical position put a collective weight of bodies, weapons, and gear atop Iman's chest. He was not sure if the pile of people or his broken ribs prevented him from taking a full breath, but he fought for air nonetheless.

"JP8!" someone screamed through terrified moans of broken bones and anguish. "Get out!" the voice called again. "Get off the bird before it burns!" the voice screamed again.

Despite all turmoil inside the helicopter, and in the face of whatever dangers lurked outside, someone had the presence of mind to incite an immediate evacuation. The team was still very deep in a war zone and slowly being covered with fuel. Any number of incoming rounds could set the entire group ablaze within a destroyed American aircraft. Those not lucky enough to die instantly would have to evacuate the downed helicopter and pray to fight on without burning alive.

Marines who could move helped others who could not. Living and able fighters assisted their wounded and broken brethren out of the helicopter. Iman finally felt the immense weight of men and packs slowly lift from his chest. For the first time in an eternity without air, he breathed in a deep and full breath of relief. A sudden flood of oxygen was enough to hoist him to his feet.

Iman, trained and ready to fight, was present. He looked upward. Harsh beams of sunlight glared against his eyes through the open hatch of the overturned aircraft. He watched Hasim's boots leave the hull of the helicopter. Iman was alone with the dead. He looked down to see the pilot and copilot lying in pools of blood and raw meat. The crew chief was mangled and soaked red. Iman didn't wince. He didn't have time to be reverent. He just respectfully tried not to step on the fallen as he grabbed packs, equipment, and rifles. He threw pieces of military equipment out of the helicopter one by one.

"Get out of there, man!" someone screamed from the other side of the metal wall separating man from certain fire. If the helicopter ignited, Iman would be consumed. Yet he remained.

Iman wanted to climb out and be free of the crash. He wanted to be free of his duties. He wanted to be free of the war. Yet he knew that their necessary weapons and equipment were precious. Surviving the crash would mean nothing if they were captured or killed because the men were unarmed. Iman knew this to be especially true of him and Hasim. Their enemy would show no mercy toward men returned to undo a cause of hate and destruction.

The well-trained Marine reached down for the last piece of equipment he knew they would need to accomplish their mission. Iman's arm ached as he gripped the handle of a heavy field radio and tried to pull it free of the carnage. A chunk of handle and the entire top of the radio tore from the mechanism with a pop of broken rivets and shredded wires. It was useless. Iman dare not burn to death for something that could not be saved, so he finally reached up to grab the top of the hull. He pulled upward and was jerked clear of the crash by Hasim and another Marine waiting for the final man's exit.

"You are crazy, brother," Hasim laughed to Iman as they stood on the upended side of the smoking aircraft.

Iman turned and simply answered in reference to the radio, "We're going to need it." They smiled, happy that the other was still alive, and leapt from the helicopter.

Hasim and Iman's boots struck the earth simultaneously to the sound of "Head count!"

# INTEL

Years quickly became decades in war. Centuries of armies moving to conquer ancient lands had long since passed. Causes for conflict shifted from land expansion to reasons of resource and protection of liberties. One authoritarian ruler was cast out for another, over and over, in an undying effort to fight for those who were either unable or unwilling to resist tyranny. Lessons learned in the Great War, and accounts of atrocity when the world fought, were being expressed across the globe. People no longer had a taste of tolerance for those who would oppress and maim the people of any country.

The United Nations, once impotent in the cause of a globalized economy, grew in strength. The United States of America was at the forefront of the movement to remove dictatorship from any table. The Human Rights Council was filled with men from places like Saudi Arabia and Sudan—places where women were publicly beaten or stoned to death for being raped—until the United States began defunding partnerships with the United Nations. The world's population watched monetary allowances to many nations dwindle as Americans withdrew from UN involvement. The people of the world then demanded a change to that which makes sense over that which was politically correct. The people's demands were answered.

Less autonomy and political control was surrendered to countries that would allow harm to its citizens. Government-sanctioned attacks and regime-funded terror organizations fluttered to minimal numbers because America took a stand against the continuation of central control by tyrants on the world's stage. The world's people felt slow but steady relief from policy changes. Aid was being allowed beyond the reaches of warlords and gun runners. India and China continued to prosper. The walls of communism in China weakened to successes realized in economic growth through capitalism. The euro recovered despite Greece and France continuing their slip into socialism. America was once again at the helm of the United Nations, and liberty began to spread worldwide. Regimes dissolved. Tyrants fell. Countries stabilized in peace and prosperity.

Despite prosperity, Afghanistan remained the last stronghold for enemy resistance. America's attempt to establish democracy there went without success. However, one president after another ensured that the United States would not repeat errors committed in the Vietnam War. American lives would not be lost in vain. There was a fight to be had, a puzzle to be solved, and an outcome suitable to support freedom for all in the war-torn country. America had no intentions of withdrawing from the belly of Afghanistan until a final knockout blow was delivered. America would not leave until the enemy was destroyed and the people of Afghanistan were given a true opportunity to thrive in a life without Islamic Sharia law.

America and her allies stood with strict tenacity. The prime ministers of Britain, Germany, France, Australia, Portugal, and Spain remained with their pledges to fight terrorism. However, alliances were tested when the United States finally ended its arbitrary approach to the War on Terror. The United States no longer pursued a fight against ideologies, but set to target tangible foes. American leaders openly identified enemy groups and their financers by name. On several occasions, the secretary of defense and the American ambassador to the United Nations stepped to the world's podium only to announce specific names of Islamo-Nazi terrorist organizations. Additionally, they provided evidence of paper trails tracing the organizations' finances to Saudi Arabia, Egypt, Iraq, Iran, Turkey, Cameroon, Ethiopia, and the Philippines.

Deeply supported evidence, presented in front of a watching world, was not well received by the accused. Countries that trickled gold, oil, cash, and weapons to terrorist organizations were identified in the open and left for unabated review by every United Nations Council. The nations identified as state financers of terrorism tried to retort that America had terrorist organizations of its own, such as the Ku Klux Klan and the Black Panthers. Feeble attempts to divert attention from reality were laughed down by the remainder of the United Nations. Responses were harsh.

Those funding terrorism did not hold enough votes at any table to sway or thwart sanctions. Enemy countries felt the full force of America's positive influence in the United Nations. Worldwide support of American action shifted, and people stood against their oppressors. To the dismay of a few, many came together in a cause of peace. The world watched as leaders set aside political correctness to denounce true heads of terror organizations. Leaders who took a stand for liberty overtly opposed those who would pay for murder. Then the world waited for backlash.

The anticipated retaliation never came. Enemy countries were stared down at the table and shied from the sleeping giant. Suspected ties were cut from terrorist organizations to preserve national economies and prevent global sanctions. Would-be insurgent groups fell to a lack of financing. Those who would do harm to civilians and Westerners were no longer able to carry out their missions in the name of any country or cause. Terror groups were left to their own wares and devices. They had to scrape for funding from isolated and small private sponsors seething from the deepest shadows of the world. Terrorists had to coil up like snakes and hibernate in the new cold they found outside their caves.

Even still, funding came through small pipelines. Terrorists with the most influence in any given area could amass enough money and weapons to carry out a single attack anywhere in the world. Much like a hidden snake, they would strike, recoil, and slither away. Secret funding was the problem facing world leaders who remained steadfast against those who sought only to kill. Such was the fight that the secretary of defense faced as he stood in front of the intelligence briefing room inside the Pentagon.

"Thank you, ladies and gentlemen," the secretary of defense said as he looked out over a thick crowd of uniformed officers in the darkened room. He tried not to smile at the brass echelon he once knew as a soldier.

For every general, there were two colonels. For every two colonels, there were two lieutenant colonels. The lieutenant colonels had two majors each. Then he looked over as a Marine sergeant shuffled quietly to a nearby table and delivered coffee cups. The Secretary thought to himself, *The heart of the fight...and he's reduced to brewing coffee for people who will never see it.* He quietly cursed his thoughts. He knew that many of the officers sitting before him were political children, but many others were war-weary veterans who knew the scars of combat. He continued.

"I appreciate all of you being here today. I know that you are very busy with the many operations in which we are involved, so I will get to the point as quickly as possible. The nature of today's brief is that of a foreign matter. However, we will not be taking this to the United Nations because there are too many who cannot be trusted...or who simply seek to sell America out." The Secretary was tired of political correctness and pussyfooting around issues. He went for the throat of any task ahead of him and bore down with a smile. He never gave a second thought to who might or might not be offended. He spoke only in facts, in refreshing truth.

"In light of that, my orders are to continue the fight at present and as planned to this date. Carry out your orders accordingly." He reiterated, "Continue the fight." He paused, then continued, "With that said, I only need three men to stay. Generals Gutzwiller and Potts, please meet with me at"—he looked at his watch—"thirteen hundred hours. The third has already been designated. Everyone else is dismissed, and again I thank you for your time and service."

The secretary of defense stepped back from his podium to the Marine sergeant's call, "Attention on deck." Each man and woman stood in military order and waited for the secretary to leave. The herd, confused by what they thought would be another military intelligence brief, shuffled out the theater doors and went about their day.

The selected generals were both Marines. They were called to the meeting on the basis of their records, the billets they filled for the Marine Corps, and because they were warriors beyond politics. Their collective service at the Pentagon amounted to that of any liaison who would administer broad-scale reports of troop whereabouts and equipment functionality. However, their service, separate from each other prior to arriving in Washington, was the prompt for their call to the Secretary. Each man would fill a specific function in a mounting plan to destroy the enemy. Each man brought with him knowledge and a skill set beyond his peers that would move America to a successfully achieved objective. Each was ready to answer his respective purpose.

# GENERAL
# KNOWLEDGE

The brass echelon of American armed forces, including Generals Gutzwiller and Potts, cleared the theater room where the Secretary once held all attention. Some officers grumbled for having their time wasted. Others whispered their questions surrounding the mysteries of carefully selected men. The secretary of defense stood idly by with his immediate staff. He listened to the confusion and assumptions the herd held in a broad exodus through opened doors.

He realized they were naturally curious, and his suspicions were reinforced. His trimming of informed personnel meant that he was able to isolate how data would be shared and disseminated. He knew that involving fewer people would reduce the risk of information leaks. He also realized that even the most current sources of usable intelligence are time sensitive and subject to instant change. America had little time for bureaucratic filters of information if his planned strike was to be successful. The old politician knew the war's momentum rested in his hands. The Secretary listened until the last officer exited to quiet sounds of intrigue, and he knew he had done the right thing.

"The room is secure, sir," the Marine sergeant called to the sec-retary and staff. The Secretary extended a mutual courtesy: "Thank you, sergeant. Carry on." The Marine, with his duty belt fitting his holster tightly to his hip and his cover pulled low over his eyes, ren-dered salute and exited the room. The senior man returned salute with an appropriate nod and considered the sergeant as a reflec-tion of the entire Marine Corps. *They are, without a doubt, a cut above the rest. God bless the United States Marine Corps.*

The Secretary turned to his staff and gave direction. His administrators were to go about their days as planned. All of them were to send word to very specific people throughout the inner world of war, men selected in the same fashion as those directly involved in the developing mission. All of the staff, trusted and held close, carried the same message with them that the Secretary was about to deliver. All of them dispersed to carry out their deeds as instructed. The Secretary set doubt aside in faith that his staff would obey orders.

A mounted wall clock banged away at the silence of the room. Seconds screamed their tick-tock call. Politicians, especially secre-taries who answered directly to the President of the United States, rarely experienced a moment of quiet still. The secretary of defense stood alone. The theater-styled briefing room brought a sudden calm. Unexpected peace, an ever-sought tranquility, gave the Secretary time to pray.

"Lord...I'm about to send men to kill..." He paused in the real-ization that every order he gave since taking office led to death in the name of preserving life. He realized that thousands of enemy combatants, insurgents, and terrorists were killed in the several wars fought across the globe. He then concluded that evil men must sometimes die so that good men may live without torment in the clutches of fear. His philosophical pause ended as he continued aloud, "Please guide me, Lord. Please show me your wisdom and strength so that I might better fulfill my duties to this country and to her people. Please protect the men I am about to condemn to war, and please let them go home safely to their families...and if their return home is not in your plan, God...please accept them into your kingdom, for they will have done good here. In Jesus' name I pray, amen."

The Secretary raised his head and opened his eyes. He was immediately startled. He tried to keep water from welling out and flowing down his cheeks.

"I'm sorry to have barged in, sir," a younger and well-dressed man spoke across the empty room. He had been standing with his hands folded in front of him and respectfully waiting for the Secretary to finish a moment with God. "Would you like me to come back?" the man questioned as he stood by for an answer.

"McKenzee, I didn't see you standing there," the Secretary said, smiling across the room as his eyes began to dry. "Come on in. I was just saying a quick prayer for what we're about to do," he explained to the younger man, unworried about being judged for his commitment to faith. Each of them smiled.

Special Agent McKenzee, with the Central Intelligence Agency, answered, "Don't worry, sir. I just did the same." They chuckled and joined in a handshake at the center of the theater.

"What time did you tell the generals, sir?" McKenzee asked as he nonchalantly glanced at his watch. He was answered as a side door opened with a loud click. General Gutzwiller, a man who would be considered wiry if not for his bold and well-decorated uniform, entered first. He was immediately followed by the broad-chested and stoutly built General Potts.

"Sir." General Gutzwiller opened his palm to the Secretary. They exchanged greetings, as did Potts. The generals greeted the

Secretary first out of obligation, but they knew who he was. After giving salutations to their senior, the generals' curiosity centered on Special Agent McKenzee. He was wearing an obviously expensive suit and stood proudly upright like a soldier returned home from the field of victory. Yet groomed ends of his prematurely graying hair rested over the tops of his ears. The placement of his hands in his pockets and failure to have every inch of his person in place let each of the Marines know that the stranger was a civilian. Even still, the stranger kept important company, and they gathered that he must have been of some equal significance in a battle plan not yet widely known.

"Hello, gentlemen. I'm Special Agent Joshua McKenzee. I specialize in human intelligence, especially in the 5th Fleet CENTCOM area," he said as he shook each of the general's hands firmly. He instantly let them know his purpose was to gather information from spies and paid informants in the Middle East. He could have continued his credentials for quite some time, but the generals just assumed he was well qualified to be standing in the same room as war-bound leaders. They also understood that McKenzee divulging his information likely meant that he was seeking to pull out of field operations and climb the ladder of clandestine success behind a desk.

The Secretary took charge of the conversation quickly. "Gentlemen, you have been called upon because of your billets prior to the Pentagon. General Gutzwiller, your command at Guantanamo Bay and continued communications with personnel there led us to you because we know you can be trusted... and we know you have a knack for picking out spies who can gather intelligence from the lowest levels of Gitmo prisoners." The Secretary spoke directly, but incidentally shed some light on the fact that General Gutzwiller's emails and phone calls were previously monitored as part of his selection to an isolated team.

"General Potts, your time in CENTCOM... and the things you did at the IMEF Intelligence Battalion bring you here because you know, firsthand, what our men are going to face." General Potts came to the same realizations that Gutzwiller experienced. They were watched and were happy to be clean of indiscretions.

"Now that everybody knows each other," the Secretary joked, "I'm going to give the floor to Special Agent McKenzee here." The Secretary opened his palm and waved to the civilian. As Marines, Gutzwiller and Potts did not trust the *spook*. They remembered the Central Intelligence Agency's failures leading to devastating attacks in New York City. The Marines still held a bad taste for the CIA and its many minions. McKenzee knew their disdain to be true and silently commended an innate Marine ability to shield any revelation of emotions. He knew they would prove to be valuable in their purpose.

McKenzee spoke quickly, but gave a great deal of information. "Since 2001, we've only been able to engage and destroy sixteen truly high-value target areas where we were able to dismantle terror networks in the area of operations. We've known about many, many more. However, every time we make a plan to kill the bastards, information gets leaked, the bureaucracy takes too long to act, or one strike disperses the many other snakes into deeper grass. Therefore, we," he pointed to the Secretary and himself, "have devised a new strategy for approach and dispatch."

"At this time, we have confirmed information for twenty-eight locations where terrorists are being quartered, armed, and trained. Six of these locations are known to be bomb-making facilities that will continue to arm suicide bombers throughout the region. We've learned that striking the locations one at a time is ineffective because these people are highly motivated and highly mobile. Therefore, we are aiming to strike all twenty-eight locations at once." McKenzee watched as the generals' eyes widened to the insurmountable task.

"Don't worry, gentlemen. Your job is to strike only one of the twenty-eight. Twenty-seven other teams just like this one have been formed here and elsewhere. No one has been identified publically, and no one has been informed as to the identities of other team members across the board. You will not have any other staff involved. You will not be able to discuss this throughout your commands. You are now isolated until Mission Accomplished. You have, at your disposal and discretion, any available asset needed. However, the assets will not be informed of purpose or mission. They will simply be tasked to complete an objective and leave. We no longer reason why. We simply do." Both of the generals nodded and tried not to grin at the agent's words.

"Priority one is to select two spies, preferably from our side, that can be trusted absolutely." McKenzee pointed to Gutzwiller, "general, I understand there were two brothers at Gitmo that you used directly... who answered to no one other than you, for the sake of getting information... a couple of Arab American Marines on station?" McKenzee looked to General Gutzwiller almost certain he would receive an elaborate answer.

Gutzwiller nodded and knew who the agent was referencing. "Where are they now?" McKenzee questioned as if he were not already aware. He was testing the general's knowledge of personnel.

"They are both still at Gitmo and mixing with prisoners in process there," Gutzwiller answered.

McKenzee nodded. "Alright, sir. Let's get them here." He pointed to the ground as if he wanted the young Marines present the same day. Gutzwiller ignored the agent's arrogance and agreed.

McKenzee continued, "General Potts, I have a file for you on the town that we are targeting. It is an encampment of heavily armed insurgents, and I need you to make a battle plan to send in two teams on ingress and egress routes. Their job will be to paint the target and call in an airstrike." The agent spoke in heavy jargon for two reasons. The first was that he knew the generals would understand every word he spoke and could save time in bypassing unnecessary explanations. The second was that he was genuinely nervous around the well-accomplished Marines despite his steady voice. He wanted them to know that he was at least well versed in matters of clandestine combat.

General Potts, logical and even-keeled, interrupted. "If we know where the camps are, why don't we just send bombing runs simultaneously and call it a day?" The question was obvious, and everyone wished the answer would be simple.

The Secretary answered for McKenzee. "That's where it gets sticky, gentlemen. These camps are set up like towns. The insurgents are there with their wives and children. The snakes are using the *women and children* aspect of media warfare as their human shield. However, we all know that these *women and children* are picking up AK-47s and RPGs with the rest of them. We know they are as likely to be used as suicide bombers in the next terrorist attacks wherever. We just need to confirm it so the United Nations does not send us a backlash for killing unarmed civilians. So, Guts," the Secretary said, calling Gutzwiller by his obvious nickname, "you are going to send the two young Marines in. They'll have to assimilate to the camp, blend into the mantra of *kill America,* and gather as much verifiable intelligence as they can while in camp."

He then turned his attention to Potts: "You will then have to extract them from the camp, help set up some sort of escape, only to send them back in with the secondary team and level the place if the women and children factor is no longer applicable."

The Secretary paused hard before continuing, "The harsh reality is that we might find peace-loving people being bullied by terrorists. If the villagers are living in fear and abiding by terrorist rule so as to not be killed, then the whole quick-and-easy mission is scrapped. However, if we find that these people are of a collective mind then they will all be sent to meet whatever version of *the maker* they choose. Either way, we have to know...not suspect, but know that we are killing the enemy with minimum collateral damage and not the other way around." He waited for everyone to nod and show their agreement.

McKenzee spoke again. "It probably goes without saying..." Potts interrupted, "Then it probably shouldn't be said." The general unveiled his feelings toward the arrogant agent for a split second before continuing, "No one is going to say anything to anyone, and no one will act until we are given the orders. Guts will get the Marines here. I will work the file that you give me." He rubbed the thick index finger of his right hand into his open left palm to punctuate his point.

The room went silent once again, but it was no longer still. The air was tense. Then the Secretary offered relief. "Good. Let's make it happen."

# GREEN

G et up and face the wall!" a Marine guard on yard duty shouted to a collection of detainees. He shouted to be heard, but his voice was calm. He was not the angered warmonger frothing at the mouth and urinating on prisoners as he was made out to be by an unfavorable American press. He was, by all standards, respectful. He was just loud. All Marines are loud. They simply have that presence.

The guard announced the order again as some stragglers were slow to move from their prostrated prayer positions. His second order was followed with "please." The detainees seemed to respond to the boisterous request a bit better than the previous order.

Prisoners of war, even those who threw wads of feces and cups of urine at Marine guards, were treated with a certain level of respect. Every prisoner was protected under conventional standards and by the political fallout that always followed any incident involving a guard and a prisoner. The detainees, Islamo-Nazi terrorists who would claw their way through the prison's concrete walls for just one more opportunity to kill another American civilian, were regarded as "resistance fighters" and "war heroes" by American media sources. The opposite side of the coin held contempt for men and women standing between terrorists and would-be targets. The Marine guard thought quietly to himself. *This world has been turned upside-down by empathy for evil...and here I am, hoping to avoid having feces thrown at me by other grown men. Strange days.*

"Please place your hands on the wall and spread your feet," the Marine called out to the small crowd of surrendered enemy soldiers. The jarhead was not alone in the cage of beasts. He stood across the fenced area from another uniformed Marine. Together, they paced half of the allotted space each. They observed, back and forth, while the prisoners moved. The guards gave their head counts. All the new prisoners were accounted for.

The detained terrorists stood a little off-balance with their hands flat on the concrete wall and their feet slightly spread apart. The intent was to draw immediate attention should any prisoner feel a need to regain his footing prior to mounting an attack on the guards. This kept the guards one step ahead of men who would just as soon kill any American if provided the opportunity.

Each of the prisoners was new to Guantanamo Bay. They were captured from around the world, having been identified as members of terrorist organizations, and brought to the cattle farm that processes murderers. They hated their whereabouts accordingly. Their newness to the environment made them unstable beyond those who had been in custody long enough to understand process. Cuban heat and humidity only made the environment that much more miserable and volatile. Prisoners and guards hated each other as much as they hated Guantanamo.

"Turn around and face the wall!" the young Marine at the far end of the cage ordered with a pointed finger. One of the detainees turned from the bulkhead to look around. The prisoner moved like a lion turning just enough to reach and paw a child through the bars of a zoo exhibit. The Marine at the far end of the cage responded to the movement by withdrawing a large canister of pepper spray from its sheath. He was ready to douse the enemy with as much liquid fire as needed to subdue any resistance inside the confines of the outdoor cell. The terrorist saw a triggered can of impending pain, and whatever notion of resistance he held simply faded. The detainee lowered his head as he returned to face the wall.

Both Marines waited, focused on every twitch made by every detainee inside the cage. The prisoners were so new to camp that they still wore their traditional and nontraditional garbs. The eclectic mix of combatants had not yet been uniformed in the bright orange jumpsuits known to all prisoners at Gitmo. They were entering into the Receiving and Processing areas of detention. This is where Iman and Hasim usually operated, before prisoners found their kinsmen within the confines of the internment camp. Iman and Hasim got to the prisoners before the prisoners got to their allies inside.

"I understand the gravel will be uncomfortable, gentlemen, but please kneel down facing the wall. Please also place your hands on top of your head." The Marine guard was still respectful and polite though he spoke through gritted teeth. "The faster you move, the faster you will be able to stand up off the rocks. Thank you." The Marines hoped for reason to settle in, but the enemy still held onto their attitudes of resistance. They decided to move when they wanted rather than when the Marines dictated. The prisoners would eventually learn to save themselves heartache and trouble, but not that day.

The Marines waited for each of the prisoners to finally kneel into the hard, pebble-covered floor of the cage. The prisoners placed their hands on top of their heads as commanded. Then they waited.

Gate 1 opened first and four more Marines stepped into the fenced purgatory between cells. Gate 1 closed behind the group of Marines and Gate 2 opened for entry into the holding area. Four uniformed guards joined the two other Marines inside. The guards quickly grew in strength and number. Intimidation previously felt by the prisoners amplified as the Marine presence increased within a tightly enclosed area. General, but silent, assumptions were formulated by the captives. They figured that if two Marines could control ten men, then six Marines could wreak unabated havoc upon them. The idea of defiance wavered in the reality of fear. The captives suddenly became compliant to every order issued.

"Do not move!" one of the Marines barked from behind the detainees. Each of the kneeling men tried not to jolt from the sudden noise. Eight of the ten captives did what they could to keep their hearts in their chests. Several terrorists mumbled prayers, not knowing that no harm was to come. Only two of the captives knelt without fear, but they were still surprised by unexpected actions.

The four Marines having just entered the cage separated into pairs. They stood directly behind two designated prisoners. "Go," one Marine ordered. The two-man teams leapt forward. They grabbed the designated prisoners, draped their heads with black hoods, and dragged the detainees backward through the gravel.

Trails cut by the prisoners' heels could be followed from the wall to the gates. Dragged backward by two men, the captured jihadists were provided little opportunity to resist. They were removed from the detention area, but their brethren decided that the deed should not go unanswered.

The insurgent who had been backed down by the threat of pepper spray decided to act. He incited avid and loud protests by the other jihadists as he tried to stand from his kneeling position. The man's first mistake was to disobey orders. He was to remain quiet, but failed to do so. His second mistake was to move. The Marine guards responded accordingly.

The Marine at the far end of the cage planted the sole of his boot squarely into the middle of the resister's back. He shoved forward, and the full weight of the man's body was planted hard into the concrete wall. Flesh met masonry with a hard thwack.

The sound of debilitating injury and loss of breath inspired the other prisoners to scream out and move from their positions. The Marine guards looked at each other, stepped back into defensive fighting positions, withdrew their canisters of pepper spray, and squeezed the triggers indiscriminately. The eight-man riot was dispersed to wailing and tears. The insurgents cursed with burning eyes and gagged at the overwhelming mist lingering about in the cage.

The Marine guards exited the holding area easily. They decided it better to wait out the clouds of pepper spray and allow the enemy a chance to recover. The prisoners' eyes, noses, and throats would burn for a few minutes, but the searing sensation would forever be burned into their memories. The Marines hoped that the hard lesson was learned, and they expected to have fewer issues with resisters from that point forward. Neither of the guards enjoyed inflicting pain on prisoners, especially given their firsthand knowledge of the sweltering agony caused by pepper spray. Each of the guards had been subjected to the overbearing chemical sting in their initial days of training, so they sympathized with the screams coming out of the pen.

Unguarded prisoners were scarce across Guantanamo. Marines held tight control over enemy soldiers there. However, the pair of guards stepped away for a moment to grant freshly sprayed foes a period of recovery. The Marines stepped around the corner, out of view of the cage, and laughed.

A senior guard asked, "You guys okay? I mean...that extraction was almost believable that time." He chuckled as the two-man teams released the two detainees previously dragged from the others.

Marines laughed quietly while Iman and Hasim pulled the black hoods off their heads. "Man, you guys could at least wash these things every once in a while," Iman complained as he looked up at the Marines standing around him.

Then Hasim cut in, "Did you really need to spray all of them? I don't know if that was really necessary."

The senior guard answered, "It's probably better for them to learn the nonlethal lesson than to have to teach them the hard way." Iman, Hasim, and the other Marines nodded. They knew the senior was right. Each prisoner in the holding cage received a valuable lesson. Resistance equals pain and continual discomfort. Compliance equals amenities and comfort. The teachable and wise would be able to avoid future discomfort at the very least.

"That was a heck of a kick, Lance Corporal," Hasim commended the young Marine who took instant control of the prisoner most obviously seeking to fight his captives.

The young Marine tipped his hat jokingly. Then he patted the other guard on the chest and asked, "You think we're okay to go back now? It seems like the choking has died out a bit." Both guards laughed and went back to their posts inside the cage. They were in control once again. Their force was absolutely felt among the captives.

Iman scratched his head, answering the remnant itch left from the hood. "If I get lice from one of these nasty things, I'm going to be really mad," he griped. The other Marines, including Hasim, laughed at Iman's jest. "Didn't you guys pull us out of there a bit soon?" Iman continued to question.

Hasim elaborated, "Yeah. I didn't get a chance to really talk to anybody in there, let alone gather any meaningful intelligence."

Hasim and Iman stood up and dusted themselves off. Their long white robes had become dingy from the dirt of the detention area. Their hair was long enough to hide the tops of their ears and stank from being unwashed for several days. Their beards were thick and unkempt. Neither of them had been provided the opportunity to brush their teeth or bathe over the two days they had been *received* along with the other prisoners.

"Man, Iman. I love this job, but I am not a fan of wearing a bedsheet while smelling like a mule," Hasim said, mocking the traditional Arab garb and their overall appearance. Then he looked to the most senior Marine. He was still waiting on an answer as to why they were pulled from the rest of the detainees so early.

Previous years of experience provided Iman and Hasim ample time to infiltrate enemy captives inside Guantanamo. They were systematically placed among the population of new captives. They were treated like prisoners, acted like jihadists, and reported back to Command like spies.

If any of the prisoners learned about the Marine intelligence mission, Iman and Hasim would have been executed inside any of the many common areas within the prison. Therefore, they became masters at blending in among the enemy.

Iman and Hasim were second-generation Americans. Their parents fled northern Afghanistan when Russia attempted to wage war there, and they found solace in the United States of America. The refuge and safety realized in America was appreciated through wholehearted assimilation. Their father embraced the country that provided his family shelter, and he taught his children to do the same. They held onto their Muslim faith and remained in practice as a family, but did all that they could to blend into American society.

Years later, Iman and Hasim made a patriotic decision to join the United States Marine Corps. At the time, every valuable billet for either man was full due to the heavy influx of volunteers following the infamous terror attacks in New York, Washington, and Pennsylvania. The brothers were almost turned away until the local recruiter received their entry test scores and learned that they were fluent in Arabic with a slight regional dialect. Iman and Hasim were physically fit, intelligent, and invaluably skilled in linguistics. Exceptions were made to ensure they were allowed into the Marine Corps. Concessions were made to ensure that they could serve together.

The exceptions and concessions made for Iman and Hasim landed the men at Guantanamo Bay, Cuba. Unlike every other Marine on base, the brothers did not shave or wear camouflage uniforms. They didn't even bathe every day just to keep their cover among other prisoners. They were not able to observe Colors ceremonies or show their respect for their ranking officers, country, or Corps. Instead, they lived among the enemy with the purpose of gathering information about mounting insurgencies and attacks at home or abroad. They were tasked to spy from within, and they proved their salt time and again, defying unspoken dangers to get useful intelligence out to American troops who needed it.

"Don't worry about the detainees," a weathered and wiry staff sergeant barked. "You two go scrape the scuzz off of ya." The staff sergeant's accent was thick with a Southern drawl. He looked Iman and Hasim over with a snarl. "Ya'll are done looking like them. Get back into regs...haircuts, shave, uniforms, spit shines. It might behoove yuns to bathe twice. Man, ya'll stink something awful."

Iman looked at Hasim, Hasim back to Iman. They were confused. The staff sergeant was following longstanding and unwritten protocols of the Marine Corps. Short, choppy pieces of orders were given in the expectation that Marines would follow blindly and without question. The big picture was rarely provided in a single setting, but Iman and Hasim felt they deserved a bit more of an answer from the staff sergeant.

"With all due respect, Staff Sergeant," Iman huffed. He was interrupted by the very man from whom he was seeking answers.

"Look. All I was told was that you two need to clean up and get packed most ricky-tick. Admin has your orders out of here. That means you clean up and get back to being Marines instead of"—the staff sergeant nodded toward the invisible enemy—"being like *them*." He snarled again when he mentioned the opposition. The staff sergeant, several tours deep into the wars in Iraq and Afghanistan, made no effort to hide his disdain for his foes.

Hasim and Iman were done asking questions. They were officially authorized to bathe, shower, and get back into their uniforms. They would get their answers from the Administrations Office after they cleaned up. Each was happy to do so and eager to look like Marines once again.

Bearded men at Guantanamo Bay were either caged or in process to be caged. Iman and Hasim were neither in process nor caged. Therefore, they were escorted by a uniformed Marine. Though the notion of having an escort might have seemed excessive to an outsider looking in, anyone inside Gitmo understood the need. Without an escort, the accurately disguised Arab Americans would have been harassed and questioned by those who guard dangerous men of like appearance.

"What's the story on you guys?" a young private asked Iman. The Marine was new to the unit and had not previously engaged the senior men in conversation. The private was privy to the back end of Iman's inquiry to the staff sergeant. However, he was not informed enough to piece together all the puzzles surrounding the spies.

Iman turned to the guard and smiled. Iman and Hasim tried not to chuckle at the naivete of the youthful Marine. Their purpose was guided by and suited for ranks much higher than private. The no-name kid in camouflaged utilities knew that he did not rate an answer. He seemed to be making small talk with the civilian-looking strangers. Hasim acknowledged the gesture and gave a simple answer to soothe the man's curiosity.

"Don't worry, kid. We're actually Marines." He patted the junior Marine on the back. He didn't offer the private any other information. Then they carried on to their barracks rooms, under escort, nearly a mile and a half away from any detention areas.

The orders to the private were simple. He was to follow the men around and make sure they were not harassed. Otherwise, he was to stay out of their way and wait until Iman or Hasim dismissed him from his duties.

The disguised were of like mind. "I don't know about you, man, but I want to bathe first," Iman said, waving his hand in front of his face toward Hasim. They laughed in the knowledge that they smelled like sweat and dirt. Bathing became their first priority. The filthy Jarheads walked at an accelerated pace until they reached the corner of their barracks.

The men walked up the stairs and down a long corridor at the barracks building. Their rooms were directly next door to each other, so the private was able to follow without having to go in different directions. Iman was hospitable and offered the younger Marine a place to sit. "Go ahead and watch a movie or something. I'm going to make sure I get all this filth off of me," Iman laughed to the other Marine.

Living in the Corps usually involved close quarters and tight spaces. No Marine was unaccustomed to having someone around him at all times. There was very little room for personal space.

Privacy was rarely considered. This was especially true of Iman and Hasim, who had been living as prisoners for months.

Prisoners lived in large groups. They bathed, clothed, ate, slept, and generally existed in herds under the watchful eyes of military police. The only moments of solitude were those just prior to interrogation. Iman and Hasim had lived as prisoners for so long and done so well in their disguised duty that newer intelligence officers would unknowingly interrogate the Marines to no avail. Existing without privacy made Iman less modest than an average person, so he shed his filthy clothes in the middle of the barracks room. He could have waited until he was behind the bathroom door, but he was not bothered by his nakedness as much as he was bothered by the smell of the dingy garb.

"Do me a favor, Marine." He pointed to the pile of semi-white cloth on the floor. "Bag that and put it out for the trash." The private nodded and complied with the request, knowing that sergeants do not make requests of junior Marines, no matter how politely an order is given. Iman then walked into the bathroom. The small room had a toilet and shower. The mirror and vanity was just outside of the door and open to the barracks room. Much like everything else in the Marines, the rooms were simplistic and provided minimal comfort.

Iman turned on the shower. He didn't wait for the heater coil to bring the water's temperature up to a comfortable degree. The filthy Marine stepped into frigid water without hesitation and watched the runoff rush a light brown film of dirt into the drain. The cold nearly shocked his breath away, but he was cleansed anew. He felt some civility return to his core as he washed.

Frigid temperatures in the shower water eventually heated. Practical purposes of bathing were fulfilled. Iman's long hair and thick beard no longer smelled of natural oil and dirt, but chemical scents of shampoo and soap. The crevasses of his arms and legs were no longer accented with dirt and filth. He returned to human form, so he was able to enjoy the massaging heat of the shower until the water ran cold once again.

Some modesty returned to the weary man. He stepped out of the bathroom with a towel wrapped around his waist. He looked to the private and laughed. The young man was still very motivated to be a part of the Marine Corps. His movie selection illustrated his spirits. *"Full Metal Jacket?* How very cliché of you," Iman joked to the Marine. The kid chuckled as he looked back over his shoulder. Iman was facing the mirror at the vanity, readying to groom further.

Refreshed from his long shower, Iman moved with more fervor and purpose. He seemed eager to return to what he felt was his natural form. He reached into the cabinet and withdrew a beard trimmer. The bearded man then disappeared to the whir of a small electric blade.

After removing the thickness of his beard, Iman used a safety razor to smooth his face. He looked himself over in the mirror and barely recognized the man staring back at him. His rough hands rubbed at his barren cheeks to make sure that no stubborn whiskers remained. Iman was satisfied that his shave would meet Marine regulations, so he wiped the sink and countertop. He cleared the area of beard remnants and trashed the entire mess.

Iman's assembly line mentality continued. He was bathed and shaved like a civilized man. Therefore, he was ready to be clothed accordingly. The refreshed warrior turned to his closet and opened the door with a grin. Each of his undershirts, boxer shorts, and socks were neatly folded and tucked into their appropriate spots. All of his uniform shirts and pants were hanging, in order and facing left, in fine Marine fashion. His boots were spit shined. His canvas belt was tightly coiled. Everything was exactly as he left it.

He was relieved at the order and organization that contrasted with his prior few months amid the turmoil of being a prisoner.

The senior Marine was dressed and ready within minutes. The commonplace camouflaged utilities that covered his body were crisp. While many Marines might have taken for granted the everyday uniform, Iman wore it with resounding pride. He was, by all accounts, a beacon for his peers to follow. His belief in himself and in his beloved Corps gave him the air of confidence that commanded respect.

Iman looked at himself in the mirror once more. He made sure that his uniform was in order, his trousers were properly bloused over his shiny boots, and his sergeant chevrons were correctly aligned to the edges of his collar. "You about ready to go, Marine?" he asked the private, who was completely enthralled by the Hollywood combat based on Vietnam lore.

"I sure am, uh..." The kid paused, only seeing Iman's rank for the first time and trying to pretend he wasn't surprised. "Sergeant?"

Iman laughed and told the private to turn the television off. He waited for the young man to exit the room and locked the door behind them. Then they walked to Hasim's room.

Iman banged the side of his fist to the flat heart of the barracks room door. "Coming in," Iman called out as he opened the hatch and entered Hasim's room. Hasim had just finished tying his boots and stood up from his seat. The men laughed at their drastic differences in appearance.

Each of the men wore the Marines' camouflaged uniform. However, the two sergeants looked less like Marines than the junior man standing among them. The private was smoothly shaved and had nothing more than fuzz for hair atop his head. Iman was shaved but had a head full of thick, curly hair. Hasim was unshaved and had locks of curled hair covering his ears.

"You didn't shave at all?" Iman questioned Hasim. The younger brother laughed and explained that he was going to let the barber do the work. They all smiled at the idea. The private smiled harder than the rest. He was amused at the idea of two Arab men wearing Marine uniforms and trying to make it across base without being stopped somewhere along the way.

"You know some Gunny is going to see us and lose his mind, right, Sergeant?" the private laughed into the room. They agreed to the possibility of having to explain themselves and left for the barbershop. Neither Hasim nor Iman could wait to have a haircut appropriate for their uniforms.

Unexpectedly, their walk across base went without obstacle. Iman and Hasim walked into the barbershop and ordered fresh, high-and-tight haircuts. The barber, a professional "marine mower" for many years, was able to whip them into shape very quickly. Hasim was then shorn free from his previous self. Hasim stood from the barber's chair and was immediately replaced by Iman. The barber ripped through Iman's thick head of hair until they were finally clean-cut and ready to go to see the administration clerk for their orders.

The brothers stood outside the barbershop. They rubbed their heads, feeling renewed by the clippers. They playfully slapped each other on the back of the head while the younger man grinned uncomfortably, unfamiliar to the two older Jarheads. They saw that the kid was out of place, so Iman nodded to the junior man. Hasim dismissed the private and the young man carried on back to his guard unit.

Hasim looked at Iman with a grin. Iman returned the gesture, and they welcomed each other back to the right side of the fence. They were anxious to see what orders were waiting for them. They were eager to leave Guantanamo Bay. Most of all, they were happy to be Marines again.

# TWO

"Would either of you gentlemen like anything to drink?" a silk-skinned flight attendant asked Iman. He smiled politely at the woman and shook his head. Then he looked to Hasim and saw that his brother was fast asleep with his head against the window. "I don't think he wants anything either," he chuckled to the woman.

Iman laughed under his breath at his brother. "How can you sleep like that?" he questioned the sleeping man, critiquing the angle of Hasim's neck. The posture was unnatural and seemed like it would be uncomfortable, but didn't stop the younger brother from dozing into the darkness of a plane window.

Leaning over, Iman gazed beyond the glare of the oval plexiglass pane. The plane's intermittent flash of red into the black sky gave no indication of where they might be. Iman knew that the flight from Florida to Washington was going to be a few hours, but he began aching to get off the flight.

He and his brother were flying under official orders, so they were not profiled at security as would be expected. They were flying in uniform, so they were treated well by the other airport patrons. The overall travel experience was pleasant and moving along without the annoyances of delay. However, Iman was growing impatient with the travels. He could not wait to get to the Pentagon. He could not wait to find out his new purpose within the Marine Corps.

"Whatever it is, I'm sure it's going to be good," Iman whispered to himself in faith that the Corps held great things for his future.

"Ladies and gentlemen, we are about fifteen minutes out," the pilot's voice chimed into the darkness of the plane. Hasim's head snapped forward as if he were coming out of a bad dream, and Iman chuckled. "We'll be landing at Dulles Airport in beautiful Chantilly, Virginia. On behalf of myself and the crew, we hope you've enjoyed your flight. Crew, prepare for descent." The pilot chimed once again to end his announcement. The flight attendant responded by making sure everyone was awake and in an upright position.

The plane descended and touched down into a new world for Iman and Hasim. Their Marine Corps prior to landing in the District of Columbia was muddy and stank of captured enemy. Their new Corps was sure to be very clean and stink only of federal-issue coffee. Hasim and Iman adjusted in their seats. Then they adjusted to the idea of a different job. Both of them were happy to continue their service alongside one another. They knew how rare it was for brothers to join together and be able to carry out their terms in the same unit. The two shared this fortune for a second time in their orders to the Pentagon, and they were grateful.

Slightly ahead of schedule, the plane landed with chirping precision as rubber tires met slick asphalt. The Marines wondered if the pilot had served in the military or if he was so well practiced that he could move from sky to ground in such seamless fashion. They half expected a hatch to lower aft allowing equipment to be swept out via deployed canopies of green fabric tethered to anchor knots. The pilot's approach was similar enough to a touch-and-go resupply that each of the Marines rendered a nod and an invisible salute to the cockpit.

The Marines, and everyone else aboard, jolted with each application of the aircraft's heavy brakes. The pilot decelerated in short, choppy power drains and energy dispersion from the wings to the wheels. Whirring engines turned to lightly whining turbines as the plane taxied runways and finally halted. Everything seemed to move slowly against Iman's eagerness to leave the transport. Airline patrons stood excitedly in a hurry to leave, only to be denied exit at a secured hatch. Finally, the door opened. Eardrums decompressed and equilibriums returned to normal as tired passengers shuffled, row after row, to the front exit. Iman and Hasim waited their turn before they disembarked and made way to baggage claim.

Exhausted from travel and shrouded in uncomfortable uniforms, the men ached to get to their destination. Their trek through terminals and corridors was unabated by the light foot traffic inside the airport. However, the ends of their toes and the bottoms of their feet burned at the confines of patent leather footwear. Hasim was still a little groggy from his nap aboard the plane. He rubbed at his eyes until he caught sight of a small boy.

The boy was visibly tired and less than thrilled to be in an airport during hours that would otherwise be deep into his bedtime. His small left hand clutched tightly to the comforts of his mother's right. Hasim smiled at the mother and child as their paths crossed. The little boy, suddenly excited and apparently raised as a patriot, rendered a salute to the Marines. Each of the men smiled back and broke uniform protocol. They returned a playful salute to the boy, and the child lit up. He was elated to have received the military courtesy as he yelled, "Mommy, Mommy! Did you see?"

Iman and Hasim forgot about the pains in their feet. They dismissed the itch of form-fitting collars and heavy ties. They discontinued their silent complaints against the heavy wool of their uniforms. Rather, they smiled with the slight bump of charging energy that the child passed to them. Hasim said, "There's a future Jarhead right there." Each laughed lightly as they arrived at baggage claim.

Distinguishable luggage drifted around the baggage carousel on a single pass as the Marines reached through a sea of strangers. People stood around the baggage claim area like hogs at a mobile trough waiting to be served a buffet of cloth and canvas. Civilians, fearful by nature, were too intimidated by the Marines' uniforms to have raised any issue of over-aggressive baggage grabbing. Iman and Hasim achieved their immediate goal. They moved within the hustle of thousands of people going here and there until they stepped out of the airport to hail a cab.

Iman whistled loudly at the passenger loading zone, and a cab stopped directly in front of the uniformed men. The cabdriver exited to help them with their bags just as Hasim noticed a young woman standing behind them. She was also in apparent need of a cab. The younger brother tapped Iman on the shoulder and pointed to the woman. Iman simply nodded.

"Ma'am," Hasim said, initiating a short conversation with the stranger. He smiled invitingly. "Why don't you go ahead and take this one?" The woman, taken aback by the unexpectedly kind gesture, attempted to argue politely. Iman insisted, "Don't worry. We'll catch the next one." He opened the door for the woman, and she thanked him repeatedly as she sat in the backseat. Iman made sure that she cleared the door before he closed it and tapped on the trunk. The cab pulled away with the woman giving a last thank-you wave to the men. Then the yellow car was promptly replaced by the next in line. "It looks like good karma pays off quickly," Iman joked as they got into the back of the cab.

"Some things just don't make sense to me," Hasim laughed to Iman in the backseat ride to a hotel. "Uncle Sam flies us out on red-eye flights to try to save some money. However, we land in the middle of the night so we don't have a barracks to check into. So whatever money they saved on crappy flights is then spent on hotel rooms and having to eat off base. Does that make any sense to you?" He poked at Iman. Iman laughed along with his brother knowing that the logic was flawed by nothing other than reason. Iman just shrugged. That was the last bit of energy he had to give to conversation for the night. He was spent from the long night's travel.

The rest of the ride was quiet until they reached a sign hanging over a brick passage. *Guest Check-In.* Iman rolled his eyes at the overdone letters etched into the elaborate wooden sign. A Marine to the core, Iman preferred things simple and functional. He had no appreciation for finer things that served no purpose beyond décor. Even still, he was happy to have reached a place to sleep comfortably.

Iman paid the cabdriver. Then the men checked into their hotel on federal vouchers. With room keys in hand and directions getting them to the following morning's complimentary continental breakfast, they bid each other decent rest. They would have to be awake and ready to check into their new command in a matter of hours. Such was the way of the Marines. Hurry up and move. Hurry up and wait.

The brothers disappeared into their respective rooms and dropped luggage at the doors. They were of like mind in equal eagerness to shed their uncomfortable uniform shoes. They peeled out of their green suits and crawled into bed before accidentally catching a second wind. The last thing Iman wanted, especially after not being able to sleep on the tubular winged prison, was to experience an adrenaline rush. He wanted nothing to prevent him from slipping into a deep slumber. He wanted only to reset. He slid into a bed that offered far more comfort than he was accustomed to, and his eyelids made no effort to remain open. He faded away cursing the prospect of an approaching morning.

Morning, suddenly, was rudely announced by the sound of a blaring alarm clock. The young Marines were awake, dressed, and ready to go before most people were rolling out of bed. Iman and Hasim were itching to leave their small rooms before the rest of the world was able to slide into well-worn slippers and stumble their way to a fresh cup of coffee. They met each other in the hotel lobby and made their way to cabs parked outside the hotel's circular driveway.

"Did you want to get breakfast?" Iman asked Hasim.

Hasim shook his head and answered, "I'm still too tired to eat." Neither of the men was accustomed to eating anything worthwhile first thing in the morning. Most of the meals they had consumed in the early hours for months prior were served while the men were held in custody at Guantanamo. Neither of them was fond of eating breakfast, so Iman offered no objection to Hasim's decline.

Hailing a cab outside of a hotel would have been an easy feat for anyone, but two Marines in uniform were treated better than either man expected. They were accustomed to lugging around their own bags and opening their own doors. They did not have to do either as the cabby catered to them curbside. "I could get used to this kind of living," Iman joked as they climbed into the back of the cab. The driver slammed the large yellow trunk over the passengers' luggage and hustled to the front door.

The driver sat down in his seat and asked, "Where to?" He then looked questioningly into the rearview mirror as the Marines stated that they were going to the Pentagon. He looked back with an initial response of doubt. Then the man looked the Marines over once more. They were clothed neatly in their uniforms, ready to fulfill orders, and each had a respectable stack of medals and ribbons on his chest. Having spent a lifetime in a cab, and really not worried about much else, the cabby knew nothing of the military decorations representing accomplishment. Yet he decided the Marines looked important and worthy enough of the Pentagon. The driver shrugged and left the hotel, headed for the heartbeat of all military operations.

Despite the early morning call to do Marine labor, traffic jams filled every street in every direction through the city. Washington was packed with people trying to get to work, and the men were worried that they might not make the designated check-in time. The cabdriver explained that the high level of traffic concentration was normal. The driver, like all cabdrivers, swore that he knew the fastest routes around town. Iman and Hasim hoped he was right because there were only two conditions Marines dreaded to ever be: dead and late.

An hour's worth of sharp turns, rapid accelerations into decelerating traffic jams, and gut-wrenching brake checks brought the brothers to their intended destination. They finally reached the Pentagon and paid the cab with chuckled protests about the expensive cost of the rolling death trap. The cabdriver offered a standard form of gratitude for their payment and the ensuing tip. Then he offered a much sincerer and much deeper felt bit of gratitude for the Marines and their service to the country that loves and hates them with equal fervor. Neither of them responded with more than a nod as the driver dropped their bags on the sidewalk next to them. He gave them a final handshake and made his way back to the throes of traffic.

Iman and Hasim were touched by the man's show of thanks. They were motivated by the reminder of why they served as both turned to the front of a massive federal building. Then they were lost. Two sergeants, standing with their standard-issue duffel bags, were sore thumbs among the hustling suits and brass. They weren't able to walk ten feet without having to render salutes here and there, so they were eager to get inside. Indoors, though they were plunged ever deeper into the strange world ahead of them, at least offered certain rescue for having to render salutes. They would be able to "uncover" by removing their uniform hats. Unlike the Army or Air Force enlisted men, the Marines would not be required to offer an indoor homage to officers.

The Marines were devoted to protocol and standards. They only fled the need to salute as to not accidentally miss an opportunity for rendering proper respect.

"Where in the hell are we supposed to go now?" Hasim questioned as they walked through the front door and into the main lobby. Iman shrugged and pointed to a security area. Several civilian, uniformed guards conducted their normal duties and chores. The Marines walked over and sought direction like tourists who harbor conspiracy theories, hoping to find out America's secrets. The guards accepted the Marines' paperwork and were then able to point the men to the correct corridor. One of the guards provided them with a suite number where they would be able to check into their new command. The men were thankful to have some sort of answer to concerned curiosity. Feelings of being lost slowly dissipated.

"This place is a *sir factory*," Iman joked to Hasim as they continued to walk by one officer after another. Marine etiquette is to greet every officer in passing, whether they were outside to render salute or inside to render a verbal acknowledgment. Etiquette was starting to chip away at the excitement of two sergeants who were completely out of place.

Iman and Hasim carried all their belongings, slung over their shoulders, because they had no place to stay for the time being. They had no room to call their own. They were, at the moment, Marine nomads in search of their next command unit until they reached their newest destination.

Hasim opened an otherwise blank door labeled "Marine Administrations Office," and the men presented their printed official orders to a clerk at the front desk. The clerk, and several others who followed, were confused by the Marines' presence.

"We don't exactly have...a barracks or anything," a female Marine said through her thick makeup. The bun in her hair was pulled so tight that it seemed to stretch her forehead into blotched areas of redness. She was as lost to the printed documents as anyone else. "I'm going to call my C.O. and hopefully get an answer for you guys," she chirped more toward the paper than to the Marines. She was very informal and the sergeants were not familiar with being talked down to by a corporal. Each of the men let her demeanor go uncorrected. They were in foreign territory and understood her to be their only ally.

The admin Marine hung up the phone and finally had some direction for the two unguided weapons. "Go up to the second floor to Room 220. Meet up with a...General Potts," the corporal directed, glancing back and forth between her notes and Hasim's face. She handed the written orders back to the sergeants. The corporal seemed to dismiss the senior Marines as she went back to work on whatever she was doing prior to their arrival. She rendered no formal acknowledgment of the seniors or their ranks. They offered no gratitude to the young woman. The men ignored broken protocols on both sides of the exchange and left the administration office.

Iman felt a little foolish carrying his sea bag through the halls of the Pentagon. Getting beyond security checkpoints with large

bags was bad enough. Then to be one of only two Marines carrying all of his belongings around started to get very old very fast.
He was relieved when Hasim pointed to Room 220. He looked at
Hasim silently asking if they were ready to enter into mystery. The
younger brother nodded and they walked into the room together.
One behind the other, they dropped their bags in the doorway and
stood at attention.

"General Potts, sir," Iman said upon their arrival, "Sergeant
Iman Sahar and Sergeant Hasim Sahar reporting as ordered." The
men stood with heels together. Their left arms were straight at their
sides with hands curled into fists. With heads up and chests out,
they offered the printed orders with their right hands extended
only from elbows set at right angles. The general accepted their
paperwork and told the men to stand at ease. Both of them moved
in unison to relax a bit, with their hands folded behind their backs
and their feet comfortably apart at shoulder-width.

General Gutzwiller looked the papers over and looked at each
of the sergeants. "I'm not Potts. I'm Gutzwiller. Potts will be in
shortly. Do you know who I am or why you are here?" General
Gutzwiller asked the men standing in front of him.

Hasim answered, "Yes, General, we know who you are. I know
we haven't met before, but you were our Commanding General
down at Gitmo for a while, sir." Gutzwiller nodded. He instanta-
neously felt more comfortable with the men he had selected for
the mission.

Gutzwiller relaxed then ordered the sergeants to do the same.
The chasm of rank between sergeant and general made Iman and
Hasim considerably nervous. Under normal circumstances, there
would be a sea of people between them and General Gutzwiller.
Yet they stood with him in direct communication. Even still, they
were confused as to why they were called to the Pentagon. Both

Marines would have been content to continue rolling in the mud with the enemy, and they hoped for a good reason to be standing so far out of place.

"I beg your pardon, General," Iman started to question, "but we really haven't received any guidance as to why we're here or what our mission is, sir." He silently begged to not have found his way into making coffee for a long list of officers. Then Iman continued, "We just received our orders and we were on a plane the next morning. Up until yesterday, we were detainees at Gitmo... So..."

Iman was quickly interrupted by Gutzwiller's chuckled response, "So you want to know what in the world you are doing at the Pentagon?"

Iman smiled. Gutzwiller was a proper man who had scratched his way through the ranks of his career, but he was approachable and friendly. He welcomed the young Marine's question and answered, "Your mission here is complicated. We'll explain what's going on as soon as everyone gets here. Then"—the general looked over to their duffel bags—"we need to get you guys a place to store that stuff."

The fact that the general used the word *store* with regard to placing their belongings let the men know that their time at the Pentagon would be limited. They would not need to get comfortable because they would surely be moving out sooner than later. It was just as well for Iman. He had no interest in being a general's administrative assistant or some colonel's coffee go-getter. Iman had joined the Marines to fight enemies destroying life across the globe. He wanted nothing more than to do just that.

Minimal conversation filled a quiet corner of the room between Gutzwiller and his newly recycled Marines. The general invited small talk and tried to get his subordinates to relax in the brass-filled environment. The air between the senior man and those in his direct command was awkward, but was finally relieved when General Potts and Special Agent McKenzee walked into the room. The sergeants returned to previously established positions of attention in meeting General Potts. The generals and Special Agent McKenzee were relaxed and seemingly lighthearted. They tried to get the junior Marines to act in the same demeanor and eased attitude until the leaders finally realized proper Marines would not rest to anything other than an explanation. The sergeants stood ready to follow orders but had deeply unanswered questions running through their minds over and over. *Why are we here? What is our mission?*

Civilian by nature, the CIA agent asserted more than his share of authority without considering anyone else in the room. "Alright, gentlemen," Special Agent McKenzee chopped into the tension, "we'll get right to it then. The reason you are here is because you are well-trained, highly proficient, dedicated Marines. You're second-generation Americans, so we can rely on your home-grown patriotism. You speak Arabic. You are practicing Muslims. And your work down in Gitmo let us know that you don't have any problems playing *the part*." McKenzee was brash in his compartmentalization of the men, but he was accurate nonetheless. The agent had an impersonal approach that rubbed people the wrong way at first, but the sergeants considered undeniable accuracy in his description. Iman ignored offense.

Hasim, however, did not turn a blind eye to McKenzee's bold comments. Rather, he glared at the special agent and questioned, "I'm sorry. Who are you?" He set aside that the civilian was standing between two very high-ranking officers of the Marine Corps. Gutzwiller and Potts at least had the decency to introduce themselves and treat the sergeants with some level of mutual respect. However, the man cloaked in his black suit made no effort to extend an olive branch to the Marines before getting straight to business. Hasim, unlike those who had clawed their way through a desert of politics to earn stars on their collars, was not able to conceal his discontent at McKenzee's boldness.

The generals remembered their first meeting with McKenzee and sympathized with Hasim. Potts cut Hasim off before the young Marine made an error in judgment by planting the agent into the floor. Potts identified McKenzee. Once Iman and Hasim heard "Central Intelligence Agency," they knew their mission at the Pentagon was well beyond that of administration and coffee. CIA. The acronym alone saved McKenzee an unexpected visit to his dentist. Hasim concealed his contempt for the agency, reentered the world of military protocol, and accepted his new fate. *Maybe making coffee and doing paperwork isn't that bad after all.* The Marine joked silently within because he knew the agency offered nothing other than dangerous missions with no true expectations of return.

# ENCROACH

**P**lausible deniability. Special Agent McKenzee's words rattled around inside Iman's head. Months of planning and training with the CIA agent chipped away at the sergeants' spirits. Their time back in their beloved Corps was short-lived. McKenzee made sure of that. Iman and Hasim had to stop getting haircuts and shaving their beards. They were no longer allowed to visit the Pentagon because they were no longer Marines. Their personal belongings were condensed further. Their assigned and quietly paid apartment had nothing more than a light, a toilet, and two bedrolls. They were allowed to keep their Korans and continued to pray. They assimilated into the minimalist Muslim culture shared by so many extremists throughout the world, the same culture that allowed terrorists to walk away from possessions and willingly detonate their bodies into innocent crowds.

Iman and Hasim found the same shared culture of minimal-living extremists as they shifted from the streets of Washington, D.C., to the deserts of southwest Asia. United in purpose, the brothers committed to their roles so convincingly that they knew how to blend into the enemy in small villages or wide-open terrain.

Iman and Hasim bounced around in the back of a small pickup truck. Unsettling soreness worked its way into the backs of their legs and buttocks as muscle battled against the metal of an old truck-bed. They were on an open trail in the vast desert of Afghanistan, well away from their empty apartment in Washington. They stared at armed militiamen riding with them in the back of the truck. AK-47 barrels wobbled around with the gunmen's bodies as the truck ran over rocks and sand. They were on fast approach to rocky and impassable mountains, unreachable by mechanized force.

*Plausible deniability.* Iman continued to think as he tried not to stare at enemy rifles. He recalled McKenzee's explanation, "You guys are now ghosts. We've erased you from the system, so only a few people know who you are. You don't have anything on record, so nothing can be hacked or given up to the enemy. Additionally, you can't be traced back to America, so Uncle Sam won't get blamed if a bunch of women and children get blown away. Your team will be the only group that can identify you once you egress. In the event of *Mission Accomplished,* you will be returned to the system and reinstated completely across the board. In the event of *Mission Failed,* it won't matter because you will be dead."

Iman tried not to grit his teeth at the memory of McKenzee's arrogant dismissal toward a dismal future. He thought to himself, *If I survive this, I'm going to kill that guy.* Then the truck screeched to a halt. One of the militiamen in the back stood and fired his rifle one time into the air. A moment later, his shot was answered by another from the hills.

"Let's go," the militiaman said to Iman and Hasim. He spoke in a harsh Arabic tone, but they knew what he was saying without a second thought. They had lived among Afghani people, in a small village outside of Mazar-i-Sharif for several months after leaving Washington. Neither Iman nor Hasim had spoken English for several weeks, so the Arabic tongue came to them naturally as they questioned where the lightly armed group was going.

The armed escorts simply poked at the undercover Marines and pointed into the mountains. The steep terrain was foreboding but held some hope of success. They would climb the mountain to find themselves welcomed into an insurgent camp or into Paradise upon their execution.

Previous weeks spent in the village seemed to have paid off quickly. Iman and Hasim arrived in the small town and posed as men looking to join the cause. They had false backstories that held very few details. If anyone were to look into their pasts, nothing would be found other than tales from unknown times and obscure places. The newcomers had no family and had to work bottom-level jobs hoping to start conversations with villagers about where to go for a fight. Eventually, word spread and Iman was approached by an armed teenager. The kid had the answer they were seeking, and he took them to meet one jihadist after another.

Iman worked his way through a tightly knit network of terrorists. He began with quiet nods in back alleys. The nods turned into quick handshakes. Handshakes finally evolved into detailed conversations regarding Iman's dedication to jihad. Iman was able to portray himself as a devout warrior and assured everyone he met that Hasim would serve with equal conviction.

Hasim, ever present with his brother, was given the opportunity to meet each of the terrorists within the small-town network as they manifested from the shadows. The Marines became regularly discussed topics among the villagers. They seamlessly plugged into a foreign stream of jihadists, and they were unsettled by the number of people who were willing and able to kill Americans.

After a great deal of consideration, the eager jihadists accepted that Iman and Hasim were holy warriors. A decision was made through a series of cloaked conversations and whispered winds. The brothers were to be taken deep into the mountains. However, acceptance was found on a razor's edge. Two United States Marines were about to climb a mountain and ooze into the ranks of a terrorist organization based on their fake existence in a real war.

Every aching step up the steep hill landed in a pool of anxiety. Iman and Hasim were unarmed and surrounded by their enemy comrades. In addition to mental anguish and apprehension, their legs burned with physical fatigue. Time spent with McKenzee training them how to be jihadists took away from the time they would have trained as Marines. They were rail-thin but were hardly fit or capable of such a climb. They ached.

Small stones and bits of sand trailed down the side of the tall mountain path as the men reached central camp. They looked around as a makeshift city of canvas tents and poorly constructed buildings came into clear view. The air was cold, but the ground reflected the sun's heat. Iman mentally noted yet another of the desert's strange occurrences.

Iman and Hasim watched as their armed escorts were greeted with hugs around narrow shoulders and kisses on dried cheeks. The men atop the mountain were rested and fed. Everyone in camp seemed to be armed or within immediate reach of a weapon. What was once suspected to be a village was now confirmed to be a militant camp. Iman and Hasim felt that they had gathered enough information to support a full airstrike. More so, they felt an urgent need to flee. Yet each knew the end outcome of leaving too early. If they were rushed and left together, the village would spook and scatter. If one left without the other, the stay-behind would surely be shot. If they were both caught, they would both be executed for their treachery against Allah.

"Are these the men?" a man of obvious command authority asked. The harshness of the Arabic language and his affinity for smoking made him sound like he spoke through a glass tube full of nails. Iman and Hasim offered their greetings, but were silenced. "How can I trust you?" the man asked. "No one knows you. No one knows your family. Out of nowhere, you find us..." He paused and stared hard at the newcomers. The man was rightfully suspicious.

Iman then answered, "Rumors. We came to you based on rumors that holy warriors were resisting the American war. We just followed the rumors until they became true." Iman swallowed hard hoping that his explanation would appease the jihadist.

The man glared at Iman. Hasim remained quiet. The brothers waited for his response. "Rumors?" The man questioned the validity of the answer. Then he nodded to the armed escorts. The rifle-wielding men poked Iman and Hasim at center spine. The men were guided by gunpoint to the center of camp. They followed the group leader until he stopped and turned around to face them once again.

"I want to believe you. I want to believe that you are true in your purpose, in the fight, in your faith..." He paused hard once again. The leader summoned someone over with a wave of his hand. A young man pushed a blindfolded teen into the makeshift courtyard and forced the kid to kneel. Then the leader pulled a pistol out of a shoulder holster dangling at his left ribcage. The older man handed the weapon to Hasim.

"How can I trust you?" the man continued. His pause was dramatic enough to invoke disingenuous intrigue from a surrounding crowd. "This boy was caught in an act of apostasy. We found him in the village handing out Bibles and speaking of Christ as a savior. He claims that Muhammad was a false prophet." The man stroked his beard. "This is punishable by death. However, only a true believer, only a true son of The Prophet, can carry out this execution." The man opened his palm to invite Hasim behind the boy. "Please," the man said, smiling devilishly, "carry out Allah's commands."

The elder stepped back as Hasim raised the pistol to the back of the boy's head. Hasim's heart jumped into his throat, and his hand trembled without control. Thoughts of survival and self-sacrifice raced around his mind. He wanted to carry out his mission and do what was best for the War on Terror, but he did not want to do so at the cost of murdering a teenaged boy. Hasim panicked as he placed his finger across the trigger. Then he looked to Iman, searching for an answer as to what he should do. Iman's heart pounded to get out of his chest as he watched Hasim aim a pistol at the base of the boy's skull. He just nodded and closed his eyes, not wanting to see what Hasim was about to do.

Hasim prayed, silently begging Allah and the boy for forgiveness. Tears flooded his eyes. His stomach turned. He wanted to vomit and flee for his life. Then he gritted his teeth and clenched his eyes as he pulled the trigger.

Click.

Hasim nearly dropped the pistol to the noise of an empty chamber. He fought to stay on his feet despite his shaking knees. He tried to keep from vomiting from fear and remorse even though the gun was not loaded. Iman joined Hasim in the fight for composure.

The old man and many others laughed heartily into the mountain air. They laughed as if Iman and Hasim were the butt of some very sick practical joke. "This," the man said, taking his pistol from Hasim's shaking hand, "this is my oldest son, Rami." The blindfolded teen removed the cloth from his eyes and stood with a wide smile. Then the man continued, "I am Farhad." His laughter dulled and he put his arm around Hasim's shoulders.

"Come. Come. We have a tent for you. You are welcome here." Farhad led Iman and Hasim to a tent tucked away from the center of the camp. The canvas flapped at the hard mountain winds, but the structure of the tent was heavy and steady. They knew that little would protect them from the elements of winters or summers in Afghanistan, and the tent certainly was not going to be enough for comfort. They hoped to be away from the place sooner than later. Farhad showed the men inside the tent. Their bedrolls were raised from sharp rocks by wooden pallets. They were provided several old blankets along with sleeping bags. A wash pan sat on top of a brittle milk crate in the corner of the large tent. In the opposite corner was a bucket that held the remnant smell of its purpose.

"Welcome home," Farhad said, coaxing them inside before giving a description of the camp's events. He described, in great detail, chores that were to be conducted on a daily basis. However, the chores were only to be carried out between prayers.

Iman and Hasim were familiar with the calls to prayer, but they were still American in their thoughts of homage. They internally anticipated grouping prayers together so that they could remain efficient in their earthly chores. However, their new brothers were devout to the idea of five prayers at five separate times of the day. There was room for nothing other than service to Allah in the camp. Everything else was just to kill time before killing the enemy.

# ACCEPTANCE

Fajr. The sun had yet to peek over encompassing mountaintops, but the camp was awake. They bowed to Mecca and prayed. Their foreheads pressed to the ground beneath their prayer rugs. They welcomed the morning by thanking Allah for a new day.

The call to prayer ended and the day's chores whipped everyone in camp into a whirl of people. Those who woke hard were still fumbling in the dark. People with early spirits moved in habit and found their way around quickly.

Hasim and Iman hoisted themselves from their prostrated positions and rolled their rugs. They stowed the woven fabric into the front corner of their tent. Then they stretched to the onset of daylight. Still relatively new to camp, their only chores were to continue their studies.

The morning prayer was their twenty-second in camp. Three weeks among the enemy gave the Marines time to at least conduct a meet-and-greet with nearly everyone in the village. The unkempt Jarheads had taken time to shake hands with every man and teenaged boy they encountered. Each tried to memorize names the way that partygoers would work a room of socialites. They teased relationships to the edge of mutual gain. If someone could not benefit their existence, comfort, or mission then the person was not committed to memory. There were too many terrorists to keep track of, all on an individual level. Farhad, his sons, the lieutenants in charge of varying sects, and the suspected bomb builders were the only guerillas deeply imbedded into Marine memory banks.

Iman's dedication to service and his ever-present drive for mission accomplishment set him apart from his brother. Hasim, devout in his faith, had to be reminded that relationships were fragile. To Hasim, everyone in camp was a Muslim first, and he found commonality with them. Iman, quietly at night and silently during the day, nudged Hasim's mindset. The people they met were false-friendly. They would execute Iman and Hasim without a second thought if the spies were found out.

Weeks spent with the mujahideen let the Marines learn a very harsh truth about the village. The place was home to no one under fourteen years of age. The women were held as wives, but wielded weapons alongside the men in the makeshift town. All the children were years into their combat training and ached for an opportunity to kill infidels. Each day brought a new realization that every person in the area was worthy of a military-driven death.

Iman yearned to be away from the jihadists. He wanted to pass the information to Command. He wanted to assemble the team that would deliver a blow into the heart of terrorism. He wanted to finish the job. Hasim, on the other hand, just hoped that death would come quickly to the people of the village.

Hasim sat cross-legged and leaned forward to the religious lecture hoisted from Farhad's gullet. Iman, deep in his resolve against the enemy, adopted a posture opposite that of Hasim. Iman sat back on his hands with his legs stretched out in front of him. Hasim was involved while Iman seemed to distance himself from the others inside the tent. The older brother went as far as a near faux pas by exposing the bottoms of his feet, but he aimed the soles of his boots at no one in particular. Farhad took notice but remained steadfast in a lecturing posture.

Despite their opposing sitting postures, Iman and Hasim looked at Farhad with an equal amount of intrigue. Iman was astounded at how Farhad could twist and contort the words of the Koran to meet the jihadists' needs. He was taken aback by the level of justification that could be derived in and out of scriptural context. Iman fought back his urge to loudly and hatefully dismiss Farhad's rationalization of evil. He bit his tongue early and often.

Farhad spoke with such fire and force that he was able to sway spirits. Hasim sat among future murderers, but he dismissed the fact for feeling. The young Marine was enthralled by the improvised imam's speeches and use of scripture. He was drawn into the call to war, ironically setting him at war with himself. Iman, watchfully concerned, sat with his brother and did not sway.

Hasim's interest in the messages of hate was not based on any willingness to accept empty justifications for violence against innocence. Rather, Hasim was taken with the thought of saving the other villagers. He knew that there was no hope for Farhad, the sons, or the most trusted of men in camp. They were too involved, too deeply buried in their own filth to be cleansed. However, Hasim looked over the rest of the village as if he were their guardian angel. He looked to the youngest men of the group, knowing they were still children. The Marine believed that if he could only reach the teenaged warmongers before they were brainwashed by Farhad, he could save them from the hell that was sure to come.

Iman began to worry. He saw how Hasim was connecting emotionally and spiritually with the rest of the villagers. Iman's concern grew each day that Hasim spent with Farhad. The older zealot seemed to have a great deal of influence over the younger brother's personal involvement in the mujahideen. Iman knew that he and his brother would have to remove themselves from the enemy. They would have to disconnect if the Marines aimed to indiscriminately destroy their foes. Hasim knew it as well. Yet the younger brother was unable to tear from the village without tearing himself apart.

Farhad's words were drowned out by Hasim's innermost thoughts. *I understand now, Allah, how the people here stand against America. Your messenger is right. This land is divided by your many tribes. However, they are united under the single call to fight invaders. I understand how so many young men would answer the call to protect their homes. I've seen the excesses and filth that American culture has to offer, and it will only drive a wedge between you and your people.*

The light in Hasim's eyes was glazing over with the notion of one-track death. Iman watched quietly as Hasim faded from a steadfast Marine to a dirt-ridden jihadist. The older brother spent more time paying attention to his brother than the leader.

Iman, exhausted from maintaining silence against stupidity, was thankful for Zuhr. The noon prayer time was sounded and would be followed by lunch. Everyone in the village would bow and pray. Then they would all sit in a sense of community and fellowship to eat lunch. Bits of goat and small portions of rice would be divided throughout the village. Iman and Hasim, as a two-man addition to the population, would spread the rations a bit thinner for another day.

After lunch, the people would return to their chores. Iman and Hasim anticipated that they would return to the religious lectures. Hasim saw the *studies* as misguided reinforcements of faith. Iman

considered the time as a means of brainwashing illiterate and disenfranchised people to carry out the biddings of evil men. Hasim
continued to hope for the village's salvation while Iman prayed for
its demise.

Farhad had observed Hasim's reception and Iman's resistance
to the messages. The leader knew that Hasim was ready to move
into the next phase of training. However, he questioned Iman's
willingness to kill infidels. The elder waited until the men were
done eating. He watched them from across the open common
area where meals and ceremonies were held. Farhad observed how
they interacted with each other and with others in the group. The
false prophet openly stared at Hasim's smile and Iman's frown. He
watched until he was satisfied.

"Hasim!" Farhad called loudly over the low roar of the community. Hasim looked up from his light conversation and met
eyes with the head jihadist. The young man stood quickly and
responded as a teacher's pet would run to the front of a class. Iman
watched as Hasim jogged to the older man.

Iman sat nervously as the two religious warriors spoke. He
made no effort to hide his stare. His curiosity heightened when
Hasim shook his head matter-of-factly before nodding toward
his older brother. Hasim and Farhad spoke outside of any range
that would give Iman the ability to hear their conversation, but he
could see that his brother was staging a request of the aged jihadist.
Iman cursed himself silently as he wondered if Hasim would give
over to the enemy.

Hasim's conversation with Farhad ended as the younger man
walked back to Iman. Farhad watched from a distance. He waited
for any correspondence between the two brothers, but was surprised when Hasim returned without Iman raising any questions.
Hasim simply sat back down, next to his brother, and continued

as if nothing happened. Farhad knew that he could trust Hasim, a man who traveled the earth with his brother but would travel into Paradise alone. The leader would grant Hasim his request.

Lunch ended. Everyone went back to their chores. All sacrificed and suffered. Yet no one suffered their labors more than Iman. His gut turned into knots with every sentence bellowed by the babbling bastards of Allah. Steadily, he endured the task. He considered his suffering as his penance for the deaths he would soon cause.

A short line of young men filed into the tent where Farhad would hold his next session of religious indoctrination. Their small bellies were full enough to thwart hunger pangs. Soon the rice from the meal would expand to its maximum potential and create an illusion of satisfaction. The undercover Marines were not strangers to hunger and could withstand inevitable pain, but they were as grateful for the small portions as everyone else in camp.

Iman and Hasim were the last two men in line, and they were stopped outside the tent's entryway. An armed guard stepped between them and the tent to impede their attendance at the next lecture. The brothers were suddenly confused and concerned within a single heartbeat. Their fears were not calmed as the rifle-wielding man seemed to look through them simultaneously.

"Move," the man quietly ordered. He nudged Iman rearward with the side of his AK-47. Any other time, in any other place, the small-framed Arab could not have bullied Iman or Hasim. Under professional circumstances, the man of little stature would have never been able to get close enough to bother them. However, the jihadist was armed with a fully automatic assault rifle. The Marines were empty-handed and surrounded by those willing to kill. They decided it best to cooperate rather than resist.

Iman turned away from the side of a rifle being pushed outward from a skinny enemy soldier. Hasim followed his brother's lead. The gun poked at Iman's back intermittently to direct the path from the indoctrination tent to a different area of camp.

Hasim had a fairly secure idea of where they were going, but had not shared the information with Iman. The older brother was relieved when he saw that they were not being taken to their execution. The Marines had been selected to join the able-bodied fighters.

They reached the edge of base, and the armed escort patted Hasim on the back in welcoming fashion. The rifle-carrying man walked ahead of the brothers. Iman waited for enough space to build between them and the guard. Then he quietly asked, "Was that funny to you?"

Hasim looked at Iman and explained sincerely, "I didn't know what was going on any more than you. When Farhad called me over, he was going to send me without you. He said that he wasn't convinced of your faith and conviction, but I told him that I would not go without you. I didn't know if he was going to send us or kill us, but we're here now." Hasim paused as one of the mujahideen approached holding two assault rifles. "Just remember that we've never fired a weapon before," Hasim reminded Iman of the alternate reality encompassed by their undercover personas.

"This is where believers meet bullets," the cloaked warrior chuckled through a mask. The man's turban wrapped around his face and veiled everything but his narrow, dark eyes. The jihadist's boots were well worn, etched from black to brown around the toes, a product of being dragged through the desert for years beyond reason. His uniform was tattered and tired. Iman looked around at the few other men in the area. Each of them was of like appearance, and he was not able to recognize any of them as being members of the base camp. He glanced to gauge Hasim's reaction and found the same questions being asked into nothingness.

"Come with me," the veiled villain ordered as he handed loaded rifles to the newcomers. Hasim and Iman accepted the weapons. Both of the Marines pretended to fumble with the bodies of unfamiliar guns. They held the tools awkwardly. Iman was on the edge of overacting the scenario, pretending to touch a gun for the first time, but he withheld the last seconds of faked anxiety. He passed.

"This is the AK-47. It is the most versatile and widely deployed weapon in the world," the masked man coached. "It is also employed by children as young as nine years old in our resistance against the American pigs that continue to invade our villages, rape our women, and bomb our wives." Iman snarled at the anti-American propaganda. The man accepted Iman's reaction as affirmation to a shared view of Americans rather than that of disgust at baseless accusations.

Iman and his only brother were inserted into the bowels of Islam in the interest of preserving innocent lives. They were risking their lives just to make sure that unarmed civilians and noncombatants were not going to be killed. Even still, Iman had to listen to some shrouded scumbag list empty propagated talking-points and nonsense in the continued brainwashing of Islamo-Nazi recruits. Iman felt his hate boil. Hasim saw the tears of anger well in Iman's eyes. He nudged his brother, hoping to bring some calm to Iman's inner storm.

The man turned away from the new recruits. Iman considered the idea of immediate relief. He could shoot the jihadist in the back. Then surrounding others would kill him and Hasim. The world would be one terrorist lighter and the Marines would be put out of their misery. He refrained.

They watched as the bandit pulled another rifle off his back. He racked a round into the chamber with a hard jerk against the weapons charging handle and fired indiscriminately at empty barrels. The fully automatic discharge of ammunition kicked dirt and rocks up all around the intended targets. The man was not showing off any real marksmanship. He was, more or less, introducing the new jihadists to the sounds of outgoing bullets. They were not as surprised as he had hoped, so he invited them to do the same.

Hasim went first. He pretended to be lost with a weapon in his hand, acting as if he did not know what to do. He pointed and clicked the rifle. "Mine is broken," he announced to the group of terrorists who, despite their character, answered with laughter. The jihadist trainer showed Hasim how to charge the weapon, moving a bullet from the magazine to the chamber and pushing the safety switch downward. Then the younger brother opened fire on the same rusted barrels. He estimated that one in six bullets actually hit the targets, but still would have registered as low-miss on a legitimate qualification range. Marines rarely shoot shoulder-fired weapons on full-auto because the rapid recoil produces more errant misses than hits. Hasim ignored the general rule of thumb and held the trigger down until the weapon ran dry. It was an ammunition-wasting mistake that only the untrained and careless would make for lack of wisdom and experience. Hasim meant to mislead the enemy and did well enough to convince the herd.

The empty weapon cued Iman to follow. Hasim stepped away from the predetermined firing line and spoke to Iman in passing. "First time," he reminded his older brother with a whispered and scolding grin. He hoped that Iman's pride would not get the best of him. He hoped Iman would have the wisdom to miss, to break the character of his usual ability to destroy targets at center-mass. He hoped that Iman would not get them killed.

Iman was usually a fantastic shot. He was capable of striking man-sized targets at the center ring from hundreds of yards away. The Corps taught him how to adjust for wind and elevation, weather, and minutes travel on moving targets. He prided himself on the honed craft. Iman knew that he could likely outshoot every man in the camp, including his brother.

A prideful and angered man stepped to the firing position. He shouldered his rifle. Hasim watched as his brother swallowed the broken shards of his pride. Iman squinted, faking fear, feigning intimidation, and depressed the trigger. Bullets flew free from the end of the rifle, and Iman missed every barreled target only a few short yards away.

Two Marine Rifle Experts stood among a chuckling enemy squad. Each of them was deafened by whining in the inner ear created by shooting an AK-47 without hearing protection. Missed targets, torturous noise, and a grinning devil at the end of an empty weapon; such was their war on terror.

# TORN

Iman was reminded of boot camp. Just as he grew weary of any single activity, he found another lying in wait at the behest of men for whom he really did not care. Farhad's guided weeks of indoctrination were followed by initial weapons training. The weeks of weapons training were followed by obligatory time in defensive positions. Every day was like the day before. They woke. They prayed. They defended. They ate. They prayed. They slept. They prayed. They defended.

The droll existence and constant barrage of reinforced propaganda chiseled at Hasim's edges. Much like a hostage succumbing to the symptoms of Stockholm syndrome, he continued to identify with the villagers. He connected with those who were otherwise disconnected from the world. He moved further from his own reality and more toward the life of a minimalist. Hasim wondered if he would be able to kill the foes or if he had developed new enemies in the course of his stay. If he held a defensive position in the event of an invasion, would he defend to the death? This was his war. Each day seemed to drive a new wedge between Hasim and America. Each day seemed to drive a new wedge between Hasim and Iman.

Iman saw that his little brother was tearing away from reason and reality. However, he only saw fractures of Hasim in small fractions of time. Iman and Hasim relieved each other in the defense immediately following Asr. Otherwise, they were separated to serve Farhad's purposes. They saw each other only in passing as one would leave base camp for the fighting holes along the ridgeline and the other would leave the fighting holes for base.

Afternoon prayers gave each man a chance to make peace with Allah before sending his brother into a world of danger. One was tasked to live in the belly of the beast they aimed to eventually destroy. The other was tasked to guard the beast from being destroyed by others. Their time among the enemy set them so far apart that they were in a constant state of turmoil. They were conflicted within themselves, with each other, and with those who would kill them.

Farhad, a maniacal mastermind, noticed the brothers' bond early on. He knew that Iman and Hasim would be invincible together. He also had a gut feeling, a diabolical intuition, that the brothers could not be trusted. Therefore, he had them divided. The leader, seeking the approval of his herd, set them apart rather than have them killed without evidence of betrayal. The old man knew that he could not order the brothers' deaths without fallout from the village, no matter how loyal the village was to their chieftain.

Farhad concluded that if they were true to the cause then he did not want to lose able-bodied fighters. If they were dedicated, he did not want to lose the chance at sending two more suicide bombers against soft targets across the world.

The elder continually lurked like a vulture circling above dying meat as Iman and Hasim relieved each other on post. He observed short conversations turn into shorter greetings. He watched as the greetings eventually turned into silent pats on the shoulder in passing. The leader watched every day until he was satisfied that the brothers were splintered. He knew his success was realized in driving a wedge between them. Their unity was gone. Their solidarity was shattered.

Iman still glared back at Farhad from time to time. Hasim no longer seemed to care enough to acknowledge either of the men as he moved from one position to the next. Farhad knew that he could finally send them on separate missions if the situation called for one man instead of two. He knew he could send Hasim to carry out a lone objective, but he still questioned Iman's commitment. Even after weeks turned into months, the elder could not bring himself to trust the young warrior Iman. Everything inside Farhad told him that Iman served a higher purpose, but Hasim's dedication to the cause cloaked the fact that they were actually American spies.

Farhad's distrust for Iman followed the undercover Marine around. Iman was given more hardship and heavier duty than any other member of the camp. Farhad kept Iman at a distance from the other members of the fight. He didn't want the young man to influence others away from an immediate willingness to obey Farhad's orders. However, the elder could not have the defiant man killed without suffering a backlash from Hasim. A brother's blood ran deeper than any call to jihad. The false imam knew it to be just as true in the eyes of the brothers he watched closely with apprehension nearing fear. Therefore, Farhad had Iman loosely followed and monitored in and out of camp.

Outside of camp, Iman's defensive position was the only one that was regularly checked. Other defenders secretly used narcotics, smoked cigarettes, hid pornography in the trenches of their holes, and carried out other ungodly deeds in their solitude. Iman knew that Farhad was looking for a way to get rid of the outsider by any means that even Hasim could not resist under Islamic law. Iman was too smart to give Farhad an excuse. He did nothing more than stand ready over his rifle and pointed into the blank wilderness of the desert.

When Iman refused to fail his faith while in the defense, Farhad had him followed inside the camp. Farhad tasked his second and least-favored wife, Rasa, to ultimately spy on Iman's activities. However, she was not to be coy or deceiving about the deed. She was ever present and was meant to report back to Farhad with anything unusual, anything at all that might lead to further inquiry of the young Marine.

Iman knew that Rasa followed him and watched him. He felt her eyes on him from the moment he returned within the guarded perimeter to the time he bedded down in his tent. She was up before him in the mornings, prayed next to him, followed him during their separate chores, and observed his every move inside the confines of the village.

Rasa, by nature, was not a nosy person. The soft woman, strong despite her frailty, would have been happy to go about minding her own business. She had no real interest in reporting Iman's activities back to Farhad. She had no interests in Iman that would serve the greater purpose of a common good. Rasa's interests in Iman were less pure. She was as forbidden to look at him with lust as he was forbidden to look at her. However, their developing intrigue was unmistakable and natural.

The American spy and the terrorist's wife were of similar age. To Rasa, Iman was the pinnacle of her physical desires. He was the antithesis of her husband. Iman was well built, young, and had gentle eyes despite his rough hands. Farhad was old, unappealing, and had evil in his eyes. Rasa hated to be around Farhad, let alone be mounted by his lust-filled body, but she had little choice otherwise.

As a young girl, Rasa was abandoned by her family. The men of her world joined terror organizations or were killed by the Taliban. Women in her family were executed for having opinions. Rasa was orphaned by a culture of war before she was abducted as an unnaturally young bride for the tribe elder. She was strong-willed at first, but Farhad spent years beating the spirit out of her. He whipped and raped her until she was broken. She served him more as a slave than a wife. His early sexual assaults left her so badly damaged as a child that she was unable to have children as an adult. She could not serve him as a childbearer. Her service to Farhad then became to watch Iman and report all things, no matter how miniscule. Otherwise, she was beaten without mercy and tasked to do better the next day.

The days Iman saw bruises and cuts around Rasa's eyes made him want to kill the entire village even more. His time there let him know that all innocence was lost. There were no unarmed noncombatants in the camp. Everyone in camp was focused on war, prayer, and conflict. Iman's sense that no good existed in the village was heightened by the collective camp reveling and mourning the loss of two young women. Farhad called them "women of Allah" when he announced and praised their deed.

The old man had ordered two fourteen-year-old girls into a market full of armed American servicemen. Once the girls were in the market among his enemy, he had their escort dial a cell phone number. The phone was attached to a bomb strapped around one of the girl's chest. The teens detonated together, holding hands like scared school kids, and murdered a crowd of people. The world news reported the treacherous affair as an atrocity. Farhad reported the bombing as a glorious victory.

Iman, the vigilant spy, continued his true labor in the face of menial tasks and Rasa's presence. The Marine would return from his chores, his training, and his defense posts. Following Ishah, he would praise Allah for another day of life. Then he would go into his tent and seal himself off from the rest of the jihadists. He would wait.

The spy waited for the world to go quiet around him. Then he spent every late evening conducting the same activities. He pulled his bedroll away from the wooden pallet. He shifted the heavy wooden pallet to the side. Then, no matter how cold or raw his fingertips were, he clawed at the cold earth until he uncovered his journal.

The leather binding was dry-rotted. Edges of the paper inside the journal were brittle and flaked away at the lightest touch. The journal was new the first time he snuck the book into the ground. It was disheartening to see the bindings decomposing with time because the journal reminded Iman of how long he had walked in the lions' den without any foreseeable hope for departure.

Each rain or snow brought with it a certain level of anxiety that Iman's many notes would be lost to precipitous weather. However, he had no other place to keep the journal from discovery. The ground gave the best disguise when he was away from his tent tending to the defensive positions. The small rat hole he dug beneath his bedroll served him well, but he continually got the feeling that his luck was nearing its end.

Iman made up his mind. He and Hasim had gained more than enough knowledge to justify the destruction of the village. The only person worth saving was the barren-bellied woman who watched Iman's every move. However, killing her would give her the peace she needed to finally rest. Iman ached at the idea of taking life from the woman he had grown to love from afar. She was as much a part of his day as the sun. Seeing her eyes beyond her veiled face became Iman's reason to wake in the morning. Her long burqa could not shroud her from his want. Yet he thought it merciful to bring her a swift death, an end that he knew she prayed for every day and night.

Asr came and went. The late afternoon prayer was done. Then Rasa followed Iman across camp. They exchanged glances, silently connecting in affection and lust. She walked at his pace as to observe him and report back as tasked. It was her front, her ruse of sorts. She really walked at his pace to watch him, to be with him.

Iman's feelings for Rasa, equally bright in an emotional flame, kept him walking slower and slower as days passed. He did what he could to prolong his time with her distant company. Her eyes told of her beauty. Iman wished he could know her completely, beyond her scars and into the depths of her being. He never held such want, such desire for anything or anyone before. At his very core he knew that Allah had put Rasa in his life so that he would know love amidst hatred. The knowledge made Iman ache at the thought of how empty his life would be without Rasa, his nosy spy, the object of his undying affection.

Rasa turned from the edge of camp and went back for her report to Farhad. Iman had done nothing unusual, but she was going to advise Farhad of what he already knew. She dared not suffer another beating if she could avoid it altogether. She hoped that Farhad would only push her away with his foot rather than kick her from his path.

Iman looked back over and over until he could no longer see Rasa disappearing into the tents. Once she was gone from him, he focused his efforts on getting to Hasim. The many days prior had gone to silent exchanges between them. He decided that their next exchange would not be the same. Iman refused to allow another dominant silence means for further impediment in communication between him and his brother.

The older Marine reached Hasim's defensive position as the sun's bottom edge met jagged mountaintops. Snow covered the ground and little protected either man from the harsh elements of winter. Iman watched as Hasim crawled out of a shallow-set grave where a machine gun and watchman rested at the camp's perimeter. Hasim was cold, distant, and quiet. He had been alone for a full day and should have been eager to discuss prior events with his brother. Yet he was removed from his surroundings, from his reality, from his family.

Iman assumed that Farhad would not dare stand out in a winter chill to watch the brothers' exchange. Hasim made no effort to resist as Iman shoved his way into the hole. The space was tightly confined but provided room for movement. Iman looked into his brother's face and no longer recognized Hasim.

"Hasim." Iman shook his brother. Hasim was jarred awake. He seemed to come out of a coma to the familiar sound of his brother's voice. "Hasim, it's time," Iman announced through chattering teeth. "It's time," he repeated.

The light returned in Hasim's eyes. Iman watched as his brother and closest friend returned to him. Hasim, the Marine, rolled his shoulders back and sat up anew. "What do you mean?" he questioned, ignorantly amused. Hasim acted as if he had forgotten his purpose there.

"It's time for us to get out of here, brother." Iman's hands dug into Hasim's shoulders with excitement. They were both eager to leave the place that held so much deceit and danger. "But it rests on you, Hasim." The happiness in Iman's voice faded to coach Hasim with a more serious tone.

The air thickened between them before Iman continued. "Go to Farhad and ask for a mission. He trusts you. He will give you a task...probably to blow yourself up. Make sure that you do not accept the task if I'm not included. Make sure that he tells us both to go...together." Iman watched as Hasim's eyes went distant once again.

Iman wasn't sure if Hasim was freezing to death or if he was so far removed from reality that the Marine struggled to continue. "Brother! Do you know what day it is?" Iman asked. Hasim just shrugged. Iman laughed, "It's Christmas!" Iman chuckled at the notion of two Islamic terrorists wishing each other a Merry Christmas. However, Iman's real intentions were to remind his brother that they were not Islamic terrorists. They served no purpose of jihad. They had no business among murderers but to destroy evil men.

Iman looked into his brother's eyes. He smiled and silently begged for Hasim to come back to him. "It's Christmas," Iman said, reminding Hasim of the American Christian tradition they loved as kids and fought to protect as men.

Iman could not hold back his tears when Hasim answered, "Well, then...Merry Christmas, Marine."

Hasim returned to his mission. He found the steadfastness he had buried in the desolation of being a terrorist. He was back and he understood what he must do. He must beg Farhad for a call to jihad, for Hasim and his brother to carry out the will of Allah. Then he had to betray the village he embraced so blindly only moments before. The Marine was back on duty and the brother returned home in war.

# RAHAB

Fear shook Iman's entire body with a trembling shiver as he knelt inside his tent. The ends of his fingers were worn into raw meat as he clawed at the earth. He hoped that some fit of exhaustion had forced him to bury his journal deeper than normal. He hoped he had simply forgotten how deeply concealed it was in the soil. He scratched at loose dirt and rock until he reached ground too packed, too hardened, for his sore fingers. Hope was lost.

Freshly turned topsoil sat in a mound around a small hole where the corner of his pallet and bedroll normally lay. Panic. Anguish. The burning in Iman's fingertips coursed up his arms and found its way into his chest. The physical pain of ripped flesh shifted into the tormented sorrow of a torn heart. The pressure of dirt crammed under Iman's fingernails became pressure inside his brain. Iman's every thought of inevitable demise yearned to be scratched free all at once. He closed his eyes, rolled his fists, and pressed his knuckles hard to each side of his aching head. Then he took a deep breath and exhaled the panic from his soul. Acceptance.

His identity would soon be revealed to the village. The camp would soon know Iman as a wolf in sheep's clothing, or more so a shepherd among wolves. Hasim, his only brother, was certainly set to die by his side. Iman tried not to cry at the thought of having failed, having led to his brother's beheading. He fought back tears for his mother. He held onto pride for his father. He shook his head for Command.

Iman's thoughts raced back and forth. *Maybe Hasim moved it before he left for his shift. Maybe I dropped it and forgot to bury it. Maybe Hasim destroyed it. Maybe Farhad will relieve us of our burdened heads.*

The thought forced a chill down Iman's spine. He was not afraid of death. Had he been afraid to travel into Paradise, he would have never accepted the suicide mission from McKenzee. Rather, he was afraid for Hasim. He was afraid that his little brother had strayed too far from faith and had been routed to hatred by enemy vessels. Iman hoped against hate, prayed for his brother, and ached to beat Farhad before Farhad had a chance to strike first.

Maghrib. Exalted tones bellowed from a broken voice through whipping cold winds. The top of the sun was disappearing behind the crest of western mountains. Iman had to push beyond the pain, past his scraped fingers, and move his things back into place. He had to do it quickly as to not be late for prayer. He had to hurry despite the fact his identity was compromised. Iman had to maintain that he was not the man who had written detailed logs of information in American English. He needed to keep his alternate identity, his terrorist self that was ready to detonate a bomb in a schoolyard. *Maybe I'm just exhausted and confused. Maybe I'm not digging in the right place. I have to hurry.*

The seconds needed to return his tent to usual order lasted through the entire first breath of prayer. He nearly dove out of his canvas prison, timing his fall to the last man kneeling east. Iman fell in line unnoticed. He successfully hid the turmoil inside his tent though nothing was left to be found other than his bedroll, pallet, and the smeared bucket serving as a makeshift toilet.

He should have been praying. He should have been begging. The sunset prayer was rushing along according to nature's quick schedule. Iman would find no protection in the period of worship. The worried man had every reason to want more time. He had even greater cause to call out to Allah. Someone held his journal. Every page of the small book gave evidence of his mission. His long hair and bearded face could no longer hide the fact that he was a United States Marine, sent by the Pentagon, to cut the head off a poisonous serpent. He should have prayed, but he knelt and waited for the snake to finally bite.

*They wouldn't kill me between prayers. That would be too outrageous even for these maniacs. I, at least, have until Ishah before Farhad sends someone for me. I wonder if he will have the guts to do it himself, or will he have one of his minions do it... What if she will do it?* Iman's calls to Allah were disrupted by his fear and innermost worries.

Iman's mind fluttered from fear and made way to Rasa. He contemplated his infatuation with her. Then he realized that Farhad was never able to break Iman's spirits, faith, or dedication to his true mission. None of the brainwashing and physical torment got to Iman. He was too stubborn and devout, too bound to truth, and too strong for Farhad to infiltrate with venomous messages. Iman assumed Farhad held a great deal of inability to use any weapon against the Marine's patriotic devotion until he realized Rasa was the weapon.

*That's it. She was my weakness. That dog used her to get to me... and I let him. She batted her eyes at me...and I fell for it. I let my guard down and she caught me...*

Iman ground his teeth as he thought wildly of what was to come. His body swayed as he mumbled his mantras of praise. Then his mind absently eased into his final decision. *She's with Farhad tonight. She is his wife and should be. However, if I'm not killed tonight...I will make sure she dies with me tomorrow.*

He stewed on the notion for a moment before reversing his anger at Rasa. He realized little else could be expected of the woman. Hasim, a well-trained and extremely strong Marine, was nearly broken by Farhad's indoctrinations. Rasa had endured a lifetime of the elder's abuse and misuse of religion, weapons, and people. Then Iman considered his previous ideas of vengeance and cursed himself. It was his duty to forgive his transgressors. Seeking revenge and yearning to kill a messenger made him like them. He knew, in the fibers of his being, he was nothing like them. He would never be like them.

The call to prayer ended and Iman had only begun to pray. He begged for forgiveness. He pleaded for absolution from the thoughts and feelings that betrayed him and his faith. His body went through the motions of standing and moving away from the common area, but his thoughts stayed with Allah. His mind and heart screamed for forgiveness until his eyes burned with unshed tears. His breaths became short in an effort not to sob. He prayed through the anguish of guilt. He prayed until he became calm.

"Iman!" Farhad's boisterous voice called across the open area. The Marine, head high, turned to face his fate. Iman's heart stopped only long enough to know that it was broken and scared. He considered the idea of running from the leader. Iman knew that armed guards around camp would tear him to shreds with their Russian-made rifles. Well trained or otherwise, no man can outrun a bullet. He knew it to be true. He simply didn't want to give Farhad the satisfaction of a check mark in the proverbial win column. Terrorist-1, Marines-0. Iman snarled at the thought.

The broken man rolled his shoulders back. He inflated his chest with a full breath despite his shattered pride. He held his head high to meet demise head-on.

Iman walked across camp like an innocent man moving in front of a firing squad. He knew he had done nothing wrong, but he was going to die for his deeds nonetheless. Farhad waited.

"Yes, sir?" Iman questioned as he continued his cover, ignorant of any concern the old man might hold. Farhad stood in the door of his large tent. Iman still hated that the "servant of Allah" served himself first, well enough to ensure he had the nicest dwelling in the village. The old man's tent was the only one in the village with a vent hole in the top, so it was the only one with a fire at the center. Farhad and his several wives, including Rasa, would remain warm through the harsh night. The rest of the village faced a possibility of being frozen to death. The men on defense would suffer far more than their leader through the snow and wind. Iman tried to avoid an arrogant grin. *This devil is no different from the fat cats on the Hill. The only real difference is they aren't as willing as Farhad to murder civilians.* His thoughts returned him to anger and turmoil.

Iman stood in the silence of Farhad's stare. Farhad stayed quiet long enough for Rasa to catch Iman's attention from inside the tent. She tossed a log onto the increasing flame at the center of the structure and stoked the fire for more warmth. Then she glanced at Iman through the open flap at the entrance. The weak doorway was nearly blocked by her husband's wide robes. Iman's face was lit by the fire, and she could see him glare. She looked back at him like a child who had just tattled on a sibling. Rasa tried to pretend that she didn't know why the Marine was in trouble.

Rasa, seemingly ashamed, looked away from Iman's stare. Iman broke his attention from her and returned it to Farhad. The old man inhaled just enough to posture himself above the subor-dinate jihadist. Then the leader asked, "Are you and Hasim of the same faith?"

The spy was not sure how he should answer. He could not deci-pher Farhad's intentions behind the inquiry. Iman was ultimately confused by the question. Does Farhad want to know if Hasim is also an American spy, or if we are of equal military character? He wasn't certain if the old man was asking about their mutual devo-tion to Islam or simply staging a philosophical question without blatant accusation. He has the book. He knows who we are. Why won't he just kill us and call it a day?

"Yes, sir. We are of the same faith," Iman answered with a lump in his throat. Then another long pause filled the air between the two men. Farhad looked away from Iman and gazed into the direc-tion where Hasim stood watch. Iman looked at the ground and collected his thoughts. He refused to surrender. Then he glared hard at the old man, almost challenging Farhad for control.

The elder spoke plainly, "Then tomorrow you will go with him." Farhad was vague. He left questions racing through Iman's imagination. The old man spoke ambiguously and gave up no further information. He simply placed his hands on Iman's shoul-ders, looked the younger man in the eyes, and spoke again. "Rest well, my friend, for soon you will be in Paradise."

The false prophet's final words to Iman left nothing to the imagination. Iman and Hasim were set to die. However, the Marine was still left with questions. If Farhad knew their true iden-tities, then he did well to hide his hand.

Iman knew that the plan had been to die. He and Hasim were either going to be killed in the line of duty, killed in an incidental raid by the United States Army working in the area, or killed on a mission set by the fake imam. Yet he stood amazed at Farhad's words. Iman was just informed that he would either be executed alongside his brother, or they would be sent into the world to die for the cause. Either case would go unanswered for the time being.

Farhad stepped into his tent and closed the flap behind him. Iman was left standing in the open courtyard of the camp. The young man was flabbergasted at the idea of being murdered by the very people he aimed to kill. His every instinct told him to run to Hasim's position and make a break for the open desert. He assumed they could surrender to the first Allied troops they happened upon and make it back home after some arduous journey through the course that prisoners of war must endure. Then he considered the fact that he had no records in any system at the Department of Defense. He and Hasim had been removed by the CIA for the sake of plausible deniability. They would not be allowed to contact McKenzee until they reached Guantanamo Bay as actual prisoners. There, the brothers would be killed by the other detainees, whom they had betrayed several times over. There was nowhere left to go other than back to his tent. He would have to wait until morning to find out what Farhad had in mind for the spies.

Iman returned to the darkness of his dwelling. Cold winter winds licked at the bottoms of the canvas walls. He hated that his last night alive would be spent in such a place, but he accepted the reality of his situation. He was relieved that he would, at least, die next to his brother with honor and pride. Their suffering would soon end.

Iman sat wrapped in his bedroll and let his mind continue to swirl. Very little time passed between Maghrib and Ishah. He was once again summoned to the outside of his tent. He bowed east and prayed. Unlike the time before, he actually prayed. He made his peace with Allah and readied his spirit to move on. He longed for the mercy of death that would settle his misery. Then the prayer finished and allowed him to return to the torments of his lonely thoughts.

Restless and exhausted, the spy tossed back and forth into the night. He had no idea what time it was, but he knew that the onset of morning was coming whether he was able to sleep or not. He forced his eyes to close. He slowed his breathing down. He dared not sleep as to not dream of what was to come. Instead, he meditated. Iman calmed himself enough to finally drift into an accidental rest. His mind did not shut down, but he was able to distract himself enough. The weight of his eyelids won in his battle against fatigue.

The alarm clock known to the village as *Fajr* screamed into Iman's tent. He jolted awake as if his feet had been plugged into an electric socket. He had not been assassinated sometime in the night. He was breathing and was not covered in blood. His slumber began and ended peacefully. Iman smiled to the new day and thanked Allah for his ability to wake one more time.

Alert to the still-dark tent, Iman allowed his eyes to adjust. He looked around, hoping not to find anyone else in the swaying structure. He knew he should have been more present through the night, but he figured that he would be best served to die having rested properly.

His eyes refocused to dimly cast early morning twilight. The sun was about to rise, cascading its glow into the lower sky. Early slivers of ambient illumination flicked beneath the bottom of his tent, and Iman saw the shadow of a rectangle on the floor. His blood turned to thick lava pulsing through every vein in his body. Burning relief soared into him as he saw his journal lying on the ground next to his pallet. Iman realized that he had fallen into a deeper sleep than he realized. Someone was able to move in, undetected by his normal state of awareness, and slide the journal under the edge of his tent while he slept.

Iman grabbed the book, frantically hoping that he and Hasim were preserved as jihadists rather than exposed as American warriors, expendable spies. It was still too dark for him to read, but he smiled at the journal's return. He smiled until he considered the calculated maneuver accomplished during the night. Someone had taken the journal, surely read it, and returned it in clandestine fashion. Someone was ultimately letting Iman know that his identity was discovered and he would soon die. Relief was replaced once again with panic.

Pre-sunrise calls to prayer were often the loudest of the day. Religious rites and practices were a superior duty to Allah, even beyond the natural duty to sleep. The village stirred and made their way out of their tents. People took their places to pray. Then the top of the sun welcomed them into the day, shedding just enough light for Iman to thumb through the journal inside his tent. He was not concerned with being late to prayer. Farhad already told him he was going to die, so he didn't bother with the thought of punishment if he missed a moment's worship.

The sunlight peeked into the flap of Iman's tent as the journal pages flicked under his thumb. He was elated that none of the pages were missing or marked. Then a small piece of paper fell from the center of the book. The scrap was folded only once, just enough to make it thicker than the other pages. Iman would not have been able to miss it.

He looked around and bent over to pick up the paper. Iman squinted in the dim light and whispered the simple words, inscribed in rushed and swooping Arabic script: "Please spare me. Rasa."

Iman's heart fluttered and his stomach twisted into jittery knots. He was right in his previous assumptions. Rasa had seen him bury and unearth the journal. She knew where it was and how she should get it back to Iman. He considered that she had not given the information to Farhad, but used the book as a way to reach out to him. He assumed she could not read or write in English, but she was able to deduce that the American was in camp for a purpose greater than that of blowing up some random market.

The young man smiled like a boy happily lost in the midst of courtship. Farhad may have beaten and raped Rasa for a lifetime, but he never broke her. The fact that she was able to write a message of hope, a plea for mercy, was enough to let Iman know that Rasa was alive. Her spirit was steadfast. She learned to read and write despite Farhad's overbearing domination of her physically. The old bastard was not able to poison her mind or her heart. She wanted nothing of the fundamentalist movement or the place where it was held. Rasa wanted out, and she found that possibility in Iman. He was her escape in fantasy and in hope.

Iman smiled with absolute joy. He silently swore to Rasa that he would get her out, break the chains binding her in slavery, before the village was laid to waste. He prayed and vowed as he moved his belongings to the side and buried the journal once again. He buried the note from Rasa as well, first into the folds of the journal before he placed it into the earth. Then he turned to join in public prayer and continued to smile. He no longer doubted his feelings for Rasa. He no longer thought of her as Farhad's weapon against him. The source of his infatuation became his drive to love.

# REASON

"I man!" Farhad called across the open courtyard of camp. Whipping winds swirled thick licks of snow against everyone standing outside of their tents. Iman wondered how Hasim was holding up in the flurried edge of a snowstorm, hoping the best for his brother.

Iman, with his face wrapped and his hands covered in shreds of cloth, turned to the older man. He made no attempt to yell back to Farhad in acknowledgment of the boisterous summons. Rather, he crunched his boots through piling snow. A deep line of footprints trailed the spy until they faded to wind and falling flakes.

The young man arrived at the zealot's tent. His approach was choppy in movement, slow in pace. Harsh winter weather impeded Iman's ability to move from his tent to the next with any form of grace. His feet sloshed and slipped. The wind did all it could to knock Iman off balance. Snow and ice stung his skin. Yet his heart was warm.

Marines, in any clime and place, will take their fight to the enemy. Iman and Hasim were men bred and forged from generations of warriors. However, previous warrior generations took to fighting head-on. They charged Belleau Wood. They raised the flag on Suribachi. They seized Hue City. They liberated Baghdad. The brothers, each regretful, were not able to share the same glory of confronting foes in direct combat.

In the spirit of their predecessors, Iman and Hasim would have preferred to move in with tanks and close-air support. They would have preferred to exchange rounds with the enemy. Yet Hasim sat freezing in a hole dug by his opposition, and Iman was preparing himself to ignore the onslaught of garbage spewed forth by a false cleric. Iman hated the people with whom he lived. He hated them because they hated his desire to live free. He hated them for their desire to kill innocents. He hated them because they misused and abused the Koran to serve their selfish purposes. He wanted to kill them all; all but one.

Iman tried to stay subtle as he looked around Farhad. He attempted to sneak a glimpse of his heart's center, but she was among Farhad's several other wives. She was buried in the struggled warmth of the large tent. Farhad's body occupied what little space he needed to present himself through the front canvas flap.

Had the old man possessed more manners in his awful soul, he would have invited Iman in from the cold. He would have given the younger man refuge from the storm slapping at Iman's appendages. Iman ached while he waited for Farhad to say something worthwhile. Instead, Farhad launched into his usually slobbered sermon before attempting to make a point based in a skewed rationale. Iman, covered with fresh snow and hardly suited for the cold, finally had enough of the old man's drivel.

"Pardon me, Farhad," Iman said, holding his hands up in half surrender. He interrupted the elder and knew that he held no established place to do so. Iman had broken in with his voice and silently begged for forgiveness with his open palms. "I'm freezing.

Is this something that can be discussed inside or be held until a time where I can feel my fingers?" Iman tried to be coy, but the gesture was not accepted. Farhad's face never changed from the resolute and stern gaze he held over Iman.

Farhad was either defiant of the interruption or so narcissistic that he thought his words were not affected by the cold, but he continued his sermon without consideration of Iman's request. He seemed to add lines and new misinterpretations to scripture. The old man spoke until Iman interrupted again. "Get to the point so I can go back to my tent and try to warm up," Iman barked over Farhad's nonsense. Such an act was unheard of in the village. It never occurred to the rest of the movement members that they could address their leader with blatant disregard, disdain, and disrespect.

Before Iman's bold barrage, Farhad was regarded and respected as the final authority on any and all things in *Jericho,* as the village was unofficially named in initial mission briefings at the Pentagon. Even still, Iman turned to walk away from Farhad's tent. The young man's insubordinate tone was answered with a belligerent silence. Farhad made it very clear that he was delaying his discussion with Iman because of the younger man's insulting behavior.

The veritable back-and-forth between enemy warriors nearly ended as Iman took his first step in the opposite direction of Farhad. "We can apparently discuss it in the morning," Iman said over his shoulder, silently proclaiming a dose of finality in discourse.

Then the head rooster crowed into the whipping wind, "Allah has tasked you and your brother."

Iman stopped where he stood. His back was still to Farhad. Iman half expected to be shot between his shoulder blades as he turned away from enemy hatred. He knew that defiance and insubordination were punishable by death, but Iman had nothing to lose. Farhad had already informed the brothers that they would soon be in Paradise. Iman saw no reason to prolong his misery. He was either set to die quickly at the hands of a less-than-worthy foe, or he was going to die in the commission of a terror attack. Either way, the young Marine had no intentions of freezing to death while waiting on some arrogant ass to blubber through guidance and direction.

Farhad continued, "Do not relieve Hasim today. I will send another to his post. When he is in, both of you come to me. We will pray together and I will give you instructions. Tomorrow, you will achieve your goals and move into the promised lands." The old man's breath froze in cold blasts of white fog as he spoke.

Mumbled gibberish fell from Farhad's lips, but Iman was elated to know that he had been tasked to carry out a suicide bombing mission. Farhad had not yet informed Iman of his purpose. However, several months in camp let Iman know the true nature of the village. The intelligence he gathered through conversations and observations led him to believe that all present were set to have explosives strapped to their chests. Every man, woman, and child was susceptible to Farhad's whim. He could point his crooked finger to any member of the camp and send a jihadist off to certain death. He could send them off to cause the certain death of many innocent people as well. The severity of damage was only contingent upon how many explosives the terrorists were able to obtain at any given time.

Farhad, unwilling to truly sacrifice for his cause, was the most cowardly man among the villagers. He was the only man in the camp falsely endowed with the powers of Allah. He picked and chose who would go and who would stay. He selected who would die and who would live. Yet he never made the choice to go himself. He always sent others to die for him. Even still, he was viewed as a glorious leader for his conspiracies to commit murder.

Despite several atrocious instances, like sending teenaged girls to bomb-laden deaths, Farhad was still viewed as a leader blessed with genius military strategies and an uncanny ability to speak directly with Allah. The old man had the collective village fooled by his masquerade of faith and devotion. He had everyone eating soiled oats from the palm of his hand, everyone but Iman and Hasim.

Iman was sickened by the jihadist headman and his antics of leadership. The Marine tried not to unveil his emotions for the sake of accomplishing his primary mission. However, he had watched as his brother started to slip away from faith and allegiance. He had listened to the reports of the villagers "successfully" detonating themselves in markets. He had seen what Farhad held with such blatant disregard, and Iman could not help but want what Farhad had. More so, Iman wanted the company of the woman Farhad favored the least among his wives. Iman hated the old man with every amplified moment that dragged on within the confines of camp. Yet he was intrigued by the elder's words of announcement.

The Marine faced the cult leader. Hastily wrapped strips of cloth enveloping Iman's face began to loosen, and snow immediately clung to his beard. His long hair was tucked tight into his turban. The burliness of hair and beard provided Iman very little protection against the need to shiver in the snowstorm. He loathed the presence of the extra hair and yearned to get back into military regulation. All the while, he was grateful to have the slightest shield against the stinging sleet.

Snow-covered and frostbitten, Iman stared at Farhad. The elder was done speaking, and Iman acknowledged the conversational pause. "What is the task?" Iman did not ask for guidance. Rather, he demanded elaboration.

Iman's curiosity would have to go unanswered. Farhad had no intentions of answering any questions without Hasim present.

The older brother would have to sit in his tent and remain in a state of standby until Hasim returned from the outer defensive position. Farhad could have answered enough to ease obvious concern, but Iman's defiant posture was not to go unpunished. The old man was already sending Iman to die, so lashing the youthful pride out of a rigid body would have been to no avail. Farhad knew that anticipation, the not knowing, was torture enough to fulfill his need for revenge.

Farhad grinned. Iman noticed the corners of Farhad's mouth turn upward under his frost-kissed beard. He wondered what might have amused the senior to such a mild degree.

The elder rudely stepped out of the cold and left Iman unanswered yet again. Iman grit his teeth and considered the idea of challenging the old man to a fistfight. He refrained. Rather than expedite his death warrant, Iman turned away once more. He trudged in concession through mounting wet piles of white. His feet plunged into the slop of snow and mud. His steps slipped unnaturally wide as the frozen and stubborn precipitation refused to stick to the ground. The air was frigidly crisp, but the ground resisted the weather's hateful decline into a saturated cold.

The young man walked back to his tent, the horrible place he had come to know as home. He tucked his chin against his chest in a feeble effort to evade the cold. Then he breached the entry to his canvas domicile. Iman shook tremendously to get the snow off his body but achieved very little success in warming his appendages.

Inside his abode was warmer than the open air. Even the flapping walls prevented fast winds from whipping at him further, and for that he was thankful. However, the tent was still cold enough for Iman to see his breath. *Blowing myself up might be a lot better than freezing to death,* Iman joked to himself simply to try and beat back at the frost with his warm spirit.

Iman attempted to figure out how much time he had before he would see his brother again. He calculated the hours by prayer time, by a sentry's walking travel time toward the defensive position from camp to relieve Hasim, and by Hasim's walk back from the armed perimeter. *Five hours.* Iman ran the figure through his brain over and over until it became a mere four hours. *Give or take some time for the snow, he'll be in soon enough.* Iman paced and rubbed at his arms to stay warm. He kept himself company with his thoughts and chattered mumblings.

He was four hours from seeing his brother. He would welcome Hasim with a hug and look his younger brother in the eyes. The piercing cold had a way of sending icicles into the soul of a man. A man torn could quickly become a man shattered in the midst of a brutal snowstorm. Iman knew the treacherous woes of having to endure self despite wind, sleet, and snow. Iman wanted to know that Hasim had not splintered from himself once again. The older sibling wanted to be certain that Hasim was ready to kill the real enemy rather than a soft target designated by a monster.

The inside of Iman's tent gave just enough protection from the painful cold. He was able to force blood back into his fingertips. His sense of smell had not returned, but his vision and hearing were returned to near normal condition. His eyes no longer blurred as he regained focus. The ringing in his ears faded to a dull throb until he could hear his heartbeat just above ambient noise. He paced, back and forth, seeking only to remain warm against low temperatures.

"Brother?" Hasim called from the front flap as a gust of harsh winter breezed into the tent. Iman considered the possibility of passing time, but four hours could not have disappeared so quickly. The cold slowed everything down, including time. Yet Hasim stood in the doorway of the tent despite Iman's calculations.

The older Marine shivered but stood with a smile. He welcomed Hasim as planned. Iman embraced his brother. Then he inspected Hasim's spirits.

Iman looked into Hasim's eyes. He observed the younger man's movements and actions. He listened to what Hasim had to say about any given subject. Then Iman announced, "Farhad has tasked us for a mission."

The older brother spoke in a way that illustrated his assumptions about Hasim. Iman presumed Hasim was not aware of the duty, but the younger of the two reacted without pause. "I know, man. Farhad told me yesterday morning. I went to him and asked for a mission the way you told me to. He tried to send me off as a lone warrior, but I told him that I wouldn't go without you..." Hasim lowered his head. The younger Marine could feel his brother's questioning judgment blazing through him. Then Hasim looked up as his confidence and dedication returned. "I'm fine, man. I don't know where I went"—Hasim referenced his slip into the idealism and extremism of *Jericho* —"but I'm back. I'm with you." The younger man nodded to the front flap of the tent. "We're going to handle this mess...then I'm going home. I've had enough."

Hasim's reference to *home* was beyond the war. He had been dealt all that he could handle. He'd had enough of the enemy. He'd had enough of the Central Intelligence Agency using him as a tool of destruction. He'd had enough of serving the ideals of freedom and wanted to start living them.

Iman nodded. He knew that Hasim was right. They would have to finish their mission for country and Corps. Then, once their mission was complete, they would be able to return home. They would be able to go back into their worlds prior to war. Each of them loved being a Marine, but they had not been given a chance to serve as Marines for the majority of their enlistments.

They were used as spies at every turn, and each man lamented the closeness of the enemy. Each would have preferred to engage and destroy vermin from a distance. Yet they were face-to-face, living among their foes in Guantanamo and Afghanistan.

Once the Marines finished their chore for the CIA, they would have to go back home. Killing the enemy tasted of familiarity and human meat. Neither Iman nor Hasim had the taste for blood they had acquired through all their many days in training. They had lived among brainwashed adversaries for too long. They were given an opportunity to meet the infantry of the other side. No warrior should be provided such an occasion as it only creates pause in trigger pull. The monsters they knew to be the opposition suddenly had faces. They had mothers and fathers, sisters and brothers, children of their own. They had lives and souls, no matter how rotten. The enemy seemed to be waiting, unaware of their yearning to be plucked from the war.

Iman and Hasim would have to escape from the camp only to come back and kill people they knew intimately. Their acute knowledge of the enemy made an attack feel like an act of betrayal rather than that of completion. The Marines had to coach themselves away from humanizing their opposition. They had to forget names and family ties. They had to become ready to destroy the people they were always meant to kill.

Hasim pumped his fists against the cold air inside the tent. Iman wrapped himself in everything he could find to get away from the bitter chill. Then Hasim quietly huffed, "We aren't going to be armed when they send us. They wouldn't want us to change our minds at the last minute." Iman nodded, realizing that his little brother had gained a bit of wisdom about the group of terrorists over their extended stay in "Hotel Hell." Their escorts would be carrying pistols or rifles. They would carry Russian surplus handguns with no more ammunition than half a magazine's worth of bullets, or AK-47 assault rifles with so much ammunition they wouldn't have to worry about spraying carelessly until they hit something. The Marines hated every facet of each thought that ran through their minds. They hated the terrorist mentality. Well-trained and well-aimed Marines sought precision engagement at all turns. Their enemy sought to destroy targets with no regard for collateral damage. Iman and Hasim would be subjected to the direction of the escorts without any ability to resist, and defiance would come with as much collateral damage as needed to end the brothers' war.

Hasim and Iman knew that the enemy was brave behind an AK-47 aimed at paper targets and empty fuel drums. However, they turned into weak-kneed cowards when time came for them to fulfill their explosive duties. Suicide bombers, set to die in a blast of metal and fire, still had to be escorted by armed guards. Leaders like Farhad and many others had to force *soldiers* into carrying out their *sacred duties*. Yet the old man showed no suspicions as to why Hasim had approached with an eager emphasis requesting an attack order. Farhad didn't question Hasim's desire to die next to his brother either. The old man was just happy to have two eager soldiers at his behest. He would be able to sentence Iman and Hasim to death. The lead terrorist knew that they were willing to go without remorse or regret. He could send them under minimal escort. Little resources would be used to get them into place, and the village would suffer little more than the loss of two defenders in their absence.

Hasim pointed to the front flap of the tent. "Watch the door." Iman moved to the forward portion of the tent without questioning his brother's motives. Hasim offered explanation: "Knowing these idiots, they are going to give some load of garbage before we pray together one last time. Then the guys with guns are going to take us away before we have a chance to arm ourselves or get our stuff. So..." Hasim paused to look around. He slid Iman's bedroll away from the pallet where it lay and stomped hard into the middle of a pallet slat. A long shard of old wood splintered into a sharp staff. Hasim picked the shard up and shoved it into the top of his boot. Then he covered the top of the makeshift weapon with the bottom of his pants.

Hasim left the bedroll to the side and moved the pallet. "You need to find somewhere to put this," the younger Marine said, pointing to the ground. Iman knew that Hasim was referencing the secret journal but was not sure if the younger man knew about the note from Rasa. Iman wasn't certain as to how much Hasim knew about the older brother's time in camp. Iman never intentionally hid his feelings for Rasa from his brother. He merely thought that emotions would serve as nothing more than deeply engrained distractions that could compromise their mission. Therefore, he made no mention of how Rasa had drawn his heart into the war. He never spoke of feelings and love, for Marines are to fight without such human responses. They were dogs of war let loose to wreak a promised havoc upon the enemy. They were to carry out any mission, at any time, at any cost up to and including their lives with a smile on their faces and blood on their hands. They were United States Marines. They were Spartans, if Spartans had been better organized and even more eager to fight. There was no room for emotions on their battlefield. Iman continued such military mantra and did all he could to curb his infatuation for Rasa. He fought himself just to continue serving others before he tried to serve himself.

"Do you love her?" Hasim asked quietly as he traded places with Iman. Iman didn't answer. No confusion or concern remained.

Hasim had seen the note from Rasa and knew that Iman was smitten with the woman. The younger brother wondered if Iman would be willing to jeopardize their mission in an effort to save the woman. He questioned Iman's ability to resist humanity and bring destruction to the tents where love hid within storms of fire.

"She's going to die, man...with the rest of them," Hasim said, reinforcing Iman's fears. The young Marine continued, "They're all going to die." Iman still didn't speak up. He just unearthed the journal and the note from Rasa. Iman seemed to ignore Hasim's plea to reason. Then he lowered his pants and used strands of fabric to secure the information while Hasim stood watch at the tent's flap. Iman tied it uncomfortably tight to his inner thigh. The frozen leather bindings of the journal sent chills through his body before he returned his pants to his waist. Iman looked to his brother for some sign that Rasa could be saved from the hell that was sure to come. Hasim offered no reassurance. There was nothing he could say or do to save the woman from her certain fate.

Iman solemnly covered the slight hole in the ground as if to cover a shallow and symbolic grave. He returned the pallet to cover the freshly turned soil, and the hiding spot was once again shielded from immediate observation. They would soon be gone from the place, but they still needed to hide their identity. Iman placed his bedroll back into normal order and looked to Hasim for an answer yet again. There was no reply to give. Hasim lowered his head sadly and asked, "Are you ready?"

Iman nodded and they exited the tent. Hasim stepped into the biting cold of the mountain air. His older brother followed, and they walked across the open courtyard together. Each man was bound for the outside of Farhad's tent. They walked unaccompanied by anyone else in *Jericho*.

Had their call to jihad come in the midst of summer, the sanctimonious prayers and sermons would have been held in the open.

However, whipping snow and howling winds beckoned the village to the front of Farhad's tent. The Marines arrived first. Others took notice of their unspoken duties to the elder and joined them. People gathered from one tent to the next before they congregated in a shivered huddle.

Hasim fought off his want to snarl. *This maniac is no better than any other leader of any other force. He thinks he is so much more righteous than us Americans and the British. Yet he is the man with the most authority and possessions in the village. Therefore, he gets to call the shots, send people off to die, and we have to stand in the snow while he remains shielded from the storm inside his heated tent. My god, I wish I could kill him right now.* Hasim involuntarily twitched in the freezing weather, but his insides burned with hatred.

They prayed. The village surrounded Iman and Hasim. They collectively called to Allah and asked him to bless the journey to come. As expected, Farhad ran his mouth without consideration for those frozen in misery. He reinforced the brainwashing of the villagers, using the secret Marines' willingness to die as support that all devout Muslims should be equally willing to follow in their steps. Unbeknownst to Farhad, Iman had strapped to his thigh the evidence that would be the village's undoing. Hasim, the more "devoted" of the brothers, was hiding a stabbing weapon in preparation of self-defense and self-preservation. They were no more willing or ready to die for the extremist cause than Farhad. The Marines were, however, willing to kill or die justly and honorably for a virtuous cause.

The counterfeit imam finally finished his blathering drivel of nonsense and repeated rhetoric. Then the crowd dispersed to seek shelter from the cold. Darkness was nearing and they wanted to regain some warmth before their next prayer. Everyone went to their respective tents except for Hasim and Iman. They were left standing in the empty courtyard. They continued to fight the wet air of winter.

Farhad stood over the men. He stared at them as they huffed and shivered in the cold. Each of them waited for one word from the others. Their breaths showed in foggy clouds of anticipation and discomfort.

Hasim kept his eyes locked on Farhad. The true jihadist, psychologically damaged and removed from reality, began to see himself as a god among men. His every order was obeyed. His followers clung to his every word. He influenced feeble people in a way that would be discouraged and pursued legally in the United States. All the while, he stood over two men who could not wait to be rid of the menace.

Rasa suddenly showed herself in the dimming light of the tent behind Farhad. The old man was so fixed on Hasim that he didn't notice Iman grinning into the small structure. No one other than Iman and Rasa were engaged in their slight exchange. For a second, only a fleeting speck in time, they were separated from the hatred of their worlds. They were together in a winter oasis, set in peace, and bound in yearning.

The young woman's face was veiled, but Iman could see the message in her eyes. He knew that she was crying for him, though she could not show her tears. He knew that she was smiling for him, but could not show her lips. Then Rasa committed an act punishable by death had anyone other than Iman seen her move. She waved her fingers lightly in a single, calm motion as to tell the Marine goodbye. She wished him well and prayed him safely along his journey. Then she turned away from the open area and disappeared into the dark corners of Farhad's tent.

Iman hoped and prayed that it would not be the last he saw of Rasa. He hoped to make her a widow. He wanted to rescue her from the place holding her captive. Something inside him boiled to make her his wife, to care for her, and to make sure she would never have to endure another day with Farhad or his kinsmen. Iman wanted to rip her away from the clutches of the hateful place, but he knew that mission priorities held more weight than personal wants. One person was not enough to thwart the American hammer from striking its crushing blow.

The Marines stood in the cold and watched as Farhad disappeared into his tent without another word. They looked at each other with surprise and caught a glimpse of why the old man retreated to warmth. Their armed escort had arrived.

"We must go down the mountain," the man ordered harshly. He was pointing an assault rifle at Iman. The Marines nodded. Down the mountain meant out of the snow. Snow would become sleet. Sleet would become rain. Every descending step down the mountain led to warmer temperatures, if only warmer by a degree at a time. No true need existed for Iman and Hasim to be escorted by armed guard. On the surface, they descended the mountain to pursue their jihadist-based mission. They walked into warmer temperatures ahead of a pointed rifle. The brothers were ordered out of the snow, and they were happy to oblige.

# DRIVEN

In a single moment, Hasim unconsciously reassured Iman that he had returned to the right side of the fight. Hasim's usual snarky demeanor came back to life as he placed the end of his index finger into the barrel of an assault rifle. He playfully plugged the end of the weapon as if his finger could prevent a shot from being expelled by the enemy escort. He jokingly pushed the man's aim away from center-mass.

"You really don't need to point that thing at us, brother," Hasim coaxed the weapon aside. "I promise you that we aren't going to resist getting out of the snow."

Hasim grinned widely to keep his nervousness hidden from plain view. Iman chuckled. The guard conceded. The man with the rifle just nudged them to face down the hill and walk. The guard did not have to ask twice for them to leave the mountain. It was all they could do to hide their eagerness. The Marines had to make a conscious effort not to sprint away from the village.

Iman smiled and slapped the back of his hand to Hasim's chest. He noticed a small car at the foot of the steep mountainside and pointed it out to his brother. They would not have to walk far before finding the refuge of heat inside the auto. The car and any idea of immediate warmth made Hasim snicker enthusiastically at the notion of getting into whichever available seat out of the rain.

The car was a pebble, a speck of nothing in their broad view of the desert. The men had to walk for nearly an hour before they could make out the true shape of the vehicle. It was a four-door sedan settled into the side of a desert road. Each of the Marines considered how lucky the driver was not to be observed by American snipers. Sharpshooters might have mistaken him for one who is set to bury roadside bombs, and he would have been an easy static target. Even still, they continued walking until the puffs of exhaust at the rear of the car became visible.

Hope for heat became the catalyst for their speed. The young men were actually Marines, so they had an unnatural ability to move quickly through open terrain. The wind still whipped against them. Snow had given way to a bitter, stinging rain. However, Iman and Hasim set a pace that the armed guard could not keep. The guard hollered out for the brothers to slow down, but they were determined to find their way into the safety of the car. More so, they were determined to get into the backseat without being obstructed. They would have the advantage of unrestricted attack positions unabated by their guard.

Iman arrived at the rear door on the driver's side. Hasim opened the door opposite to his brother at the rear right. They swung the car doors wide against piercing rain and startled the driver awake. Had the driver been armed, they would have likely been shot. They frightened him, triggering his instinctive urge to put to fight or take to flight. However, the man sitting behind the steering wheel was not holding a weapon. Therefore, the Marines remained without mortal wounds beyond their wet and frostbitten appendages.

"Where is Fa'iz?" the driver asked. The armed escort's location was of chief concern because he was not with Iman and Hasim, men he was supposed to force into the car. The Marines looked at each other and shrugged childishly. They were becoming arrogant and defiant in their exodus from enemy-held territory. Then Fa'iz, the escort, opened the right rear door of the car. He looked inside and saw that Iman and Hasim were already seated. The guard immediately yielded any advantageous position over the other jihadists. He was exhausted from tying to keep up with the brothers on their downhill hike away from camp.

The guard gave up at the sight of younger and stronger men occupying the car's rear seat. He turned and crawled into the front seat, huffing to catch his breath, with his rifle muzzle pointed downward. The end of his weapon was jammed under the bottom edge of the dashboard. His response to sudden resistance from the backseat would be delayed before becoming a matter of futility. The escort would only be able to shoot at the floor should any need to pull his trigger arrive. The unarmed driver was a proverbial sitting duck.

Fa'iz, breathless and tired, slammed the car door out of frustration. He turned to curse the soon-dead soldiers for making him look foolish. All the men chattered their teeth, having battled against the cold, all except the driver. He chuckled at their plight and Fa'iz's eagerness to bicker with the condemned.

The driver shifted his rickety car into first gear and turned on the headlights as he pulled forward. Night had since fallen. They missed the evening call to prayer, but doing so seemed acceptable when moving to answer a higher calling to die. *I wonder if they skip prayer because they think they're going to be talking with Allah face-to-face,* Hasim joked silently to himself and let only the slightest smile curl at the corners of his mouth.

They drove into the desert night for an hour. No signs of civilization or life had come about in the sixty minutes' time. "Where are we going?" Iman asked, but no one answered. Iman then repeated the question, but staged the query in different form. "Are you allowed to tell us where we are going?" Again, he was answered with silence. However, Iman persisted. He wanted to know where their intended target was and who they were aiming to kill. "Guys, where are we going?" Iman's harsh Arabic tone presented the question with its intended sense of belligerence.

The guard had enough of Iman's inquisition and disposition. Fa'iz turned to Iman, just over his left shoulder, and answered, "You don't need to know where we are going. You just need to sit quietly and worry about obeying orders." The guard barked like a father irritated with his children on a road trip. Then he turned back to face the windshield once again.

Iman looked at Hasim and nodded. They had traveled far enough into the open desert that the car was well out of the camp's view. Fa'iz unknowingly had spit his last words on earth. Hasim, seated directly behind the guard, reached nonchalantly into the top of his boot. The younger brother withdrew the shank he had taken from Iman's former bedroll pallet. Undetected, Hasim reared back then crammed the point of the wood shard deep into the bottom of Fa'iz's skull. The splintered tip broke off, but Hasim was still able to stab forward through meat and spine.

The top of Fa'iz's head snapped back with the force of the blow. Triangle-shaped wood ripped through the guard's brain stem. Every inch jammed flesh and organ further apart. The man's mouth opened to the wedge of wood being shoved through his spinal cord. Hasim gagged at the spit- and blood-covered atrocity splayed open by his hands. Then he twisted the spear to quickly finish the job.

Fa'iz's spinal cord was severed from the bottom of his brain. The fatally injured man did not twitch or stir. He blinked and gagged at the pressure of a wooden foreign object over his tongue. He choked on blood before his lungs and heart failed without communication to the man's brain. His every organ quit simultaneously. Fa'iz was no more.

Chunks of blood and tissue sprayed back onto Hasim before the driver could react. Gurgles preceded Fa'iz's last gasp just as the driver swerved in response to the attack. The man screamed out of confusion and fear as his friend was stabbed to death in the next seat over. Then Iman wrapped the crook of his elbow around the driver's throat and jerked upward. The driver's hands flew from the steering wheel in a desperate effort to claw for life. Every inch that the man fought for was taken from him as Iman wrenched with all his strength. Iman's elbow became the hangman's noose, stretching the driver's neck from his shoulders.

Time in camp, fatigue, and malnourishment had robbed Iman of his previous power. He was not able to break the man's neck to end a suffocating misery early. Instead, the driver's foot pressed hard onto the gas pedal and sent the car swerving in a large pattern over wet desert dirt. The driver tried to push his legs against the car's floor just to lengthen himself under Iman's pull. He tried to relieve the crushing pressure at his throat, but to no avail.

The driver's life faded with every constricting second that he was not able to take a breath, but the seconds it took to kill him seemed to drag on well into forever. A high rate of speed and erratic swerving were heading them toward an imminent crash if someone, anyone, was not able to regain control of the vehicle. Hasim realized the lurking dangers, and reacted.

Hasim reached over Fa'iz's limp body and pulled at the dead man's rifle. With lightning speed, the young Marine pointed a blood-splattered rifle muzzle at the side of the driver's head. He yelled, "Clear!" Iman reacted without hesitation. He knew that Hasim was telling Iman to move clear of an outgoing bullet. The driver was nearly strangled to his demise, but Iman released him anyway. Hasim buried the muzzle directly above the man's right ear. The jihadist escort was not able to regain full consciousness before Hasim pulled the trigger.

A high-velocity rifle bullet penetrated and exited the man's skull instantly. Sudden cranial decompression sprayed into a fountain of blood, brains, and bone fragments. The smell of death filled the car. Gunpowder, blood, and internal organs created a stink that gagged both living men. However, they had no time to react to any level of stench. The car was careening out of control at full tilt.

Iman took charge. He dove over the remnants of the driver's open head and slid through blood and gore. Inverted over the driver's body, Iman shoved the dead man's foot off the accelerator. Then he crammed both of his hands down hard on the brake. The car's tires nearly buried in the sand before the transmission choked to a gurgling halt.

Hasim recovered from the mental shock of killing for the first time. He reached forward and forced the shifter into the neutral position as the car slid to its awkward halt. They stopped safely, in the middle of an unknown desert location, having killed two militiamen. They knew that divine intervention was at the core of their survival. They were thankful.

Iman slithered backward until he was upright once again. He landed in the blood-pooled seat between two fatally wounded terrorists. Fa'iz, the dead escort, sat with a shard of wood protruding from the back of his head and through his mouth. His teeth bore down on the spike with an unnatural pressure originating at the base of his skull. The guard had a look of surprise and fear on his face lingering in death's presence. Iman then looked to his left and instantly regretted glancing in the direction of the driver. Nothing remained of the driver's skull or face. The bottom half of the man's head made a red-filled bowl of meat soup. He was no longer recognizable as human. That which held in place showed no signs of a man having just fought for a last breath.

Iman flinched away. His stomach churned, but not nearly as bad as Hasim's. The younger brother could not hold back at what they had just done. He flung open the rear door of the car and hurled himself into heavy desert rain. He hoped that water from the heavens would rinse him clean, but he knew better. He knew that no amount of water would cleanse him of this deed. Then the feeling became too much. Hasim doubled over and purged his hatred and fear. His stomach emptied in the burning sensation of war and turmoil. He ached and retched until his gut was void of any liquid or solid. Then he recovered with a long wipe of his lower lip against his wet sleeve.

The older Marine had since climbed over the dead to exit the small car. He grabbed the driver by the front of his shirt and jerked him clear of the front seat. Then he yelled over the still running auto at his brother, "Are you okay?" Hasim merely waved his hand as if to confirm he would be alright. Hasim didn't speak his answer right away because his throat still burned with bile and adrenaline.

Iman then sat in the driver's seat. The back of his pants slid against bloody and wet vinyl. He leaned across the car and opened the passenger door. He placed the flattest part of his boot to Fa'iz's ribcage and shoved outward. The dead man's upper body flopped hard to the ground at the passenger side of the car. Yet Fa'iz's feet had not cleared the door. Iman's hope to allow Hasim a means of avoidance was dismissed by the bottoms of Fa'iz's legs. The dead man held on just long enough to torment Hasim one last time.

Hasim recovered control over his gullet and turned back to the car. He wrenched his fists into the back of Fa'iz's jacket and pulled the man's body away from the open car door. The younger Marine joined his older brother in the front seat. He squished into place among enemy blood and brains. Avoidance was impossible against the slime that covered the transport's interior, so they swallowed hard and carried on.

"What do you think our best route will be?" Hasim asked as if they were two college kids on their first road trip away from home.

Iman answered with a shrug. Then he remembered. "McKenzee said just to head east if we broke loose." Iman inhaled hard and sighed, "So...I guess we go east. The only thing is...we don't know who's out here. We're probably going to run into some roadblocks. I'm really hoping we just get captured by American troops. Pointing our guys back to two dead jihadists will be a whole lot easier than admitting it to the other side."

They laughed and Iman threw the shifter into first gear. The transmission let out a quick grind to his lack of practice behind the wheel. The tires tore into saturated desert floor before regaining traction. Then the older brother barreled along a broken roadway with reckless abandon. He was not worried about preserving the vehicle's tires or engine. Farhad was expecting a report back about their successful detonation within a matter of days. They knew that such a detonation would not come. Therefore, they had to exit the area quickly and rejoin their unit before Farhad had any chance to uproot and move camp. Their time among the enemy would slip into a vain nothingness if they lost track of the camp, so Iman charged east. He drove the car as hard as it would go until he saw lights ahead of them on the road. Then he drove the engine to its maximum capability. The motor whined for a couple of hours before they found hope.

A young soldier, once defeated by the rain and wind, stood atop his post and came alive yet again. "Inbound! Inbound!" he screamed to the other watchmen on guard. The youthful and adrenaline-filled man readied his machine gun. Every soldier on duty gasped at the fast-approaching car.

Iman's expedited drive toward the guard post fit nearly all standard means of suicide bombers seeking to attack hardened military targets. The enemy charged in vehicles and detonated themselves on impact. They destroyed roadblocks and took as many casualties as possible, so American soldiers were on edge any time a fast-driven vehicle was headed their way.

On the other side of the coin, many people in-country simply drove like they had no cause for caution. Deciphering terrorists and average bad drivers in Afghanistan often proved to be difficult. An overwhelming inability to determine friend from foe was especially true on rain-drenched and cloud-darkened nights. To avoid killing potentially innocent people who held an affinity for the gas pedal, soldiers turned massive floodlights on approaching cars. Blaring brightness from the lamps was enough to blind any driver, so people not seeking to reach the post with an explosion would naturally stop. Those seeking to detonate would continue to drive despite the bright lights and would then be torn to pieces by machine-gun fire. Each of the soldiers on post had suffered the onslaught of fast-approaching cars. Several were unfortunate enough to have experienced a stop enforced by bullets. All were on hard-edged trigger fingers and willing to kill to stay alive.

Iman jammed his right foot into the car's center pedal, slamming the brakes into a loud screech. The vehicle skidded across choppy blacktop on a slick road until the auto kicked slightly to the right and halted. Iman was blinded by overbearing white lights and obliged the implied order to stop.

An announcement was broadcast in Arabic: *You have entered American-held territory. We are the United States military. Please turn around and leave this area.*

Iman and Hasim yelled back in unison, and in Arabic, "We surrender!" They simultaneously realized they were screaming in the harsh-sounding native tongue and were not furthering their cause of identifying themselves as Americans. Hasim chuckled. Then he threw the rifle he commandeered from Fa'iz out the passenger window.

The disguised Marines sat still as soldiers yelled out scattered calls of "Weapon, weapon!" All the soldiers watched with heart-thumping fear, though they would not have been so worried had they known the hurried men were Marines. Yet Iman and Hasim were dressed like the enemy, looked like the enemy, and maintained rapport with the enemy. Furthermore, they were covered in blood and stank of months in a terrorist camp.

The two Arabs, still incognito, exited their car with hands high up in the air. Neither of them could see outward because of blinding lightbeams focused into their eyes. They were not able to determine what type of barricade they had happened upon or how many men were aiming weapons at their hearts. However, their every move could be seen within the enveloping light cast upon them from an American military post. The soldiers watched as Hasim stepped aside. He opened both of the right doors and the trunk. Iman opened both of the left doors and the hood. Then they stepped forward of the vehicle, casting shadows in the car's headlight beams against far greater illumination from the opposing direction.

They were already soaked with rain and drenched in red. Each man knew how confused and scared the young soldiers were. Iman and Hasim had no desire to come so far, accomplish so much, in their mission through the desert only to be killed by their own. Each of them screamed, in English, "We surrender! We surrender!"

Iman acted first. He lay flat on the cold and wet ground. His arms were straight out from his sides. His legs were spread apart. His head was turned to the right with his eyes closed against the rain. Hasim did the same. He spread out over the ground and did not move. His head turned to the left so that he could face his brother. They lay in wait until a boisterous and bold voice ordered, "Private! Go check them out!"

The two men waited until they were met by soaked and scared soldiers. "We're Americans," Iman stated as he was being zip tied and patted down.

"We're United States Marines on a SpecOps team. We surrender, and you have our cooperation," Hasim reiterated their compliance. They understood that the soldiers were rightfully amped up about the seizure and detention of two Arabs claiming to be Marines.

"Ain't no Marines I ever seen," one of the Southern boys on post retorted as he zipped Hasim's cuffs, plastic against skin. Iman turned to Hasim and chuckled, "Seems to be the same everywhere we go." They both laughed as the soldiers jerked them to their feet.

The Arab men were officially captured as prisoners of war and brought to the post for a more detailed pat-down search. They knew an interrogation was on the immediate horizon. Hasim was void of weapons, information, and stomach content. Iman, however, was strapped with intelligence pertinent to his mission. The soldier, a very young private first class, was not sensitive to the nature of Iman's journal or Rasa's note found tethered to Iman's leg. The soldier pitched it aside and forced the Arabs to their knees.

Iman announced through his beard and long hair, "We are United States Marines. That journal is full of intel that must be pushed up our very short, but very distinguished chain of command. I understand and appreciate your concerns that some long-haired rags are in your area of operations, but I cannot explain how important this is to our mission here in Afghanistan. I need to speak with Top most ricky-tick. Do you understand me, troop?"

If Iman was an enemy combatant, he had the junior soldier convinced otherwise. His banter and military-speak were clear. The demands were made by someone who clearly outranked the subordinate soldier. The troop saw no harm in calling his ranking first sergeant to speak with the captives. The Arab men looked and smelled like the enemy, but they sure didn't speak or act like the enemy.

The soldier used his best judgment and great instincts to get higher command involved rather than push two more captives into the system. Then a military-styled waiting game ensued. The first sergeant, more an administrator than a fighter, took his time getting to the men on post. Several shivering soldiers and their prisoners, even if temporary in status, had to wait for their senior staff non-commissioned officer to yield his time.

A squatty old man bellowed as he approached, "Who in the hell is dragging me out of my rack for a couple of hajis that should already be on a bird to Gitmo?" The chubby, bedridden soldier was typical of the anti-grunt. He boasted like a war hero but rested like a civilian. He readily engaged in war stories over hot chow and in the comforts of his tent. His stacks of paperwork were taller than any rifle he had ever seen. He was belligerent in his want for battlefield grandeur that was answered only with pencil and paper.

Iman and Hasim stood from their kneeling positions. "I'm Sergeant Iman Sahar and this is Sergeant Hasim Sahar, 1st Marine Division. We are on special orders...as you can see," Iman said, referencing their beards and attire. "Our orders are classified, and we haven't been living as Marines for the better part of eight to ten months. We need to get on the horn with 1st MarDiv Ops Chief. You can verify us. Codeword: *Jericho*."

Dirty and tired, Iman gave the first sergeant every ounce of information he was allowed to divulge. The Army first sergeant ultimately didn't need any further information. Had he simply made the radio call as requested, the Marines would have been confirmed without further obstacle. Iman and Hasim would be out of zip ties and in the showers. However, the first sergeant decided to start a proverbial pissing contest with two questionable men.

"You're in no position to make any demands, haji. This is my post and I'll say what goes in and out of the radio around here," the old soldier said, grinning arrogantly at the captives. However, his grin disappeared as quickly as it arrived.

Iman stepped forward as to be heard only by the first sergeant. He tried to whisper so the senior soldier could save some dignity with his men in clear line of sight and hearing distance. "Listen, Top. Do not impede this process. Get 1st MarDiv Sec Ops on the horn now. Verify *Jericho*. My brother and I are on a team that report directly to the SecDef." Iman let the first sergeant know how important a call to Division headquarters really was. "So, if you want to play this game, we can see to it that you don't get an ounce of pension when you are dishonorably discharged on some trumped-up criminal charges...or you can make a radio call-out and verify us. If we don't check out, you can beat me senseless and lock me away forever...but if we do check out and you block us further, that will be your butt in a sling for the rest of your days...*Top*." Iman finished his threat with a sneer and tried to maintain some means of mutual military respect for the ranking enlisted man.

The overbearing Arab spoke in the intimidating fashion known only to Marines. The first sergeant figured that Iman and Hasim were either on a legitimate mission, or Iman had simply found his way into a fit of lunacy through the haze of a widespread killing field. The Marine was willing to kill or be killed and would pay any necessary price later. Either way, the first sergeant decided not to roll the dice against a man claiming direct communication with the secretary of defense.

The first sergeant ordered his captives back to their knees. The Marines complied without resistance. They knew the tides of situational control would turn following a single radio transmission. Their time wasted submitting to the will of a round-bellied and pompous rank holder would soon be at an end.

The armed guards waited for Top to walk away before they started asking questions. "Somethin' big is fixin' to go down. Ain't it?" one of the soldiers asked. He was an eager kid who seemed to grin at an oncoming fight. Iman and Hasim were amused by the Southern kid's drawl. They found the thick accent to be heartwarming. They were once again among Americans and celebrated cultural and ethnic diversity. The Marines smiled.

The kid showed a respectful distance with his posture and where he aimed his weapon's muzzle. Under normal circumstances, he would have pointed his weapon directly at captured enemy soldiers and stood over them to ensure minimal resistance. However, the soldier trusted the Arab men without any reasonable explanation beyond insight and instinct. He was not worried about them attempting to flee or fight. He, like the kneeling Marines, waited for the next order.

Top walked into the guard shack and demanded the radio. A soldier on watch handed the senior man a headset and stepped aside. The first sergeant then called in, "Bravo 2, Bravo 2. This is Post 43." He waited for register then requested a relayed message to the 1st Marine Division Headquarters. The first sergeant felt as if he were about to find himself at the butt-end of a bad joke. He was calling in a big order all the way to the top of a dangerous food chain. He hoped that his reputation would not be tarnished by the transmission.

"Roger Bravo 2," the first sergeant paused after receiving radio traffic. Then he continued, "Need to verify...*Jericho*," the chubby soldier huffed into the headset. He was matter-of-fact in his attitude of dismissal. He was fed up with the notion of the call before any relay was made from Bravo 2 to 1st MarDiv. The first sergeant's eyes widened with fear when the message was classified as *Net Priority One*. The once arrogant man listened as the codeword set into motion a flurry of transmissions to confirm *Jericho*. Then an unfamiliar voice came across the radio. "Post 43, Post 43. This is Omega. *Jericho* is confirmed. Treat them like they were your own. Out."

Top handed the radio headset back to the watchman. He was speechless. His bloated ego deflated despite the remaining width of his belt. Then he turned and clumsily sprinted the short distance from the guard shack back to Iman and Hasim. The older soldier personally helped Iman and Hasim to their feet and cut each free of their restraints. He puffed as he moved, trying to catch his breath against the cold air and his portly shape.

"Welcome back, gentlemen," Top said, changing his tone. "Sorry about the initial contact. I'm sure you can understand given how you look and everything." Iman and Hasim agreed wholeheartedly. They were dressed like insurgents, had full beards, had unkempt hair, were in possession of an AK-47, and were covered in blood. They undeniably looked like trouble. Then the Marines commended each of the soldiers for their discipline and restraint throughout another odd situation in a warzone.

"Thanks for not killing us," Hasim joked to the crowd of sentries. The group chuckled and greeted the men with handshakes rather than butt-strokes from the backs of any weapons. Natural curiosity and a desire for information led the soldiers into a series of questions. Iman and Hasim knew that they could not speak of any details surrounding their mission. They knew the soldiers did not have appropriate security clearances or a need to know what had occurred over months prior. Therefore, the two newcomers provided vague answers and surrendered nothing to their sudden allies. They smiled and accepted a nearly overwhelming return from the enemy's grasp.

One of the soldiers announced, "Well, you've got bigger balls than me. Even if I was a haji, I couldn't take smelling like that." He waved his hand in front of his nose as he mocked the unbathed men. A collective chuckle turned into a barrage of banter among brothers-in-arms.

Iman and Hasim were happy to be back with their true kinsmen. Though they were still miles from Marines, they had returned to camouflaged utilities and combat boots. Unlike miscreant jihadists in the hills, Army guards were properly suited in body armor. Their weapons were clean. Their gear was appropriate for the dank desert setting. American soldiers were the direct opposite of those formerly surrounding the Marine spies.

Hasim lifted his arm and sniffed. "It's not that bad if you dig your men musty," he joked with the others. They all laughed before a low-ranking soldier was ordered to escort Iman and Hasim inside the post. The Jarheads were shown to the showers first. Then Top ordered that the Marines be taken care of as if they were dignitaries come to visit. They were given soap and towels. The soldiers provided the Marines with uniforms and boots. All items necessary to one night of survival on post, shy of weapons, were instantly issued to the brothers. They were then fed better than either had eaten in a very long time. They ate until their stomachs were uncomfortably full, in the comfort of an American-held territory, and under the guard of men they could trust. *Jericho* was confirmed.

# RAGE

Special Agent McKenzee swiped his arm hard against the front flap of a large canvas tent set in the center of Army Post 43. A dank must, the smell that only old and worn military equipment could make, filled McKenzee's nostrils. Rows of cots lined each side of wobbling, drab green walls. Wind kicked at the bottom of the tent and allowed a slight but piercing breeze to enter the large space. Packs and personal belongings were neatly staged, but small bits of trash and letters were scattering about in the winter draft. The tent was well kept by most standards but showed the signs of an Army post not common to those held by Marines.

All the gear was new and seemed unused. Sleeping bags remained on top of cots rather than being rolled and stowed. Vacant boots were set at the foot of each cot with the laces loose. Only two cots stood apart from the others, distinguishable by being occupied and kept in better order.

Iman and Hasim, true to the core of their Marine ethos, had their boots placed beneath their racks. The toes were turned to the underside, left side dominant, with the laces pulled tight and tucked neatly into the tops of the leather. McKenzee smiled at the sleeping Marines. *I'm surprised they aren't sleeping at the position of attention.* McKenzee's lighthearted thoughts fled the tent in a sudden chill. He realized that waking the men, considering their current state of rest and their prior engagements with the enemy, might be like poking a stick at a sleeping lion. The beast might simply stir to roll over if he was well fed and too tired to fight, or he might pounce to life and cut the man's throat.

McKenzee cleared his throat loudly from across the tent, well outside of arm's reach. Neither of the beasts stirred. They were resting, truly resting, for the first time in what seemed like a decade. The agent held no doubt that they were dreaming of time away. He shuddered at the nightmares they must have faced every time they closed their eyes. His skin crawled at what they must have seen. His heart ached for the things they had to endure just to get back home. Then he pondered in sorrow the idea that "home" was a war.

"Rise and shine, gentlemen," McKenzee said in a waking tone. Both Marines sat up scared. The unfamiliar environment put them on edge, and they were ready to fight. McKenzee was thankful that they were not armed and he had the foresight to stay out of reach.

Iman saw Hasim. Hasim saw Iman. They were instantly comforted in the fact that they were still alive, but each man took a moment longer in registering the relative safety of the tent. Finally, they looked to McKenzee and realized safety was assured. Neither of them was doomed to live out the twisted dreams of the enemy. They were away from *Jericho* and among friends. However, McKenzee's presence only meant that relative safety was set to end sooner than later.

"Give us a second." Iman rubbed his eyes as he spoke to McKenzee. The Marine's reaction to a familiar face was unnatural. He should have been excited to see the agent. He should have wrestled out of his warm sleeping bag and rushed to hug the operation leader. Yet he barely acknowledged the man.

"Do you have any gear or anything?" McKenzee inquired as to whether the spies were able to obtain any enemy equipment.

Hasim smiled. "Just what we borrowed from our Army brothers." He waved his hand over the cots and sleeping bags. They were both drab in their unpressed Army camouflage uniforms. Their loaned boots were barely black, having been without polish for quite some time.

"Let's make it quick. The bird's waiting." McKenzee clapped his hands once as he informed the Marines that a helicopter sat idle on standby. The Marines responded. They hastened their pace but refused to leave until they were set and ready.

Each man was happy to have so few items to handle. They rolled the borrowed sleeping bags into tight barrels of fabric and tied them appropriately. Iman and Hasim then folded their cots and stowed the equipment in a neat pile at the tent's corner. McKenzee was mesmerized by the Marines for the few minutes taken to put things into place. They were clearly exhausted and had a golden ticket to walk away from minute responsibilities. They had permission to leave the mess for someone else to handle, but they were Jarheads. McKenzee could never understand why the Marines were compelled to leave borrowed equipment in a better state than when it was issued to them. To the agent, they were wasting time. To Iman and Hasim, they were leaving a lasting impression on their Army hosts. To the Corps, they were touching the dirt of Chosin and the cinder blocks of Hue.

The gear was properly set aside. The Marines bloused their tight-laced boots. Then they marched. McKenzee, in charge of a huge operation, remained intimidated by the warriors he did not fully understand. They were of a different breed, and one could only watch the men in awe as they moved. Their fists were curled tightly at the ends of their arms. Their shoulders were rolled rearward, and they were proudly erect with their heads up. They were exhausted, yet they scowled through gritted teeth and squinted eyes, ready for war.

Iman was the first to reach out and shake McKenzee's hand. He gripped the agent's hand and gave it a single hard shake. Then, as if to unburden himself, Iman handed his journal over to the CIA. "This is a record of our daily events," Iman grunted to the civilian. Dust and earth from the book puffed against McKenzee's chest.

Hasim added, "We both wrote our accounts in there. We were on alternating schedules in camp, so you might have some questions about the mismatched notes...but it's all in English and all pretty self-explanatory." The younger Marine reassured their leader that nothing was left out. McKenzee held all the information he needed for the remainder of their mission. *Mission accomplishment* was bound in cracking leather, covered in dirt, and weathered with hatred.

"Is this everything?" McKenzee asked while waving the book lightly.

"Yes, sir," Iman lied. He held onto the folded note from Rasa. The brittle paper rested stiff against his thigh from the inside of his pocket. He withheld Rasa from the facts of the mission. He did not subject McKenzee to the idea of weighing one innocent life against the masses of evil in *Jericho*. Iman knew that the agent would pretend to consider halting the mission to save Rasa. He would do so out of moral obligation to humanity, to normalcy. Then he would reconsider the reality of war. He would surrender to the undeniable truth that innocent people die on the battlefield. Innocent people, those who do not leave the field, do not remain untouched by conflict. Iman had no inclinations to give McKenzee a reason for feigned pause.

Rasa's note was impertinent to the overall mission. Therefore, the paper held no value for the Central Intelligence Agency or to any military unit in zone. However, Iman held it dear. The words, written by an unbroken woman, were his priceless treasure. The paper was something that could not be used by the Central Intelligence Agency or the Department of Defense, so it would be discarded. Iman knew that the message could not be replaced, so he withheld it from McKenzee, hoping only to hold onto Rasa forever.

"You'll be debriefed at the command post," McKenzee coached as he turned to exit the tent. Winter winds relentlessly slapped sadistic sand through the air. The special agent was well suited for the harsh occasions of weather. His thick coat protected him from winter's angry sting. Iman and Hasim did not have the same luxuries of warmth and protective equipment. They tucked their chins into the tops of their borrowed camouflaged shirts. The Marines did the best they could to deal with the bitter cold. They knew they were expendable assets and were treated accordingly. They had no delusions or hopes for comfort in their near future. They could not wait to get back to being Marines, and they knew that any delay was going to be insufferable. They yearned for standard-issued anything that would provide some protection from the weather, from the country, and from the war. Each man hoped for the best the Corps would offer them once they arrived back in the command center.

Propellers chopped at the frigid air. Small bits of rock and heavy clouds of sand surrounded the bird as it lay in wait. McKenzee hunched over and ran to the side of the helicopter. Iman and Hasim followed in form. They ducked downward and jogged forward until they reached the helicopter's side hatch at mid-hull.

The flight chief handed each of the men a Kevlar helmet and a flak vest through the open door as they approached the helicopter. Standard procedure called for everyone to travel with body armor because flying machines seemed to be magnets for small-arms fire all over the country. Iman and Hasim hated the battlefield all the more, but they appreciated having extra layers of gear to drape over their thin camouflaged utilities.

Collective hatred toward discomforts in the war zone amplified as the helicopter took to flight. The noise level pierced into the Marines' eardrums. McKenzee covered his ears with headphones so he could communicate with the pilot and crew. Iman and Hasim marked the headphones in the same category as McKenzee's coat. The agent was well taken care of while the Jarheads went without. They were left to shiver and stew in the silence of their thoughts.

Hasim's teeth clenched as if his molars were engaged in a bitter battle against each other. He thought of the months spent away from the Corps. He was removed from the war and sent into a snake pit. For that, he blamed the Central Intelligence Agency and the minion with whom he had immediate contact. He tried not to glare at the face of the agency as McKenzee smiled and chatted with the pilot. Hasim tried to disguise his disdain for the civilian by looking away.

Instead, Hasim stared at the floor and continued in his thoughts. He had known that the snake pit was full when he volunteered to go in. He knew that the pit remained as full of venom as when he first arrived in Farhad's world of hatred and misguidance. Then Hasim considered how many times he had been bitten.

Poisoned words from a false prophet, the head viper in the pit, still burned through the young Marine's veins. Hasim remembered the messages of jihad. He remembered the ideology being forced into the minds of the uneducated and disenfranchised people throughout the camp. With his teeth attempting to crush each other through jaw-clenching opposition, Hasim grew more and more infuriated at the idea of rabid beasts operating in similar fashion all over the world. *Such a waste of energy and faith...putting so much effort into something so fruitless.* He cursed himself for ever having let go of his true principles.

Hasim began to question the depths of his resolve. He wondered at his moral courage to always do the right thing. The Marine, like many, was too strong to go with a current headed in the wrong direction. Yet he lost himself among people who would have killed him without a second thought, and smiled having done so. He had assimilated into the ways of a terrorist organization, so deep in his cover that he almost adopted their collective fate. Hasim knew that he had strayed from himself and would have been lost forever if not for his brother.

The young man cursed himself aloud, but no one took notice. The noise of the helicopter drowned his misery as propellers hacked at the air loudly above the hull. He buried his eyes to the floor and prayed for forgiveness. He begged for mercy. He was ashamed of what he had thought and felt while in camp, while away from his brother in the defense, and while away from the public war. Then he turned his hatred away from himself and was relieved to have killed the jihadist escorts in the open desert. Hasim felt, if nothing else, he had destroyed his portion of the enemy in penance. Tears filled his eyes, and he choked back a sob before regaining his composure.

Boiling inner turmoil nearly got the best of Hasim in the troop transport section of a bitter and cold helicopter. However, he was able to maintain a hardened shell of himself. His warrior exterior returned to shield his human interior from conflict. He looked to his brother, wondering what Iman must have been thinking against the noise of the flight. Hasim held his fist out to

Iman. Iman answered. Their knuckles collided with assurance that no matter the course of the war, they would fight it together.

Hasim's acknowledgment distracted Iman from his personal torment. Iman's mind raced back and forth between his duties and his heart. He knew that they would get back to base and be debriefed. They would be required to give up every detail about the camp, about the routines and defenses, about the weapons and personnel. He knew that there was nothing to report other than bomb-making materials, a few crew-served weapons, small arms, a vast enemy, and a willingness to carry out any act of jihad ordered by Farhad. There was only one decent person among them worth saving.

The older brother's mind stayed with Rasa. *Please find a way to run before we return. Please get out of there before we have to come back. Please, in the name of Allah, stay alive.* He begged without a word, willing the woman to escape. Iman's tortured spirit shredded in a disheartening reality that Rasa shared the same fate as the rest of the camp. One person, a woman unimportant to anyone other than Iman, was not enough to justify calling off the critical mission. She was forced to take a journey that led only to Hell Fire missiles and shrapnel-laden death.

Iman tried with all his conviction to keep his stomach from churning in misery. He prayed and considered the spiritual philosophy of the imminent attack. *I feel that...I know that we were meant to be together.* He silently sent his thoughts to Rasa. *Allah put us on the same path for a reason. He put me in your life for a reason. You saved my life...and I know that it is my duty, to him, to save yours.*

The older brother was not able to shroud his inner thoughts the way that Hasim had done. Anguish and worry spread across his eyes. His brow wrinkled, and he tried to prevent burning tears from flowing down his cheeks. He was in pain, and Hasim saw his brother's agony.

Hasim tried to reassure Iman that everything would be okay, shoulder-nudging him to calm his nerves. However, they both knew that Hasim was lying to himself and to his older brother. The village, and everyone in it, was going to burn. The Marine spies would not be able to halt the impending attack without sacrificing need for want.

Iman swallowed hard and prayed again. *Please...if it is your will to make them suffer...let Rasa go quickly. Show her your mercy. Please give her peace.*

Iman and Hasim looked up from their plight-filled thoughts as the helicopter touched down with a bounce against a make-shift landing pad. The desert floor was unforgiving to the aircraft's sudden and heavy descent. They had arrived. They were back among Marines, but they were strangers to base and most who resided within. Neither of the men recognized any of the faces in the landing zone. Their previous unit had been cycled out of rotation. The only remnants were the Marines on their team, men they had not yet encountered face-to-face. Men with whom they would travel into combat were to become their closest allies in a very short time.

Like all things in the Marine Corps, an air of hurry-up-and-wait surrounded them as soon as they landed. McKenzee was in a hurry to get the spies back to the command center. However, they arrived and the agent placed them on standby. They were left waiting in the cold, outside of a canvas city full of potential warmth. Once again, the brother Marines were stranded without the most basic provisions of comfort.

McKenzee ran from them to find whomever, but in his rush he dismissed the fact that they were still not in Marine form. Each of the men had long hair, full beards, and had not been clad in proper uniform for quite some time. They looked like jihad-driven terrorists, were clothed in United States Army uniforms, and had remnant blood in the crevasses of their faces where limited shower waters could not cleanse them of their pasts. They were out of place and found themselves growing more nervous among friends than they were in the midst of the enemy. They were nervous because Marines are far more dangerous to their foes than the untrained and undisciplined side of the fight. Marines, when threatened, would not hesitate to drop their targets into warm piles of wet meat. Each of the brothers stood out in a uniformed crowd, and they hoped that none of the surrounding warriors would suddenly feel ill at ease by an unfamiliar presence.

Iman and Hasim stood with their arms crossed, praying to keep some body heat from escaping their chests. They shivered. Their teeth chattered to slicing winter winds. Their entire bodies ached to the cold as their blood ran to ice.

"Who are you guys?" a boyish-looking lance corporal asked as he walked up from behind, surprising Iman and Hasim. The young Marine flung his heavy coat around Iman's shoulders. A private first class, another junior Marine from the local unit, did the same for Hasim. While the brothers could not rely on their immediate superior to provide for them, they could rely on their fellow Marines.

The junior enlisted Jarheads saw two unarmed and freezing civilians standing outside. No one was under attack by anyone or anything other than the weather, so the Marines showed compassion for their fellow men despite obvious differences in appearance. The two boys-turned-men had no idea who the bearded newcomers were, but they shielded the weak and weary anyway. Iman and Hasim were quickly reminded why American heroes, especially those brave enough to serve in the United States Marine Corps, were such a phenomenal and effective force all over the world.

They fought the enemy like fanged beasts from hell, but they cared for people with angelic compassion. While the enemy used civilians as human shields, Americans served as the shields separating the innocent from imminent harm.

The four men, a suddenly compiled mix of Marines, stood in a small circle trying to share their body heat. Iman and Hasim offered to alternate times under the protection of the heavy coats, but the subordinate Marines surrendered their warmth to protect others. "We're...actually...Marines," Hasim forced through a shiver.

The younger men laughed at such an outrageous claim. One of the youthful men gave a light tug on Hasim's beard like a child at play. "I can tell. So, should we salute you, too?" The four of them laughed heartily together. The lance corporal and private first class assumed they were helping unknown civilians. The older Marines laughed at how ridiculous they must have seemed: out of uniform, out of regulations, their full beards swaying in the winter wind, and without any identification.

"It's true. We're sergeants," Iman chuckled with a certain audacity. Then he was interrupted.

"Actually, gentlemen," General Potts said as he snuck up on the group, "you're staff sergeants now." The four huddled Marines snapped to attention. None of them saluted in the war zone despite the officer's high rank. The lance corporal and private first class reported themselves to General Potts.

"We were just trying to keep these men warm until we figured out who they are, General," the lance corporal explained.

Potts smiled boldly. "I appreciate that, Marine. You did well. However, I'd prefer it if you didn't worry about who they are at this time. I'll take them from here." The young Marines stood at attention again in the realization they were being relieved of their duties to the civilian-looking men. Iman and Hasim returned the coats to their rightful owners and thanked the men immensely for the temporary relief from stinging weather conditions.

The young men turned and said, "Good day, General. You too, Staff Sergeants." The coat providers finally hustled in retreat back to the warmth of wherever they came from.

General Potts looked Iman and Hasim over. He initially took notice of their diminished weight, how their eyes were starting to sink deep into their sockets, and their overall lack of basic hygiene. He chuckled at their ragtag mix of equipment and appearance. "Let's get you guys inside. We can debrief you while you clean up and get proper again." Hasim and Iman smiled widely at the thought of being able to wash jihad from their bodies and spirits.

# STANDARD
# ISSUE

Rome may not have been built in a day, but that's just because you Marines didn't have anything to do with the construction," McKenzee laughed to an oddly mixed group of combatants. "Good luck, gentlemen," he said as he clapped his hands together and turned away. The agent jogged from the Marines as they staged on the edge of their pickup area.

Iman and Hasim stood alongside a small team of special warfare Marines from 1st Force Reconnaissance. The hardened veterans were masters of moving in and out of enemy territory without detection. They habitually infiltrated jihadist-held areas, gathered intelligence, and wreaked havoc upon armed insurgents when the mission dictated a need to deal death. The men were known as ghosts, demons sent to slay firstborn sons, and lived under the only purpose of destroying their targets by any means.

The Force Recon Marines waited for their lift into another combat zone within twenty-four hours of being briefed alongside Iman and Hasim. There was nothing new to the special operations Marines about being tapped on the shoulder and receiving a kill order. However, the sudden additions to their tightly knit team were unexpected. Iman and Hasim made the combat-ready Marines more nervous than the thought of approaching the armed foes in the battle space.

Special operations units exist in a sense of brotherhood regardless of military branch or country of origin. From the day they volunteer for indoctrination training to the day they deploy, the men of special warfare assignments live on top of each other. They share barracks rooms in garrison. They are isolated from general populations in berthing areas aboard ships. They go to chow together. They dare not sleep unless their brothers stand watch. They dare not breathe unless enough air remains for all of them to inhale. Yet they stood with two strangers in their midst. The Force Recon Marines questioned if the greenest of the group could be trusted in the field.

Outsiders, hardly welcome in the same area in garrison, were certainly not welcome on Force Recon missions. Iman and Hasim met every qualification of *outsider* by Recon standards. Yet they stood ready for deployment in the field among the Force Recon team.

The two spies had taken part in several intelligence briefs building up to their launch order. The team was informed that Iman and Hasim lived among the enemy and would head the mission, but no other information was divulged about the newcomers. Therefore, the close band of brothers excluded Iman and Hasim from banter or reassuring fist bumps. The team made it clear to the spies that a proverbial welcome mat was already worn thin. However, the team was allowed no input as to who would tag along on the mission. Their orders were handed down by two generals, and no one among them was brave enough to argue.

Lieutenant Gibson, the officer in charge of the team, felt it necessary to reiterate the importance of Hasim and Iman following specific guidelines. The officer was concerned that the strangers would do something stupid in the field. He was worried they would make too bold of a move or accidentally make too much noise. Any activity outside of patient and calculated maneuvers could compromise the entire team and get them all killed. Gibson nearly begged the brothers to be mindful of all things at all times. He worried less about mission accomplishment and more about the welfare of his Marines. Lieutenant Gibson, unlike many other junior grade officers, did not regard his missions as opportunities for medals. He only prayed that he would not have to send any letters home to grieving parents.

As far as Gibson was concerned, Iman and Hasim were nothing more than observers from Intelligence Battalion. They were along for the ride despite his request to leave them behind. He had dismissed the fact that the spies had already lived among the enemy. Regardless of how the lieutenant felt, the brothers were not observers or hitchhikers. They were invaluable assets that he would soon need. Gibson might not have appreciated how important the new Marines were to accomplish a critical mission, but Iman and Hasim understood their purpose within the team. They did not have a need for acceptance into the unit. They needed only to move into *Jericho,* destroy the enemy, and ensure Farhad would never spread another word of hate again.

Harsh winds kicked dirt into the painted faces of the team. The Arab brothers had full beards only a day before, so the stinging sand was new to them once again. They were freshly shaved. Their hair was once again cropped and field-ready. Their uniforms and gear were much newer than the issued equipment of the war-ready Force Recon Marines, men who had regularly deployed their instruments of warfare for nearly a year in-country.

Gibson continued to bark meaningless orders and elementary guidance until he saw a helicopter approach the landing zone. The lieutenant turned to his men and yelled, "Get ready, boys. Here she comes." He nodded to the inbound bird and started to step away from Iman and Hasim. However, his departure was interrupted.

Iman reached out suddenly and grabbed a fistful of the lieutenant's sleeve. The men were already at full charge with adrenaline. Their every sense was amplified. Each of them was looking for a fight, but none of them was looking to turn the skirmish inward. Iman took hold of the lieutenant, breaking all Marine protocol in the respect for rank, only to get the man's full attention. However, Iman was harsh when he jerked the officer in for an insubordinate verbal exchange.

"We aren't some pencil-pushing punks reading out satellite imagery. We..." Iman let go of Gibson's sleeve when he realized he was bordering the edge of assaulting an officer. He pointed to Hasim and himself. "We were the spies. We were the eyes on the ground gathering the intelligence. We are the source of your mission, and we certainly don't need to be talked down to." The noise of an approaching helicopter kept Iman's words held privately between himself and the officer. The staff sergeant continued, "We are very well trained and well equipped for this job. You are in support of us, not the other way around. Sorry to grab you like that... sir, but if you want to take issue I certainly suggest you take it up with General Potts or Gutzwiller...or the Central Intelligence Agency."

Gibson stood speechless at Iman's brazenness. Under any other circumstances, the lieutenant could easily bring Iman up on insubordination charges under the Uniform Code of Military Justice. He could have the Marine stripped of rank and privilege. Being that Iman grabbed the ranking man's sleeve, Gibson could have had him thrown in the brig for assault. Instead, Gibson stood in awe of Iman's boldness.

STANDARD ISSUE | 137

Iman knew that he was wrong to grab the sleeve of any officer under any conditions. However, he had finally reached his breaking point with finding roundabout ways to circumvent rank. Iman and Hasim answered to a very short chain of command. Iman grew weary of not receiving needed support at every turn in his mission. Gibson just happened to be on the final receiving end of the staff sergeant's frustration.

"Let's go, Marine," the lieutenant said, trying to assert his last bit of authority over Iman. Gibson might have outranked the spy Marines, but it was their mission. Iman made the issue abundantly clear, and Gibson could do nothing more than accept that the unknown Marines were backed by very important people. The spies were tied to the Pentagon, and the Force Recon Marines were assets at the CIA's disposal.

Gibson was running from Iman as much as he was running to the helicopter. Hasim chuckled, patted his brother on the shoulder, and ran to the bird. Iman considered his actions for only a second longer than the others. He knew that he approached Gibson with reckless abandon and could have paid a dear price. Yet he got away with the infraction. Then he ran to the waiting helicopter with a chuckle and rejoined the team.

The heavily geared Marines piled into the back of a Super Stallion helicopter. They methodically dropped their packs to the deck and settled with their equipment between their feet. Each of their rifle muzzles pointed downward. They had magazines inserted into their weapons, but no rounds were charged into the chamber.

Hasim reached over and took Iman's rifle. Iman sat back and strapped a canvas seatbelt across his lap. The buckle hooked then snapped. He gave the belt a solid tug to make sure it was secure. Then he took the rifles from Hasim. Hasim fastened himself in the same fashion. Both men were satisfied that they were locked into place and ready to go. They would be safe against turbulence or any other unforeseen problem midflight.

The rest of the Marines followed their lead. Most crew chiefs would not give a thumbs-up to pilots if the troops in transport were not strapped to the seats. However, Force Recon and other special operations units were accustomed to foregoing basic safety requirements. They so often had to get off helicopters deep in enemy territory that expedited exits were expected and encouraged. In-air precautions held little weight against the need for pilots to evade certain areas quickly. Belted Marines would have just an additional step to disembark the bird. The extra step translated to more time on the ground. Additional time on the ground created a greater window of opportunity for the enemy to shoot down an American helicopter.

Even still, Iman and Hasim kept to their most basic training. They would unhook the safety straps upon the chief's two-minute warning preempting arrival, but a lot of time would lapse between takeoff and roping into the enemy zone. Ample time to be shot down by some rogue insurgent, armed with the right equipment, filled the air around the helicopter. Every man knew the reality that helicopters make for tempting targets to the enemy. They all would have preferred to punch in on the ground, under the cover of night, but time constraints trumped that which was preferred for that which was mission critical.

The operation's clock was set from the secretary of defense's order to execute. He issued a universal attack order and set all the twenty-eight strike teams in motion across the globe. Groups similar to Iman's were mounting counterinsurgency warfare in a well-orchestrated series of assaults on several international terrorist organizations. The enemies' names—Al Qaeda, Hamas, Hezbollah, or any other identifier—were irrelevant. Jihadists all over the world were set to die in a simultaneous slash at the throats of Islamo-Nazi beasts plaguing the world.

Iman's stomach flipped over as his body sank into the bench beneath him. The Super Stallion's powerful engine whined. Long propellers chopped hard at the air until the bird bounced its fat body off the ground. The helicopter jumped free from the earth and defied gravity as it thumped into the sky.

The airborne machine swayed to the torque of its top rotor. The tail rotor stabilized in the thick air of initially low altitude takeoff. Iman's stomach eased as their altitude increased. The air thinned and the helicopter vibrated less against reduced invisible friction. Higher passage was less turbulent. The men understood firsthand why the large bird was known as the "Cadillac of the Marine Corps." It made for a smooth ride, or at least smooth enough to rival an old Coupe DeVille with blown shocks and too much weight in the rear end.

Hasim patted the back of his hand on Iman's chest. Then he pointed to the hatch at the aircraft's rear. The ramp was opened only slightly to the sky until the bird pitched into a steep climb. Iman smiled at the optical illusion of being thrown to the ground from an incredible height. Then he considered the probable safety of the ramp relative to the hole in the floor that would soon drop out from beneath them. The Super Stallion's *hell hole* would relieve the bird of its cargo. Bottom hatches would create the open space needed for the Marines to fast-rope to their destination. However, that time was not set to arrive for a while to come.

The helicopter was traveling at over a hundred knots per hour, but they had more than two hundred miles to go. They would be in the air for some time yet. Iman knew that the pressure on the backs of his thighs was going to force his legs to sleep. He knew that the impact from his landing was going to hurt, so he tried to think of less foreboding issues. He thought of killing the enemy and being done with the war. He thought of his mother and father. The young man wondered what his father must think of his Marine sons. He knew that the old man was proud. Even still, Iman contemplated the complexity of his situation. He was an American. He was a Marine. He was an Arab. The trinity of his being was constantly in conflict. Americans cursed Marines. Arabs and Americans killed each other. Marines cursed and served them all.

Hasim looked at his wristwatch. *Soon. We'll drop in, patrol to the southern defense, kill them, and have a line of sight on target by tomorrow morning. Tomorrow...this will be done. It will finally be behind me...a memory I will spend the rest of my life trying to forget.*

The younger brother then looked to Iman. Hasim felt sorry for his older sibling. While the fight might find its way behind Hasim, Rasa's death would sit with Iman for the rest of his days. Hasim knew that his brother was going to be tormented into eternity. Then he wondered about duty and sacrifice. He understood their duty was to win the war. He questioned the notion of sacrifice.

Iman's sacrifice was obvious. He was to let Rasa slip into Paradise. Hasim hoped, for Iman's sake, that lost love would be found on the other side of death. He understood that such a reunion would be the reward of a just and loving God. He smiled at the idea. Then the younger brother began to consider what his call to sacrifice would be. Hasim initially thought he might have fulfilled his sacrifice. He considered the possibility that his sacrifice of self, while in Jericho, was the loss he had to suffer before coming back to the side of the just. He wondered if losing himself in the bowels of Islam was enough.

Hasim looked at his older brother. He could see that Iman was deep in his own thoughts and might need some reassurance. Hasim only assumed that Iman's mind remained wrapped around his heart. He knew that Iman longed for Rasa, but she was lost to the war. She just didn't know it yet. Hasim nudged Iman, hoping to send some sort of condolences through the thick tension.

Hasim realized that the sacrifice he previously pondered was neither real nor enough if he had to question its validity. He returned to question what his sacrifice would be just as he received and sent a message down the line. Two minutes. He held up his index and little finger. "Two minutes," he tried to yell over the noise of the helicopter. "Two minutes," he repeated to the next Marine in the row.

The obligatory correspondence was done. Hasim and Iman returned to their worlds of distraction. Their moment of pause let them flee the war. The younger brother retreated home. The elder stayed with his love. Then their retreat into self was interrupted.

Blaring red lights inside the troop compartment flashed. The buzz of a warning mixed with screams and prayers suddenly more audible than the helicopter's roar. Hasim's eyes were wide with fear. Iman prayed. The helicopter trembled, smoked, and plummeted into a dark spin.

# RESCUE

Sergeant Thompson, a young squad leader from Tennessee, called out, "Twenty-four! We're two down!" He looked around trying to identify the dead. Iman, having been the last one out of the downed helicopter, knew the answer. He yelled to Sergeant Thompson, "Calm down. It's Lieutenant Gibson, and I think maybe Perez."

Corporal Perez, surprised to hear his name called out as a casualty, answered back. "It ain't me, Staff Sergeant. I don't see Jackson anywhere though." Everyone looked around for the missing Marine, Corporal Jackson. Perez was accurate in his assessment. Corporal Jackson and Lieutenant Gibson were the barely recognizable figures that lay mangled in the back of the helicopter. Iman was able to identify Lieutenant Gibson because of their previous close encounters conducted with discontent and limited respect. However, Corporal Jackson's remains left little that might have allowed Iman to recognize the broken man. Meat hung from bone. Death twisted Jackson's face, and Iman was sorry that he had not known the Marine better. Iman was sorry that he and Jackson had not met under more favorable circumstances. He was sorry that Jackson had to leave so badly torn that his mother would not be able to look at his face for a final goodbye from an open coffin. Iman swallowed hard.

"Sorry about that, Perez," Iman answered. He sat down involuntarily. The staff sergeant had a sudden sharp pain at his side. *Yeah, they're broken.* Iman agonized over the fractured ribs on his right side. He winced and grimaced but maintained his ability to lead.

"Are you okay?" Hasim moved to aid Iman once again. Iman sat up the best he could. He ached to the splintered bones but was able to continue breathing. No bone fragments pierced his lungs. He was not yet sentenced to death. Iman considered the pressure in his chest, wheezed, and grunted against the invisible bricks piled onto his sternum. He was hurt, but he was alive.

Iman looked around. He and Hasim were the ranking members of the team. They were to take charge and carry out their mission. Injured or otherwise, they had the most stripes on their collars. They knew the mission. They knew the enemy. They knew how to proceed. Therefore, their intentions were to carry on despite the crash and the loss of good Marines.

Losing Marines did not sit well with any member of the team. Iman huffed in pain but disguised his discomfort as disapproval toward the losses. Iman's injuries were invisible, but Hasim did not share any such luck. Blood trickled out of Hasim's helmet. The gouge in his forehead left a piece of flesh hanging limp. The tip of the skin strategically dripped red trails around his eyes, but not through them. He was still able to see despite the wound.

Iman could barely breathe. He needed a moment to catch his wind. "Contact!" one of the Marines yelled. The rest of the able-bodied fighters pointed in the same direction as the screaming and shooting Marine. Then the rest of the team squeezed their triggers until nothing remained of an approaching imminent threat.

Hasim and Iman assumed control of the two squads. They directed one man from each team to go check the dead enemies. The junior men responded. They sprinted to the slain advancers and confirmed the teams' kills.

One of the men was carrying a rocket-propelled grenade launcher. The tube was empty. The Marines assumed he was the one lucky enough to have shot down a helicopter with an unguided weapon. The insurgent had killed Marines. However, the man was not lucky enough to live his days in false valor. The insurgent and his partner dripped the last bits of their lifeblood into the desert floor. The dryness of the sand slurped at the red liquid until the enemy faded to nothing.

Iman gave an order through a grimace. "Sergeant Taylor...if that fuel hasn't gone up by now...it's probably not going to. Let's get the bodies out and move them away from the bird. Camo the dead so we can recover them later if possible. If the bad guys know a bird went down, they are going to come looking. We don't want to see our brothers on the Internet."

Sergeant Taylor understood the order and grabbed several other Marines for the task. One by one, they pulled the dead free from the crash. Iman watched the men work only for a moment. Then he asked Hasim to go and identify the dead enemy combatants.

The older brother hoped against fate. He knew there was a low probability that two jihadist camps would set up right next to each other unless it was by accident. The dead were most likely from *Jericho*. Iman turned to Hasim and softly ordered, "We should check those men." He pointed at the fallen enemy lying in the desert sand. "See if they are from our target." Iman identified the jihadist camp under a military identifier rather than reiterating its codename.

Hasim rushed to the dead insurgents. Hours of training and preparation eluded him momentarily. He nearly rolled the bodies left and right to search their remains. He refrained. Hasim did not move the bodies. In a last second of reason, the younger brother realized his task was not to check the dead for intelligence and weapons. He was only beside their limp bodies to identify the men and determine if they were from *Jericho*.

Both of the dead men were lying face-up to the desert sky. The Marines had done well to tear the enemy soldiers apart. The former jihadists were splayed open and shredded beneath blood-splattered holes in their flesh. Hasim smeared coagulating pools of red from the insurgents' heads and necks. He looked at their hollow faces and did not recognize either man. He decided the slain were either newcomers or they were of another tribe. Yet he still did not move their bodies in search of more information. The spy knew that many of the terrorists in the area would set booby traps with their dying breaths simply to kill any Marine sent in search of the deceased.

Hasim left them unstirred and ran back to Iman. He then gave a report of his findings. "I don't know them," Hasim huffed, "and tell everybody to leave them. I didn't check them for trip." Hasim panted as he used Marine jargon to inform the others the bodies were dead but not cleared to kick out of the way.

The idea that two rogue terrorists were running around the desert passed through Iman's head. Then he realized the thought was foolish. Survivability was next to nothing without the protection and provisions of a nearby village. He knew that Jericho was a beehive, but he worried that it might have only been a single hive in a colony of enemy wasps.

*We must have fallen by some village we never knew about,* Iman reasoned with the presence of unknown jihadists. He was familiar with the tribal warfare that ran alongside international conflicts. The men who shot the Marine helicopter down might have done so as an act of jihad. They might have also shot the bird down to fall into Farhad's good graces, thus saving their village from pillaging marauders later on. The laws of the land were primal. The people were savage. Social evolution skipped the ways of life in Afghanistan. The tribes there were doomed to forever contort in the throes and woes of the most powerful village of any area.

*What are we doing here?* Government-funded terrorism was no longer a matter of concern to Iman. Patriotism and a call to duty no longer held weight in his heart. *There is no saving these people from tyranny.* Tears flooded Iman's eyes. *We can't save them from tyranny because we can't save them from their own savagery.* The older staff sergeant felt defeat despite his ability to win. He felt his heart break and his stomach burn as humanity clawed its way out of him. Then he swallowed hard, devouring the human, and returned to the war-hungry beast that is the United States Marine. He yearned for war and no longer sought reason.

Reason was lost to reality. "Three-sixty on me," Iman ordered the Marines. Their dead were staged and hidden well enough to evade any distant observations. The living Marines, including Iman's younger brother, circled the senior leader and faced outward. They were in a defensive formation that protected them from an attack originating in every direction.

"They'll be coming for their kill soon enough. Let's not let them find us here," Iman coached. He spoke as he faced north. He called out only loud enough to be heard by the men circled around him. Then he paused. The quiet surrounding them caused him to exercise sudden caution toward the volume of his voice. Iman knew that only the ill-trained and ready-to-die become the tallest things in a lightning storm, or the loudest things in the middle of a field operation. He waited before he continued, "We have to carry on north from here." The senior Marine pointed ahead to the cap of a nearby hill. He knew that was their destination. Their planned encroachment patrol would have to be expedited. The team was compromised far too early to have been engaged by Farhad's defensive positions. Iman was, therefore, forced to consider two prominent possibilities.

The first was that Farhad received word of Iman and Hasim's escape only days prior and decided to move camp. The information gathered over prior months would be void. They would have no means to verify if innocent people had been adopted into the herd. They would not have the ability to stop Command from making headlines around the world that the United States of America was openly killing women and children. Iman tried not to grit his teeth to the blatant propaganda used globally to defame the greatest nation in the world.

Secondly, Iman considered that another terrorist organization was in the surrounding, and uncomfortably close, area. The presence of another jihadist camp might mean that *Jericho* would receive reinforcements in the event of a firefight with wounded and weary Marines. In either case, the Marines needed to evacuate the crash site quickly.

Their mission was either compromised and would go into history as a failure, or Farhad remained in place and would die as planned. Iman was determined to pursue the objective to its end. The Marines surrounding him, war-ready and eager to destroy demons, were determined to do the same.

"The only comm we have is the laser." Iman pointed to the bulky equipment staged nearby as he thought of improvised means to annihilate *Jericho*. "Any volunteers to hump it?" Iman asked as a challenge to their bravado and taste for machismo endeavors. The Marines looked, one at the other, unaccustomed to anyone asking for volunteers. They better understood orders. They were given orders. They blindly followed orders. The concept of volunteering for excess weight never occurred to them. No one volunteered, so Hasim picked it up first. He decided to lead from the front on the issue.

Iman continued, "We're headed north. We are going to get into position and paint the target. My plan is to cycle through and laze the target every fifteen minutes until we get a marked response or can no longer use the equipment. However, we are also looking at the possibility that no devastating response is coming...so we might just run the cursed thing until there is nothing left in the battery or nothing left of Jericho. I'm hoping that the frequency and comm checks will catch the laser. If not, we will move in for a good old-fashioned gunfight...because we'll be dead anyway. In short, gentlemen, we are playing it by ear until we play it by the general rules of destroying the enemy by any means."

# REASSEMBLE

I man stood at the center of the tactical three-sixty, the circle of kneeling Marines with their weapons pointed outward for protection in all directions. Each Marine surrounding Iman peeked back and stood in a hunched position. They waited until the leader shook his hand north. He gave them the silent order to continue their march into combat. The Marines stepped back into the war wounded, tired, unable to communicate with Command, and with little hope for reinforcement. They moved north searching for nothing shy of a bloody fight to an inevitable end. They pushed onward in a heavily determined spirit. *Victory or death.*

Iman looked to his right as the tattered team parted the area. He lowered his eyes from the dead. Bludgeoned and bloody bodies were crudely covered with whatever brush and dirt the Marines could find just east of the crash site. The living had done well enough in haste to conceal the fallen, but interment was far from complete. Yet the covering of combat Marines was done with a proper amount of respect and admiration. The living honored the dead despite very little provisions for burial and no time for last respects. The sentimental were thankful. The dead were impartial.

The men who had given their lives to the mission temporarily rested behind a large rock in the open desert. Very little of their bodies and equipment remained visible to any potential passersby. Iman and the others had no doubt that anyone stopping at the crash site would be more interested with the downed aircraft than anything else. Dead bodies would have been of little interest beyond the valuable equipment and resources to be found inside a destroyed helicopter.

"Let's go," Hasim said, urging the Marines to move quickly from the area. The Force Recon warriors were not comfortable with stomping through open terrain in blatant disregard for concealment. They were masters of sneaking around in the backfield of the enemy. They were stealthy, quietly lethal. However, their whereabouts had long since been broadcast to the enemy. The helicopter smoldered and smoked without flame, sending signals into the air for anyone in the area to see. Noise from the crash and recovery echoed through every valley in every direction. Lack of cover and concealment in the wide vicinity made for a panoramic view of what remained and who was present to defend anything or anyone on site. The staff sergeants knew that threats were imminent in all directions, including the direction that might lead them back to friendly-held territory. The team was isolated from the next nearest American force by an unknown number of very involved and very dedicated enemy troops. Therefore, Iman and Hasim prodded the other Marines to run from the crash zone. Every man experienced a renewed sense of urgency to evade looming threats that would stand between the team and their mission.

The men of Force Recon turned into machines. They were no strangers to hard runs under the weight of their full combat loads.

Some of them even preferred a pack run for the sake of getting a decent workout in garrison. However, what would be a *decent workout* in rear echelon became an impossible venture in deep sands and rocky hills. Iman vomited twice on the long run en route to *Jericho*. His heaving gullet only crushed his broken ribs further into the tissues that allowed him intermittent and sharply painful breaths. Yet he pushed on.

Hasim's legs gave out beneath him several times. The previously hard pace set by the point man slowed to a painful shuffle. Too many broken bones traveled too many miles by foot, under heavy gear, and in the direction of chaos. Every man hurt, but they kept on. The Marines made up distances lost in being shot down south of their intended landing zone. Each of the hardened men splintered and bled. Skin between their toes ripped to flattening sands and rolling rocks. Wide straps of every pack rubbed their shoulders and necks into raw blisters and peeled skin. Calluses on their hands tore open from the enthusiastically desperate grips they maintained on their rifles. Every lip split and bled with cracked dehydration. Every nostril was filled with the desert glass created by finite shards of sand settling on thick mucus. Their helmets rubbed the tops of their ears until there was nothing more than red strips of raw meat at the sides of their heads. Inner thighs chafed and burned from the incessant rubbing of fabric against tender skin. Spit congealed at the backs of their throats and coaxed out what little food they had stored in their stomachs. Even still, their legs remained in motion. One foot in front of the other, they trotted to war without hesitation. They jogged without pause. They pursued the fight like wolves chasing deer for a swift kill.

Late afternoon faded into falling night. The hills ahead of the team looked like poorly painted silhouettes rather than ridges of knife-like rocks and hatefully thronged bushes. Night was upon them as was the cold. Every ounce of sweat that poured into the Marines' camouflaged uniforms for hours prior threatened to build a sheet of ice over their clothes. Every thorn-covered bush reached out with eager blades of nature's discontent to tear into the already exhausted men. The desert, black in night and in soul, yearned to devour the Marines, not knowing that they were too tough to chew. Any beast that dared meet them in the night would lose its sad existence either in trained silence or flurries of ferocious fire. The Marines cared nothing for the land, the creatures, the natural threats, or the enemy. They cared only to win so they could leave what they considered to be a preview of hell.

They all hated the place where a fight waited to be found, even though they so desperately sought conflict. All illusions leading to a collective belief that things could not get worse were proved wrong with every step deeper into the desert. Iman's stomach muscles involuntarily clenched once more. His body heaved again as he ran. His stomach was too empty to ease the pain. His wretched vomiting produced nothing more than a painful dribble of spit and agony. Iman finally conceded to the natural need for water and rest. Hours of running through fatigue became too great, and he called a silent halt. He wanted to surrender to the desert. He wanted to die. All the Marines shared the same sentiment. Yet they held onto something within them that no other could understand. They held onto their ethos, the hot coals of hate within, even when they could maintain nothing else.

Iman raised his fist into the air. He could hear flattened feet grinding into the rocks and sand behind him. Those who expelled the contents of their stomachs were required to do so without sound. No cough or gag could be heard beyond stomach fluid splattering to the dry earth. They were marvelous in their plight.

The long distance once separating the team from their enemy

was finally found short. Clouds in the night sky parted and Hasim used a beam of moonlight to identify their first destination. He squinted to confirm their location, and his eyes rested on the nearby mountain's edge. He was certain as to where they were bound.

The younger brother moved to the unit leader. He tapped Iman on the shoulder and pointed north-northeast. Iman regained his composure through the cramping in his gut and the pain in his ribs. He could not draw a full breath for the pain piercing through his lungs. Even still, he looked up to where Hasim was pointing rather than wince in front of his Marines. Iman remembered the area and recognized the point of an impassable hill. It was the site of *Jericho's* southernmost defensive position. Iman grinned. He did not smile in relief. He only gave a smirk as a lion would, licking his chops as he crouched in high weeds just before taking prey.

Hasim and Iman knew the position well. It was the least fortified fighting hole with the fewest amenities for comfort. They knew a single machine gun rested there. They also knew that the hole was not deep enough to conceal a man completely. Anyone doomed to the cold defensive position would be hunkered down behind the shallow walls in a desperate search for refuge against piercing winds. Dedicated but undisciplined, the jihadist guard would likely be asleep in the hope that Farhad and his lieutenants would not brave freezing temperatures for a perimeter check. The sentry on duty was probably stretched out along the base of the wall, away from his weapon, and resting in a false sense of security. The guard likely put his faith in the idea that no one could possibly sneak up on the impassable defense to *Jericho's* south.

Bipod-mounted, shoulder-fired machine guns could be found in pairs at every perimeter site around Farhad's camp. Other positions were concerned with avenues of approach that had to be monitored constantly, day and night. Multiple machine gunners and spotters had to observe their fields of fire from nearly every route because of perceived weak spots in and around the camp. However, the southern defense required only one guard and one machine gun.

The machine gun's bipod rested on top of seven sandbags facing south. The weapon was moved so rarely that divots formed in the tops of the canvas bags beneath the gun. Iman and Hasim wondered if the barrel had become frozen in its near-vertical position. Then they dismissed their mocking ideas toward the enemy. If they were to assume anything, they had to assume that the threat was real and should be respected accordingly. The brothers returned to Jericho in the name of destruction, not ridicule. Each of the men had to coax calm and steady willingness back into their minds so that they might be able to kill men they knew.

The lead Marines also knew that Farhad's men took for granted the southern point's natural defenses. A rugged and steep hill separating the militant post from the valley gave guards a fallible impression that the camp was impervious to attacks from its bottom edge. Hasim and Iman cycled separately behind the vertical machine gun in the south several times when they walked openly among the enemy. Each of the men found the on-duty guards asleep or hiding from the snow on all occasions. They hoped to catch the enemy off-guard once again, only from the opposing side of the fight. They hoped to assume control of the fighting hole with minimal resistance. However, hope alone would not be enough.

Reassembling and resuming their patrol formation after the long and hard run, the Force Recon team reasserted its combat-driven presence. Iman and Hasim recognized their surroundings. They were just north of where their original landing zone was intended prior to being shot from the sky. They were officially at the original mission square one. Iman knew they could find cover behind some rocks directly to their north. They would be able to find giant stone formations with ease even in the blackness of the night. The entire team would also be able to establish a line of approach into the southern defensive position from cover, hidden by the massive boulders.

Iman straightened the fingers on his left hand and pointed his flattened palm in the direction of the large stones. The other Marines squinted through darkness and could see his waved motion. They acknowledged and followed his lead. No one spoke. No one made a sound louder than the weight of feet slowly pressing into rock-laden sand. Every strap and buckle on their gear was wrapped with green or black tape. Any piece of metal that might make contact against other metal or plastic was secured tight with the same adhesive strips. Their canteens were either completely full or completely empty as to prevent sloshing noises. If the Marines had to breathe, they did it through their noses to keep from sending a cloud of fog around their heads. None of them carried flashlights anywhere that a button might accidentally be pushed. They did nothing to broadcast their position to the enemy.

The grinding patrol pace slowed even more as a last sliver of twilight faded to black. The men naturally tightened the formation so as not to lose sight of one another in darkness. Iman was able to see that they were only fifty meters from the cover of massive rocks. However, the fifty-meter stretch was wide open. A chasm of land spread before them and provided no concealment from enemy view. Flat earth stood between the Marines and their ability to hide or seek cover from direct fire. The sparse area gave Iman a great deal of reserved pause. Then he panicked in fatigue. His mind went blank. He should have been able to make a command decision instantly. He should have been able to push forward spitting in the face of danger. He should have been able to defy ordinary logic and go with his Marine gut. However, the leader was not able to deny his instinct for self-preservation and his human desire to survive.

Iman silently summoned down the line for his brother. Hasim slowly and quietly eased forward to join the patrol leader. The younger man raised his head rearward to silently ask what Iman's problem was with their current position. They had a straight line of sight on a likely sleeping enemy just beyond the refuge of large boulders. Iman, slightly ashamed at his sudden memory lapse, pointed to the southern defense. Then he formed his hands like he was holding invisible binoculars. He silently asked Hasim if the enemy guard might have night-vision goggles.

Hasim smiled and shook his head. Then he held up his thumb and two fingers, shook his fist twice, and held up three fingers forming a "W." *Three hundred meters west.* Iman translated the gesture to himself. He understood and remembered. One of two night-vision goggle sets in Farhad's camp was allocated to a weaker defensive position three hundred meters further west from the team's approach. The enemy's defenses were separated by a large rock formation between fighting holes. Iman saw shields of darkness and stone as the framed window of opportunity he needed to lead the team once again. The Marines could move directly north without being spotted by enemy troops to their west. It was a straight line from their concealed position, to the next point of cover, and onward to the first target.

The older brother then silently cursed himself. He was the one who had briefed McKenzee on equipment available at each site. Iman was the man in charge of choosing patrol routes based upon natural layouts and covered approaches to each of the enemy's fighting holes. He should have known where the night-vision goggles were. He had all the information he needed to win the battle against opposing combatants, but he was quickly losing his personal war against fatigue. Then he started to question his ability to lead the mission.

Hours of running through a frozen desert, followed by hours without food, drove the men to equal doubt. Exhaustion, another formidable enemy in any battle space, was one of the most horrible things the Marines had to face. If they dozed off, they could be killed without ever having put up a fight. If they closed their eyes, they would be visited by their nightmares. They would break noise discipline and surrender their whereabouts to their foes. Iman wished he could be asleep. He yearned for rest but knew he would not be able to shut his eyes until *Jericho* no longer existed.

Iman regrouped his senses. He gritted his teeth and soundlessly stirred himself awake. He was present on the battlefield once again. Iman pointed his flattened hand across the void between him and promised cover from enemy machine-gun fire. Hasim and three other Marines acknowledged Iman's order without a word. They ran on feather-light feet until they found the protection of large stones to the north. Iman then guided the next small group of warriors across the open area. They ran and made it safely across as well. The process continued until Iman stood alone.

He was on the edge of open terrain. Logic and reason told him to sprint. The wise warrior within knew that being exposed, even at night, was an extremely dangerous endeavor. He paused for a mere second longer then put his concerns aside.

Iman ran across the fifty-meter field. His feet smashed into frozen soil and sent crunched echoes of announcement into the night air. The leader was no louder or lighter than any other member of the team, but he could hear every amplified step as his heart thumped in his ears. Finally, he finished the journey safely and approached the rear area of his team's new rally point. The moon gave Iman barely enough light to conduct a quick head count as he arrived. He squinted to confirm everyone was present. All men made it safely across. He was relieved by the small success.

The leader's relief was not dictated by the fact that he had guided the team back to mission priority despite a horrific crash. Nor was his respite sigh given in the fact he was able to account for every living Marine lucky enough to have survived the fall. Instead, he felt the relief of being back on mission schedule, the window of time that determined who would live and who would die.

Iman and his team arrived at the rock formation only two hours behind their intended time. Command understood the woes of combat even before the first shot was fired, so the unexpected was taken into account when creating operations timelines. No expectations were set to-the-minute in basic consideration that variables cause delays. While the team did not have communications with Command beyond a laser designator that Iman recovered from the crash site, they did have an achievable timeline to arrive on target. Iman and the hardened warriors, set to cut a destructive path through the heart of the enemy, met operational deadlines and would be able to achieve their objective. It was a minor accomplishment to be recognized, but one integral to any hope of success. Had they been too far behind schedule, Command would assume them to be dead. No one would monitor any communications networks or target designators. No one would see desperate smoke signals being sent out by the forward Marines.

Mission success, as on any other day in the desert for Jarheads, took precedent over personal comfort. Tight windows of limited seconds provided the team no room for rest as previously planned. They would have to forego any last bits of ease. They had no time to find relief from hunger pangs or the muscular burns flashing throughout their bodies. Even still, they were ready in place and looking to fight. They were hungry hounds of hell frothing at the mouth on the edge of confrontation.

Each of the Marines had his weapon pointed north. They were stacked on top of and around the rocks providing them broad cover. The Marines could engage enemy combatants while presenting minimal targets for return fire. Hasim then took charge as predetermined in the flow of operations to strike at *Jericho*.

The younger staff sergeant moved down the firing line until he found Corporal Sanchez, a razor-edged Mexican American from south Texas. Sanchez finished Scout Sniper School more than three years prior to deployment into Afghanistan with Force Recon. He had been deployed in urban sniper missions several times, battles throughout Iraq that he had fought and won. The corporal had even carried out missions that he could not disclose to any other member on his team. Sanchez had the skills needed to cover those who would inflict hatred upon a clueless enemy.

Hasim lightly patted Sanchez on the shoulder without saying a word. Then the staff sergeant moved away to let the young corporal get to work. Sanchez understood the gesture. The sniper eased out of his pack and withdrew a night vision capable scope attachment for his bolt-action, long-range rifle. The sniper's lethality would not be limited by darkness.

Sanchez thought for a moment and remembered distances he studied on operation-centered maps at the command post. He knew they were back on schedule and back on their mission of destruction. *Three hundred and twenty-two meters,* Sanchez thought to himself as he set the elevation on his scope, one click up from his battlefield zero. He scanned the area to the left and to the right. He searched ridgelines and rock contours until he found his target area. The locale was still. No winds would impede a shortly lofted shot into the center-mass of any villain vapid enough to become visible against the night sky.

A machine-gun muzzle jaunted upward into the air. The bipod was spread wide, but no one rested behind the weapon. No guard stood ready to pull the trigger on any advancing foe. Iman's hope to catch the enemy off-guard was intact. The gun was unmanned. The enemy, poorly trained and undisciplined, was blind to the approaching Marines.

Sanchez gave a quick nod to Hasim. He let the senior Marine know all was set. Sanchez was ready to take a shot at anyone unlucky enough to be on post that night. Hasim moved away to rejoin Iman as Sanchez steadied deeper into his prone position. The sniper was eager, but steadfast in control. The team's fail-safe was in place. Any two men tasked to advance on the southern defensive position would be covered by an acutely accurate marksman. However, Sanchez was only meant to fire on orders from the unit leader. Any shot ringing out from his large-bore sniper rifle would allow the team to *go loud,* but would give away their position sooner than planned. Then there would be no hiding from an overwhelming enemy. An ensuing fight would rage until the last living Marine fired his last round of ammunition. Iman hoped to avoid such sudden conflict so as to accomplish maximum impact on the collective enemy.

The Marines were not afraid of an expected fight. They simply worried about mission success above all else. The American warriors were heavily outnumbered by armed jihadists. The terrorists could quickly compromise any ability to complete the mission, so the Marines remained quiet and still. They waited to move and would only do so if ordered out of their hushed positions.

Iman took another moment in the silence of the night. He collected his thoughts and considered the next step in a shaky battle plan. With Sanchez in place, Iman knew the next thing to do was tap Perry and Jackson on the shoulder. They would cross a wide area where they held cover between the rock formation and the southern defensive position, approach the likely sleeping guard, and cut his throat. The only problem impeding a *next step* was that *Murphy* visited the team with the full force of his law. Jackson was lying shoulder-to-shoulder with Lieutenant Gibson. He was miles behind the team and far too dead to carry out any assault on a machine-gun nest.

Hasim remembered who had been selected to carry out the two-man task just as Iman was considering Jackson's replacement. Perry could have strolled into the defense and handled the problem by himself. However, the younger staff sergeant realized what he must do in the interest of their mission. Hasim decided the best course of action was to volunteer himself as Perry's support. No other candidate was as well suited as one who had worked in the defense prior to moving into the offense. He knew just where the guard rested, the best way to get in and out of the fighting hole, and where not to step to avoid making noise. Then Hasim considered that Perry was actually going in support rather than it being the other way around.

Perry snaked out of his position and assumed a kneeling hold while he waited for Hasim to join him. A sudden and tight grip found Hasim's forearm as he started to move toward the enemy. *Maybe this plan wasn't such a good idea when the CIA came up with it.* Iman projected his innermost thoughts to Hasim with nothing more than a sorrowful look. Hasim grinned sadly and patted his brother over the top of Iman's hand. *I'll be fine. Stop worrying.* He reassured Iman without a sound. Hasim then looked at his older brother and realized how false the reassurance was.

The younger staff sergeant joined Perry. He knelt next to the Force Recon Marine and patted him on the shoulder. He gave the universal sign that he was ready to move in on an unfortunate enemy sentry.

Iman watched them move until they faded into darkness. He slid the shoulder straps of his pack down and off his arms. The edges of the pack dug into his fractured ribs, and he winced involuntarily. However, the toughened man remained quiet as he withdrew his night-vision goggles from their sheath. Iman alternated between watching Hasim cross the three hundred meters and looking for the defenseman to show any sign of life. Iman watched nervously as Hasim hemmed his way through rough brush and steep rocks. He hoped that his brother was able to remain silent despite nature's noisy traps. Then he hoped the same for Perry.

Like any big brother, Iman wanted to protect Hasim from bullies and threats of harm. However, the younger brother had slipped too far out of Iman's protective reach. Iman watched helplessly as Hasim slithered closer and closer to the enemy. Iman knew that the kill had to be quiet and quick. Otherwise, the next defensive position would come alive from behind the rock formation that shielded the Marines from an increased enemy force.

"Good man," Iman whispered so quietly that no one else could hear him. It was more of a heavy breath than a whisper, but it was still too loud. He needed to remain silent regardless of his pride for his Marines. He cursed himself again.

Iman watched as Perry slipped to the southwest corner of the enemy fighting hole. He grinned when he saw the Marine pull a stick out of the hole. Iman knew that stick-looking figure appeared harmless in the green of the night-vision goggles, but it was actually an AK-47.

Hasim and Perry successfully moved in undetected. The sentry was either asleep or unaware of the Marines' presence. Either way, the soon-to-die guard was without his assault rifle and out of reach from the bipod-mounted machine gun. Iman grinned and watched a horror film unfold before him.

Perry slid the rifle out of enemy grasp. Then Hasim slowly and surely stepped into the hole. He disappeared from Iman's line of sight. Iman's heart stopped. His inner voice screamed at him once again. *I should have gone. I should have been the one. Hasim...he was too close. He'll carry this with him forever.* Iman's inner voice screamed louder than any noise made by a dying man only a short distance away. No one heard a sound come from the enemy position.

Suddenly, three infrared flashes blinked across the night sky. Then three more followed. It was Hasim's signal. The fighting position was clear. The team could move into place for the final violent act of their mission.

Iman stood into a low and hunched posture. He was still on patrol despite the black night and the unabated approach to the southern defense. *Surely Farhad knows that we deserted by now. He has to be informed about the escorts' bodies found in the desert, the missing vehicle, and the fact that the suicide mission went to nothingness.* The senior Marine was distracted from his environment. *I hope he did not find out that Rasa discovered us. If so, she is dead, and I'm happy to bring hell to this place.* Iman gritted his teeth as his feathered touch eased his boots across the harsh terrain.

The team moved without having to be told a single command. They etched their way across rocks and sand with precision. They moved like a well-armed and highly motivated drill team. Every rehearsal and practice run prepared them to sneak in, attack, and withdraw from an enemy that would never know of Force Recon's existence in the area. They were magnificently quiet, deadly in their hardline discipline.

Hasim was unstirred by the team's sudden appearance. He had assumed a defense in the captured position and focused all his energy toward Jericho. Perry aimed his weapon at the enemy post due-west of their location, but acquired no targets on account of the rocks between them. Hasim pointed northwest where he knew the main camp to be.

The canvas tents were still eight hundred meters away. Hasim did not anticipate any enemy encroachment without the Marines being able to acquire and eliminate targets quickly. Darkness lingered and the morning hour was still too early for Fajr. The pre-sunrise call to prayer would not sound for a few more hours. They finally found a moment of pause on the battlefield.

"Easy," Iman whispered to Hasim. The younger brother seemed to whip his weapon around in search of targets outside of the fighting hole. Hasim's adrenaline was pumping electric currents of fear and excitement from his head to his toes. "It's dead out there for now," Iman reassured through the lightest of sounds.

Hasim relaxed and faced northwest once again. However, his demeanor had changed. He was distant even in the closeness of the fighting hole. Iman wondered what might be on Hasim's mind. Then Iman accidentally kicked the reason Hasim had suddenly developed a new chasm in hatred.

Iman's curiosity got the best of him. He knelt down and turned the dead body over. Iman tried for a moment but could not recognize the slain guard. Hasim had not simply killed the man. Rather, he ensured that the kill would remain silent. The younger staff sergeant pierced into the right side of the man's neck and sawed all the way outward until blade cleared clinging flesh. The jihadist's throat was splayed open like a butchered animal. Then, out of rage or need to quiet the dying man's gurgles, Hasim stabbed into and around the guard's face until there was no noise. Iman was sickened by the brutality of Hasim's attack at first, but considered the means necessary. Hasim had to silence the enemy, or silence his rage within. Iman accepted the justification by both accounts. The sentry was dead and the Marines held a high-value position.

Iman stood up from the body. He looked at Perry. Perry, still facing west, continued to glance over at Hasim. It appeared as if the subordinate Marine was in awe of the staff sergeant. Only a day prior, the Force Recon team assumed that Iman and Hasim were nothing more than spooks set on ruining a perfectly good mission to kill the enemy. Perry had not previously needed to know what the Arab Americans were capable of in combat. However, any doubts he had for Hasim's willingness to kill were put to rest and sent to hell with that dead terrorist.

*Who is that?* Iman questioned silently to himself. He tried to determine if the dead man was someone with whom he or Hasim might have shared prayer time, or a meal, or a weapon. He wondered if he had been gone from the camp long enough to have forgotten names and faces. He tried to determine if his connection to the people in camp was even real. Then he thought of Rasa. *Could I even pick her out in the crowd? What was I feeling? Did I love her or was I infatuated by the lack of threat?* He paused. Then he reveled as his heart fluttered to the thought of her name. *I love her...I hope that she will find me in Paradise if only to forgive me.*

# MOVE

**E**ight hundred meters was an insurmountable distance in the dark. However, the abyss between Marines and their enemy was set to disappear as soon as the sun lurked over nearby mountaintops. They would soon be successful in their mission, or they would be discovered and killed. Even still, the devoted heroes refused to die without expending their every bullet for the sake of killing as many of them as possible.

Every Marine cursed the opposition. They dehumanized their foe, making it easier to kill the enemy. Perry wished his bullets were made of pork in a simple and snide attempt to ensure none of the bad guys found their way to Paradise. The Marines readied for a fight. Their fangs gnashed. Their snouts snarled. Their eyes blared. Their trigger fingers twitched.

Hasim remained in the corner of the fighting hole. Perry stood to the senior Marine's immediate left. Iman was steadily opposite both of them. The rest of the team fanned out into a staggered line lateral to the established position. If the enemy engaged, the American warriors would present a much bolder face than what was true to their number. They would answer small-arms fire with an array of weapons and hate. They would win at least two skirmishes before being overrun and killed. Every man was sure of their initial successes long before the first shot was fired. The Marines carried with them confidence as sharp as their sheathed blades and as deadly as their loaded weapons. They readily waited for the fight and tried not to grin.

*Eight hundred meters?* Iman's thoughts betrayed the mission once again. He hoped and prayed that McKenzee would keep to the plan. The long distance in the dark was certain to reduce in the light. Eight hundred meters between Iman and Farhad would soon be swallowed in gunfire or earth-shattering explosions. Every ounce of Iman ached for a swift end. He and Hasim had been in the fight for so long, torn from their kinsmen and themselves for so long, and dedicated to destruction for so long that Iman did nothing shy of beg for finality. The conclusion, the inevitably bloody end, would only be realized if McKenzee kept to the plan.

The team was to set sights on the camp with a laser designator, their only remaining connection to any other Americans in-country. Air support would then respond with Mark-82, five-hundred-pound bombs. However, McKenzee wanted to make sure that no one escaped the gate to Hades. He wanted to make sure everyone in camp died and that no one could be identified for propaganda later on. The operations leader decided that one bomb simply would not do, so McKenzee's kill order called for six.

According to the plan, none of the bombs were to be dropped further south than the northernmost point of the laser. The massive explosions were meant to end the jihadist camp but spare the Marines designating the target. The Force Recon team hated the idea of surviving a helicopter crash and a raid only to be killed by friendly fire from the sky. Then a thought occurred to Iman. They had been without communications to Command since the helicopter crash. No doubt remained that McKenzee was aware of the downed bird. Iman then considered the scenario as it would have played out in the command center.

*McKenzee gets word that the bird is down. We are Mission-Priority One, so he would have sent Para Rescue or TRAP...Tactical Recovery of Aircraft Personnel. Why can't they just call them Pilot Go-Getters?* Iman smirked to his coy mocking of Marine acronym complexity. *If he sent TRAP, then they would have found the bodies to be a team shy of complete. He's either going to assume we were captured and call off the mission...or he's going to give the go-ahead and sacrifice the team. In any case, he's probably having somebody monitor for laser signals in our area...I hope.* He was distracted by fatigue. *Man, I'm tired.* He rubbed his eyes. Then he signaled the next Marine over to his right side.

Iman put his fists together, end over end, and held them to his eye like a sailor looking into an old telescopic lens. He was calling for the laser designator. Rodriguez, the next man over, understood the command and passed it down the line.

The message carried like an elementary game of telephone. However, the request was received clearly on the other end. The game ended with Sergeant Ingle. The sergeant turned from his position. He slid from the right flank and behind the line of prone Marines with a medium-sized equipment box in tow. Ingle tapped the boot of every man he passed. He silently told the other Marines that he was on the move. He also kept his bearing in the dark to make sure he met the unit commander without unnecessary delay.

Ingle slipped into the fighting hole, never increasing his shadowed silhouette from a downed position. His face was as black as the night, covered with camouflage paint and dirt. He was invisible even in close proximity to Iman. Ingle was trained to move without being detected. He knew that Marines who followed their training stayed alive more often than those who did not. He was an ambassador of what fighting men should do in the field.

Iman nodded to the dark figure that slithered into the former enemy-held hole. Ingle understood Iman's head motion as being the go-ahead to remove the laser designator from its heavy plastic case. Such a feat would require finesse in the blackest hours of early morning. The case was made of thick industrial plastic that banged like a drum when accidentally struck by any object. Metal snaps on the case clicked and popped loudly into the silence of the night if not twisted loose with the lightest of touches. Burdensome and loud, the equipment carrier was an albatross seeking only to give away the Marines' position and intentions.

Sergeant Ingle's fingers eased the metal butterfly clips open at either side of the case. He considered how loud a metal-on-metal click would be in the void of night. Then he wondered why the equipment designers had not created a more silent means of opening the box. *They might as well have covered the edges with Velcro and put a car alarm in it.* Ingle's humor remained silently intact as he nervously opened the clips. He moved like a man disarming a bomb. He was careful to avoid making any sudden or wrong moves.

Once the clips quietly popped open, Ingle was able to remove the top half of the box. The laser designator was held securely in place by thick foam. The box was much larger than needed, and the foam was broad enough to keep the weapon system from getting damaged in the event of a sudden collision. Considering the laser designator was the last piece of communications equipment the team had after an unexpected bang of a helicopter crash, Ingle was thankful for the cumbersome box and the excessive padding inside.

Ingle withdrew the laser from its foam surroundings. He flipped an accompanying low-profile tripod open and readied the weapon guide. Then he looked to Iman for further orders.

Iman signaled for the Marine to move across the fighting hole. He knew that Hasim had a direct line of sight on the main camp. Hasim, in his wisdom of the place, had chosen the most optimal position to obtain as many kills as possible. The younger brother seemed pressingly full of vengeful desire, more so than ever before.

"Excuse me, Staff Sergeant," Ingle whispered quietly. He requested access to Hasim's position, but he did so in reverence of the senior fighter. Ingle saw the slain guard's body jammed into the corner of the fighting hole. The dead man's shape was barely recognizable in the darkness, so he glared harder to adjust his vision. He saw the destruction that Hasim wrought on the man. Ingle looked to Hasim in a new light, that of Spartan pride and victory lust. Any doubts that Ingle might have held about Iman and Hasim dissipated.

Hasim moved aside just enough for Ingle to take place. Ingle, having only used the designator a few times in training scenarios, acted as if it was part of his daily routine. The Marine mastered the tool quicker than any of his immediate peers, living or dead.

Back home, Sergeant Ingle was ultimately out of his element. If someone were to put him behind the wheel of a car with a street map, he would be lost forever. However, he could pick up an ancient compass and a topographical map to find his way anywhere in the world. Scopes, radios, satellite communications, and computers all became as natural to Ingle as his rifle or sidearm. He found his niche in pieces of military gear, operating them with more comfort and ease than the common man operating a toaster.

He was one of very few Marines that instantly became proficient with any technical equipment ever handed to him. Therefore, he was the resident target acquisition expert. Ingle spent many missions serving as part of a two-man Forward Observation post in Joint Task Force missions with the fast movers of the United

States Air Force. His efforts in Iraq were recognized in the destruction of several enemy bunkers and the payoff of many high-value
targets. There was no better man in Iman's Marine Corps suited for
the job at hand.

Ingle embraced the mission and equipment wholeheartedly. He stood in the corner of the fighting hole facing out from
his team. Any observant enemy soldier would be able to see the
highly exposed equipment and the Marine behind it at first daylight. However, Ingle hoped against day and observation. Then he
used the night-vision setting on the laser to acquire his target. He
pointed north-northwest and found his mark.

"On target, Staff Sergeant," Ingle breathed only in a whisper
to confirm his aim. Iman would have missed Ingle's impossibly
quiet words in the mountain's winds had darkness not been so still.
However, the air was thick and heavy. No morning breeze came
about. The previous days' snow melted away in wet pools of sloppy
earth. Living vegetation lapped at the precious water in the sun's
heat throughout previous afternoon hours. Water then refroze in
the dropped temperatures of night. Even desert sand felt like shards
of ice as Iman placed his hand at the edge of the fighting hole.

Iman acknowledged Sergeant Ingle then paused. He inhaled
deeply and with a soft and firm order. "No matter what happens
next, you keep the target painted. You hear me?" The staff sergeant wanted confirmation of his order before he made any further
move. "This mission is now in your hands, Marine," Iman reiterated through chattering teeth and a heavy whisper.

Ingle nodded while looking over the top of the laser designator.
"I understand, Staff Sergeant. They'll have to kill me to move me."

Ingle didn't see Iman smile. The younger Marine was too
focused on his task. He stared too far off into the eight hundred
meters between him and what he hoped would soon be lit with

fire. Iman countered, "You don't have permission to die on this team, Sergeant."

Ingle didn't miss a beat. He simply answered as if there was any realism to Iman's comment. "Aye-aye, Staff Sergeant."

Iman patted Ingle on the back. He barely knew the young man but was proud of the sergeant all the same. Iman counted Ingle as a brother. He was readily willing to give his life so that the younger Marine could follow the ridiculous order to stay alive. Iman had no doubt that Ingle would do the same in return.

The staff sergeant looked at his surroundings. He tried not to tear up with pain, exhaustion, and emotion. Iman knew that the team was made of men who were cut from a different cloth. They were, in fact, cut directly from the Marine Corps flag. They were crimson and gold. They were the beings that protected friendly dreams and haunted enemy nightmares. Iman reveled at the professional devotion to their tasks, to mission accomplishment, and to each other. *If only the rest of the world could know what it is like to be one of us, the few.* Iman pondered the idea in the dark.

Silence. Darkness. Boredom. Emptiness made an awful foe to face in the fog of war. Fatigued and fight-ready Marines had to battle sleep. They had to remain alert even though the average brain wandered and dreamed of other things. The Marines defied their bodies' urges to move from one distracting subject after the next before disappearing to sleep. Their only duty was to remain awake, and for normal people the task would have been too much.

Iman knew that he should be more alert and more focused toward his mission. However, he took the time to distract himself from soon-to-come horrors with any thought that came to mind. He could not stop thinking of other things or he would begin to think of her. Rasa was always at the forefront of his mind. He could not shake her from his daydreams and fantasies of a peaceful life together. Every dull moment between mission-pertinent actions and orders were brightened by Rasa. She was his addiction.

The senior Marine was glad that the desert was so dark. No one in the immediate area could see him smiling like a fool with tears in his eyes. He was a schoolboy in love. He was an infatuated teen chasing the prom queen. He was somewhere thousands of miles away, working in a cubicle, and watching the clock to see when he could get back home to her.

A light chuckle escaped his distracted smile. His inner thoughts broke free from his lips and violated noise discipline. *I never even got to see her face. How can I love her and I've never seen her? How will I know her in Paradise? I'm certain that Allah does not want his most beautiful creatures to be covered. I need to see her. I can't die without ever having looked into her eyes to tell her.*

Iman suddenly committed an unthinkable act. He placed his flat palms to the edge of the fighting hole and hoisted himself out of the earth. He sprang upward like a random weed that appears in a well-manicured garden. His silhouette sprouted an unwelcomed shadow amidst prone Marines.

The team was stunned and distracted by the noise. Bold motions in the defense were unheard of. If a Marine had to relieve himself while in the defense, he peed his pants rather than get out of his fighting hole. He did not leave his piece of dirt unless tapped to go on patrol. Only then would he move from his position, and only to the call-and-challenge of passwords set by other defending Marines.

"What are you doing?" Hasim turned quickly to snap at Iman through a near-silent hiss. He wondered if his older brother was sleepwalking or if Iman had simply lost his mind to the boredom of waiting for war. "Get back down, you idiot," Hasim screamed through a whisper.

Iman didn't pretend that Hasim's scolding went unheard. Instead, he acknowledged his brother. He turned to Hasim at the corner of the shallow hole where warriors sat uncomfortably eager. The older man knelt so that he could whisper even quieter than needed. "I have to..." Iman paused. He wondered how ludicrous his next words might sound. Then he continued, opinions be damned. "I have to see her. I have to see her face before either of us dies...before both of us die. I cannot imagine living another day without knowing her face."

Hasim looked at Iman, intent, angry, and confused. Then he looked into his big brother's eyes and understood how serious Iman was about going back into the snake pit. Iman was going to see Rasa. Their attempts to remove themselves from the raid and act only as professional Marines fluttered away. Nothing was ever going to be more intimate than the attack on *Jericho*. They knew every single person in the camp. The brothers had walked among the enemy. They knew names and family histories. They would be haunted by the faces of *Jericho* for the rest of their lives. Hasim knew it to be true and wholeheartedly embraced Iman's thoughts.

"I'm going with you," Hasim whispered back. Iman tried to shake him off, but Hasim leapt from the fighting hole just as the elder had done.

"Whatever you are doing, do it quick. Get away from us before you get us all killed," Ingle whispered to the exposed staff sergeants.

"Ingle, you have command," Iman spoke softly in response. He handed mission control over to the next ranking man, the most proficient behind the laser designator. Then he looked over and shook his head to Hasim.

"You don't have to do this," Iman said, trying to coax Hasim out of the suicide mission.

Hasim shrugged. "If you get to see Rasa...then I get to kill Farhad." A wave of understanding filled the air between the brothers. Neither of the men could disavow emotional connection to the village and the people within. Iman was connected to Rasa through love. Hasim was connected to Farhad through hate. Iman then patted Hasim on the shoulder. They gave one last look to the Marines before turning to the enemy.

The patrolling Marines remained behind a shield, a stone wall separating them from other defensive positions, so they could travel the eight hundred meters in a straight line unabated by enemy gunfire. The brothers were able to move quickly without having to exercise extensive tactical maneuvers. They were also endowed with the firsthand knowledge of the trail between the southern defense and the main body of camp.

Only two hours remained before Fajr. One hundred and twenty minutes would tick away like seconds. The morning's call to prayer would soon alert the entire village of the Marines lurking about. An inevitable fight was upon them, so the men wasted no time disappearing into darkness on the trek north-northwest. They moved through the night to bring war directly to the devil's doorstep

# PAINTED

**E**ight hundred meters over hard terrain, void of light, would have been too much for a commander to ask of any man under any other circumstances. Yet Iman and Hasim were able to cross the distance without issue. They broke the cardinal rules of patrolling enemy territory. Rather than take to the high side of the hill at their eastern flank, they walked the trail. There was no sense in braving the needled brushes and deep holes in the hillside for the sake of carrying out a suicide mission. The men willingly risked a quick death. They thought it better than being injured following patrol procedures and limping to the same inevitable demise.

Each of the men had walked the trail from the southern defense back to the main camp so many times they were able to do it blindfolded by night. They remembered where to step and where they dare not place their feet. Iman and Hasim remembered their every observation of the trail, where they would have been visible to an observing enemy had clouds not covered the moon, and where they would be able to encroach the camp undetected.

Even though the Marines were at ease on the trail, they never relaxed from their patrol postures. Both hunched over their weapons and kept ready to fire. Their fists wrenched tightly and desperately into the rifles' handgrips. They scanned left and right nervously. The many previous days and nights walked over the trail no longer brought an empty sense of safety. Security, or the illusions thereof, became darker than the fading night sky. The Marines were back on the other side of the combat line. Disloyal to the jihadists' cause of hate, Iman and Hasim would be killed on sight. They could no longer leisurely stroll by any standing guard under the assumption that the Marines meant no harm. They were present and held with them a clear purpose of destruction.

Marine camouflage utilities, covered with body armor, draped in special operations gear were tell-all signs that Farhad's enemies had come. The prophet, false in faith, was accurate in a portion of his sermons. Americans were coming to destroy his way of life. Iman and Hasim, former sons of jihad, were coming home to kill the father.

Hasim covered the left side of the trail. He paced, pointing forward and scanning left. The younger brother tried to prepare himself, mentally and physically, to down any target on the left side of the rocky path.

Iman was set to the right side. He scanned and moved forward as Hasim's mirror image. They continually checked over the tops of their weapons. They aimed high, low, and straight ahead. The enemy was omnipresent and would not hesitate to kill any intruders. Gunfire would not come as a surprise. Yet the direction from which the bullets came was difficult to determine in the remnant dark. They were vigilant.

Iman's mind raced. *Surely, they had to have changed something. How far removed from communication are they if Farhad hasn't heard of our escape? This has to be a trap.* Iman did not trust the ease with which they approached the main camp. No one was present. He suspected that they were being lured into a snare. Iman anticipated Farhad, or any of his lieutenants, would soon spring the ambush and the Marines would be killed.

Concerned reservations set in with the staff sergeants as they considered rapidly diminishing concealment from enemy troops. The pile of boulders separating the southern Marine-held position from the western enemy-held hole no longer provided cover from the jihadists on post. Iman and Hasim entered into the slight clearing at the end of the trail. They walked into the open, standing between sleeping watchmen to their west and the main camp to their north. They were suddenly unnerved.

Iman feared for his life, and for that of his brother, but he remembered his accompanied walks when he lived as an insurgent. It was the part of his daily stroll from camp, his chore to defend the village, that he loved the most. It was the only time of day when he and Rasa were nearly alone. It was the only time he was able to appreciate her presence and understand their bond. He remembered glancing at her, wanting to touch her despite the forbidden contact, and felt the connection to the alluring woman once again. Iman suddenly felt as if he were a young man, a pilgrim, returning home to his sweetheart. Then he parted from the area and from Rasa for the moment. He was back to war.

Hasim signaled to Iman. The route was clear. Iman crossed the trail to the left and they approached the southern edge of a canvas tent. The area would have been silent if not for the heavy breathing and snoring of deep sleepers. The Marines anticipated an imminent wake-up call. Hasim tried to keep track of their time spent on approach and infiltration.

Time, precious minutes, were dwindling into grains of sand through an hourglass. Iman hoped that they could retrieve Rasa before Fajr. He prayed that the laser designator's call to destruction had not yet been answered by Command. He silently begged McKenzee to delay. *Just a little longer. Don't send the zoomies yet, McKenzee.* Iman tried to communicate his plea despite the radio missing from his hand. He willed the thoughts to McKenzee with nothing more than desperation in his heart. Then he prayed. *Please don't let me die here...please don't let me die without her.* His blood ran red-hot through his veins. He tried not to tremble at the idea of a coming fight. Iman knew they had to move quickly if there was to be any chance for survival.

Iman arrived first at the rear corner of a quiet tent. He made a quick check around the edge and found no guard anywhere along the row of canvas pop-ups. He hoped no one was out of sight, between the flapping structures, that could surprise the intruders as they approached Farhad's impromptu house.

A rifle muzzle protruded into fading darkness as Iman turned the corner with his weapon at his shoulder. He swept away from the walls of the large semi-structure so as not to trip over tension lines tethered between roof and grounded stakes. The shivering Marines looked over the dark tent and envied its promised warmth.

The morning air became crisp. A slight breeze pushed winter into the creases of their camouflaged uniforms. Chilled temperature drops were the first sign of an approaching sunrise. Fajr, the morning call to prayer, would be on them just before a swarm of jihadists. Iman prayed that they would be lucky enough to be killed quickly in a firefight. He considered the comforts of swift death as an alternative to being forced into surrender within the camp. He dared not think of what Farhad would do to them, especially the devout Hasim, if they were captured. Then he measured the ultimate exit. Iman decided that he would swallow his sidearm before being confined by the village. He regretted his decision to encroach for the sake of an emotion. He lamented the idea of dying for a woman he did not know, but he was committed to his word. He made a vow and was willing to face death in the name of honor.

*Spare me. Spare me. Spare me.* Rasa's written words haunted Iman as his boots pressed over desert-defining sediment. Rasa's note flew around in Iman's brain. *Spare me. Spare me. Spare me.* He could not back out of his personal mission.

If he was successful in the unsanctioned raid, he would be court-martialed with a smile on his face because he would live out his days with his love. If he was not successful, then military legal matters would no longer be of concern as he would be dining in Paradise. *Spare me.* Rasa's unbroken but quiet spirit called to him.

Irony churned in the pit of Iman's gut. He returned, taking the southern defensive position to bring fire into the village that he once protected. He returned to the village bringing war to Rasa. He returned to destroy life, but he yearned to save it. Then he set philosophy aside and moved forward.

Hasim followed Iman's sweeping route around the tent's lines. Iman cleared gaps between the tents ahead of his younger brother, but Hasim repeated the motion. People are mobile beings. Hasim understood that Iman might have had a clear area, but that would not prevent a guard from stepping into place as the older brother passed. Hasim took nothing for granted among known hostiles.

The younger man was not confident in the overall success of their mission. Without communications gear, a lone-standing team of Marines would only be as useful as the ammunition they carried. The men could only bring destruction a few bullets at a time. They would kill more than a hundred insurgents before ammunition ran dry.

Hasim was confident in the team's ability to fight, but he doubted Command's ability to pick up the laser signal on an unexpected broadcast from men considered lost to the war. *We were shot down and written off for dead. They aren't coming...but I'll see to it that Farhad doesn't live another day.* Hasim's inner beast clawed out of him with hatred and revenge. He quickly laid his reservations to rest. He no longer regretted their presence on the outer edge of the village.

Hasim was happy to help his brother extract love from hate. He had fantasized about getting back to the United States. He dreamed of living on a cul-de-sac next door to Iman and his wife. *Uncle Hasim. That has a nice ring to it.* Hasim fought back a smile as his distracted mind remembered to clear the next area between tents. Then he shifted his thoughts back to war.

Iman reached Farhad's tent just before Hasim. Then they silently evaluated the best way to enter without being heard by the sleeping inhabitants. The lower edge of the tent was held in place with several sandbags to prevent a winter draft from causing any discomfort inside. Hasim turned outward to watch for troops while Iman removed the sandbags one at a time. Iman squatted and moved quietly.

Hunched over, Iman finished the job. Sandbags were stacked aside and the bottom flap of the tent opened enough for him to slide under. He secured the tent, sweeping his weapon from left to right, and found that no one was awake. He looked to the heavy-set man wrapped in blankets upon a cot. Farhad was in a deep sleep and likely enjoying his last minutes of rest before prayer. Then Iman looked for Rasa.

The younger brother interrupted Iman's search as Hasim slid under the tent wall. A light scraping sound announced Hasim's arrival as combat gear dug into the sand. Hasim slowed to a silent crawl until he was able to return from the prone position. He joined Iman at the back of the tent. They stood together in the heart of the beast, but they had different objectives. Iman was there to save a life. Hasim was there to take one.

Rasa would be easily identified. Iman knew she would be separate from Farhad's several other wives. Hasim scowled as his older brother searched for his love. Farhad's wives slept in an intertwined pile, a godless harem. They were naked beneath their twisted blankets. The women weaved into each other for warmth or for affection from the night prior. Hasim hated Farhad more. The hypocrisy of Farhad's self-proclaimed righteousness stewed in Hasim as he stepped to the elder's cot. He hovered over the sleeping man. Hasim's heart raced. His breaths became a heaved notion of anticipation, but he waited.

Iman stepped to the outsider among the women. Rasa was not mingled into the heap of wives. He tried not to think of the deeds she was forced into the night before. To him she was pure, and he wanted to hold onto that notion alone. He knelt next to Rasa and placed his hand over her mouth. Iman worried that she would scream in a waking fright. She would not recognize him without a beard or turban. His hair was cropped short. He was in Marine form. She would react to the weapons and gear, to the darkness of his shadow, to the paint on his face, to the war in his eyes. She would be right to do so. He was an intruder coming to take her away.

Rasa's eyes sprang open, and she stirred only for a second. Her eyes caught Iman's, and they exchanged their familiar glance. Her heart crashed loudly against the inside of her chest, first in the fright of the sudden wake-up, then to relief. Iman watched her face flood with tears. Then the captor bent down and breathed lightly into her ear. "Iman," was all that he whispered and all that she needed to know. He had come for her.

Iman nodded and Rasa returned the gesture. His war-crazed eyes softened. His nerves settled. He removed his hand from her mouth and stood. He helped her to her feet. Finally, he looked to Hasim.

The older brother held up one finger to Hasim's eagerness. *Just one minute.* Iman pleaded for patience. Killing Farhad was the younger brother's main focus, but Iman wanted to remove Rasa from the coming blood. Iman lifted the bottom of the tent wall and slid out first. He made sure that all was clear before lifting the tent once again. Rasa shivered as she hurried from the warmth of the tent into the morning air. She leaned into Iman for comfort, for warmth, for his protection as she joined him in the war.

Hasim waited until purity was gone from the canvas room. Then he quietly unsnapped the sheath on his chest. The blade was still coated with coagulated blood from the man he had slaughtered in the south, but it cleared the leather case without obstruction.

Lurking in the shadows of the tent, Hasim stepped closer to Farhad. The Marine wrenched his fist into the old man's blankets. In a single motion, Hasim jerked the fabric clear of Farhad and stabbed his knife down hard into the side of the old man's throat. A gurgled yelp dissipated into the cold morning. Farhad choked for life, but could not scream for help. The steel blade entered the left side of the old man's neck and exited the right. Hasim sawed through flesh and wind-giving tissue as he was trained to do. He cut so deep, so fueled with vengeance, that he tore through the cot's fabric beneath Farhad. The tip of his blade clinked against the cot's metal frame. Hasim hoped it was not enough noise to cause a stir. The gurgling and choking, the kicking struggle, and the clink were far more than what should have been produced. Yet Hasim was resolved to make sure Farhad died an uneasy death. He served the false prophet a swift dose of penance. No man would ever be sent to his death, to murder innocent people, or to carry out orders from Farhad's forked tongue ever again.

Farhad's eyes widened with glazed fear. His jaw slacked open. His throat was left agape. Hasim was satisfied. He watched the light in Farhad's eyes quickly match the darkness of the tent. Then he moved away to join his brother outside.

Hasim turned his back on the pile of women as he bent down to lift the bottom of the canvas exit. Bending down saved his life and nearly cost Rasa hers. Hasim ducked and tumbled under the tent wall. His body surged with hot pain and forward momentum created by gunfire and adrenaline.

A single shot was fired from inside Farhad's tent. One of the wives was roused by the noise of her husband's brutal death. Initial shock from the sight of a violent shadow wore off quickly. The woman reached for her nearby pistol and tried to kill the dark figure looking to make its exit. Her bullet tore at the flesh of Hasim's shoulder. Tumbling metal missed the edge of his body armor and met exposed meat on his right arm. Then the bullet carried through canvas and almost struck Rasa in the back of the head before disappearing into oblivion.

Hasim dove under the tent wall to the sound of women screaming in panic. All the wives were startled by the shot. The wife with a pistol in her hand began to fire wildly without aim into darkness and despair. She hoped to hit anyone on the other side of the wall. Another of the wives made a final, fatal error of sitting up during a gun battle. She was struck in the side of the head at point-blank range by the woman indiscriminately jerking on a trigger. Panic fire ensued and the entire village was brought to fright-filled life.

Iman and Hasim answered the panic fire. They aimed their weapons at the tent and sent hot bullets into the direction where they thought the wives would be. The brothers killed two without ever having seen the damage done. Then the renegade trio fled from behind Farhad's tent.

Noise discipline was gone. The camp was alive with rifles and rocket-propelled grenades. Every man, woman, and child was outside of their tents trying to assess the direction of fire and assert their defenses accordingly. The war had come to the village. The terrorists, young and old, were prepared to defend the small patch of land they knew to be home.

Iman's left hand gripped to Rasa's right so tightly that her fingers ached. He had to make sure that he did not let her go. He knew that rocks and difficult terrain were going to tear Rasa's feet into raw meat, but it had to be. There was no time to better prepare for their flight from the camp with shoes and warmer clothing.

They reached the edge of the outermost tent in the village confusion. Iman led with Rasa in tow. Hasim pulled up the rear. Just on the other side of the thin structures, jihadists screamed at one another trying to figure out what had happened. Several insurgents fired blindly into the hills thinking the shots came from outside of camp.

Iman and Rasa stepped out from behind the corner of the last canvas-wrapped pergola and came upon their clearing. The spot that once held so much peace for the paired lovers was filled with nothing but fear. Iman knew that they would have to cross in the open, in front of the entire village, before they could reach the trail heading south. He hoped that the discombobulated mass would still be too distracted to see them run for the path.

Hope was lost. Iman and Rasa broke for the trail just as one of Farhad's wives crawled from the front of the leader's tent. Her naked body was brought to light just as the sun appeared over the lip of the mountains. She was covered with bullet holes and trails of seeping blood. She was dead despite her ability to crawl.

The woman's theatrical exit drew the village's entire attention toward Farhad's tent as Hasim tried to cross the clearing behind

Iman and Rasa. He was caught in an array of gunfire before arriving at the mouth of the trail. Hasim's body armor broke to the several bullets that hit him in the back. The force knocked him from his feet. Iman looked back from his sprint and saw Hasim fall to the ground.

"Hasim!" the older brother screamed against the noise of incessant gunfire. Panic filled Iman's heart, but he was well trained. "Go!" Iman yelled to Rasa in Arabic. "Run to the south position with your hands all the way up. Surrender to the men there!" He prayed that Ingle would not be the first to see Rasa on approach. Ingle was a warrior, bloodthirsty and ready to kill any outsider on approach. He knew that the young Marine was disciplined on the trigger, but Iman and Hasim had already informed the men that there were no friendly forces in the camp. Ingle would have no reason to think that Rasa was not running at them strapped with a bomb.

There was no time to worry. He had to get to Hasim. Iman left the shelter of the trail's edge and sprinted back to his brother. He returned the enemy gunfire with fast pulls on his trigger. Two insurgents dropped from sight, but they were quickly replaced by three others. Iman was thankful that the jihadists were not able to shoot with any accuracy as bullets bounced all around the Marines.

Suddenly, two men from the weaker defensive position at the southwest appeared wielding their rifles. They opened fire on Iman and Hasim from the west. Then they turned to Rasa with a direct line of sight on the sprinting woman. One of the men shot Rasa just before she disappeared behind rocks along the trail's edge. The bullet entered her right side, tearing through flesh and breaking bone. The weight of the bullet's impact tripped her to the earth. Iman screamed "No!" and immediately regained the western guards' attention.

Furious and fearful, Iman lobbed a hand grenade as far as he could. The fist-sized explosive detonated directly between the two encroaching guards, and they disappeared into a bloody mist of shrapnel and flesh. Then he turned to the approaching village and repeated the motion. He threw every grenade on his belt until he had none left to give to the enemy. Then he threw Hasim's.

The grenade attack was immediately successful in casualty and suppression. Several men and women were blown apart or wounded enough to be drawn out of the fight. Others slowed their approach and tried to take cover. "Get up! Get up, brother. I need your help!" Iman begged Hasim. However, Hasim could not move. He was not conscious.

Iman knelt behind his brother and turned to face the enemy again. He placed well-aimed shots into the center of any target that presented itself. Then his rifle ran dry. He flung his rifle back on its sling and transferred to his pistol. Shot after shot, the villagers dropped to plumes of blood and dust.

"I'm up. I'm up," Hasim announced into the ground. He regained consciousness and realized he was down in the fight. Facedown, the young Marine was scared for lack of the rifle in his hands. He could feel the percussion of Iman's pistol firing over the top of his back, so he picked his head up only enough to locate his weapon. The rifle lay only a couple of feet away, resting naturally where it had been dropped when Hasim was shot in the back.

The younger Marine slid on his belly to reach his rifle. He found comfort and security in the pistol grip of his assault weapon. Hasim rejoined the fight. He forced himself over and shot in the direction that Iman was pointing. However, his shots were errant. He let loose in panic as he came back to life. Hasim was suffering the temporary lapse of balance and control following a period of unconsciousness.

"Can you move?" Iman asked through the noise.

"Yeah! I think so," Hasim reassured him. Iman gripped his brother by the wounded shoulders and hoisted the younger man to his feet.

"Let's get the hell out of here then!" Iman screamed as he turned to run for Rasa.

Iman ran to the eastern edge of the southbound trail and turned to face the enemy again. He had not reached Rasa, but he could not leave his wounded brother without cover fire. Iman opened into the enemy once again with hot metal. Hasim shuffled and tried to run farther south down the trail. Hasim sprinted in the opposite direction of Iman's aim. The younger brother tried to run for cover. He would kneel and set himself to suppress the enemy in Iman's egress. Hasim hustled to a small pile of rocks in the hopes they would protect him from enemy fire. Then a single bullet outran Hasim.

The projectile pierced the back of Hasim's neck and exited his lower jaw. Hasim's brain stem was severed from his body. The narrow gap between his plastic helmet and the collar of his body armor served as the slightest window of opportunity for a kill. Such opportunity was answered by an insurgent who was shooting wildly at one Marine and accidentally hit the other. Iman returned the favor and shot the insurgent through the heart.

Iman moved from his crouched position to retrieve Hasim. He saw that Hasim was gone. There was nothing left of him to save. Iman's eyes filled with water as he accepted that his brother was gone from him, from the world of man. Then his thoughts turned to Rasa. He hoped that he could still save her from the village.

Bullets and rock chips bounced around as Iman arrived at her limp body. She was laid out on her left side. The woman, struck through the ribs, gasped for air. Iman regretted that he did not have time to treat her wound. He knew that every second counted toward any lifesaving efforts, but the village was still coming down on top of them. The enemy was full of vengeance and hate for what happened to their spliced leader. They would not show compassion for a wounded woman or a mangled Marine.

Iman reached down and scooped Rasa into his arms. He was defenseless as he ran along the trail away from the enemy. The weight of Rasa's small frame slowed him down. A few jihadists caught up in pursuit to get a line of sight on Iman. They shot wildly. Their bullets were uncontrolled and missed all around the escaping lovers.

One of the insurgents ran out of bullets without ever hitting near his target. Rocks and sand kicked up all around Iman and Rasa. Another misfired and struggled to clear his weapon. The third insurgent spent his rounds to the south before his head ruptured open.

The man's skull decompressed and sprawled to a heavy sniper round sent overhead by Sanchez. Iman realized he was in sight of his Marines. He had a renewed hope, a new faith that he was going to be able to make the run and save Rasa. He prayed to get her to Doc in time.

Yet Iman was still not safe. The insurgent with the jammed rifle was able to clear his chamber. Then he stepped out and opened fire again. One bullet made its way between Iman's plates of body armor. The round cut through the staff sergeant's back and exited his chest inside his vest. Small shrapnel pierced through the top of his right lung. The upper right lobe collapsed to the decompression of Iman's chest cavity. He fell with Rasa in his arms. He was wounded, but he refused to drop his love. His elbows and knees dug into the sand as he absorbed the force of the impact to the ground. Rasa remained cradled in his grasp.

Sanchez did not let the opposition's shot go without revenge. The sniper acquired the new target and fired. The insurgent tumbled backward as his heart exploded. Then the world went quiet for a moment.

Iman huffed. He was still alive. He couldn't seem to hear anything, and he struggled to breathe. The Marine felt every ounce of suffocating pressure under his collapsed lung. He was drowning in his own blood. However, he continued clinging to hope. He knew that he could save Rasa. *Save her. Save her.* He mumbled to himself over and over through blood and pain. *Save her.* It became his mantra, ringing out louder than the struggled heartbeat thumping in his ears. *Save her.*

He ran with Rasa quickly fading in his arms. Both of them were unable to breathe. Iman's legs burned with fatigue and lack of oxygen, but he kept on. He pushed until he could see the faces of his Marines become clear in the onset of daylight. "Doc!" someone screamed from the hole.

Iman looked up and saw Sergeant Ingle waving him away. The wounded man stumbled into the path of the laser, an ill-advised move to shorten the intended distance of the airstrike from the Marines' area of operations. Iman staggered aside to clear the line.

"Doc!" someone screamed again. Doc Troy, the Navy corpsman with the team, ran from the safety of his prone position. He was not a Marine, but he had the heart of a lion. He was the only sailor any of the men ever cared to acknowledge. On the battlefield, he was their best friend. In the event of a wound, he was their medical messiah. He was Doc, and they knew he would forever put the Marines before himself even in the most futile of attempts to save a Jarhead from an injury that no one could survive.

Doc Troy sprinted toward Iman and slid on his knees to catch Rasa as Iman's legs gave out. "Who's worse?" Doc asked in an immediate attempt to triage their wounds. "Her...her," Iman was able to muster without a breath.

Sanchez fired again. The large-bore rifle kicked rearward into the sniper's shoulder. A heavy bullet spiraled down range until it found a bursting impact into the center of a terrorist's chest. The pursuer's left leg kicked out straight in front of him, removing any remaining balance from his body. It was a sure sign that Sanchez's bullet severed the man's spine. The Marines then finished the insurgent off, lobbing several rounds into the insurgent's body. Overwhelming accuracy from the Marines' shots suppressed the village remainder with fear of what might happen to any jihadists that became visible in the field of fire.

The encampment was fully armed and nearly at full count when the jihadists started pursuing Rasa and her two Marine escorts. They were able to kill one Marine and wound the other. The villagers intended to chase their enemy until nothing remained of the external threat. However, the terrorists had not anticipated running into a wall of hot lead coated in steel. The villagers withdrew from pursuit and tried to regroup in the safety of their tents. They recoiled like a frightened snake. The Marines held. Ingle's laser stayed aimed, ready on target.

# SMOKE

She's gone, Staff Sergeant." Doc Troy seemed to repeat the words to Iman with heartfelt remorse. Doc tried to make eye contact with Iman, but the senior Marine was a million miles away. His eyes were glazing over with the distance between him and life-giving breaths. The staff sergeant didn't respond. He was slipping in and out of shock, aching for his brother and clinging to Rasa. Iman had his arms wrapped around Rasa's shoulders. He embraced her with his ear to her chest. He silently pleaded for a heartbeat, any sound, any proof of life; but Iman was nearly deaf from the gun battle. The ringing in his ears drowned out all sound. He would not have been able to hear Rasa's motionless chest even if her heart was still drumming an announcement of her well-being.

"She's gone, man!" Doc said again, trying to reiterate that Iman no longer needed to hold onto the dead woman. The corpsman grabbed Iman by the shoulders and shook the senior enlisted man back to reality. Iman could hardly hear Doc Troy's muffled words beyond the overbearingly high-pitched tone in his ears. "She's dead," Doc yelled to Iman. "You have to get back in the fight!"

Farhad had not ever considered any possibility of the southern defensive position being turned inward on the established camp. Therefore, no contingency plan was made for the ingress and egress between the main camp and the south. The Marines were in a secure position. They were dug in and ready to fight in all directions, but the Marines pointed all of their fury north-north-west. The enemy, if they dared to approach, had to go through a funnel into the tip of a heavily guarded trail. The Force Recon team stood their ground like mighty Spartans hacking at an invading mass. Every insurgent that appeared in the corridor was struck down and remained in place as a lump of dead flesh. Other insurgents were not willing to risk their lives for the sake of extracting wounded men and women. The terrorists stayed hidden until they could work up enough courage and pop out for a quick shot at the Marines. The American warriors responded with lethal accuracy and heavyhanded kills.

"If they keep showing up, there won't be anything left for the airstrike," a voice called out in jest from the right side of the line. A series of chuckles and war cries carried into the morning air. The team dismissed any need for noise discipline. They taunted the eager-to-die. They laughed, screamed, spit, and cussed to the camp while they dared the insurgents to show something worth shooting. Iman knew better.

Doc Troy was finally able to convince Iman away from Rasa's body. The corpsman did what he could to patch the holes in Iman's back and chest. The field dressings soaked before they provided any damming relief. Doc could only try to keep blood inside Iman's body. Iman felt himself fading. Daylight dimmed despite the onset of late morning. Air was scarce no matter how hard he gasped. He struggled to stay awake. He fought for life with the same fervor that he used in battle. He was a warrior determined to win.

Iman, patched and weary, broke from Rasa. He remained present on the battlefield. He tapped the Marine to his right on the shoulder. The young man, Corporal Middleton, looked at the wounded staff sergeant and surrendered full attention. "What's up, Staff Sergeant?" the corporal asked. The young Force Recon Marine was worried for the dying leader. Middleton listened intently, as if Iman were pulling together his parting words.

The senior Marine pressed on the hole in his chest. He tried to stabilize the pressure in his body, allowing his lung to inflate. He was unsuccessful. Drying blood cracked and flaked at the corners of Iman's mouth. "Flank," Iman said, pointing to their right side. Iman knew there was a broken trail leading to the high side of the hill next to the Marines' position. The enemy would eventually make their way around and flank the Marines. The jihadists would gain a downward angle on their foes, and the Marines would be lost to the exposure of unabated gunfire.

"Roger that, Staff Sergeant," Middleton acknowledged. Then he barked out an order to the two corporals at the end of the line. "Make your way to the top of the hill there," Middleton said, pointing, "and make sure they don't flank us. Keep them pinned down as long as you can."

The corporals responded blindly to the order. They stood up from their prone positions and charged up the hill fearless of any enemy presence. They went looking for a fight and would hold until they won or died trying to win. Iman watched the Marines fade to the top of the hill. He wished them well and mentally marked the time. He guessed that the men would need relief or resupply by the middle of the night. *Just hang on until then, boys. We'll send you some support...eventually.*

"Hey, Staff Sergeant," Ingle took pause. He broke from his rifle long enough to check the laser. It was still on target. However, the battery was fading fast. "What are the chances you packed a backup battery for this thing?" Sergeant Ingle looked over his shoulder to the superior. Ingle imagined seeing Iman's battery light fading like the laser's indicator. Iman just grinned at the lost cause.

The laser designator was the team's last desperate grasp to contact Command. The Marines prayed, and did so aloud. Every man called out to God, either through mumbled lips or announced prayer, and begged for a miracle. Then the top of the hill at their right flank erupted into small-arms fire. Iman was right in his assessment of the team's position. The terrorists were coming to attack the Marines from the trail on the high side of the hill, but the corporals held the insurgents off in a hail of bullets and hand grenades.

The Marines fought well into the brightness of another snowy day. The men holding the hill killed three more jihadists before the village recoiled once again. Iman knew too much to leave a hole in his fight. He was privy to too many intricate details of the camp and surrounding trails. He was the Marines' most valuable asset.

A full morning of fighting led to a sporadic afternoon of skirmishes. Then the night became long with waiting to fight. Jihadists proved to be inept during daylight. The insurgents were worse off at night. They crashed loudly against rocks. Their weapons rattled. They whispered too loudly from one man to the other. Every action that gave away a position was answered with a hand grenade or a burst of gunfire from the Marines.

A few jihadists made initial attempts to attack the Marines early in the night. Most who made an effort did not experience the luxury of returning to their camp. The village never realized Iman was in command of the American unit. They had no idea that one of their own returned to destroy them. Iman used his knowledge of the place to ensure the Marines had an advantage in the fight at all times. Every Plan B the enemy could muster failed as quickly as it came about. The insurgents withdrew to regroup again and again. They fell back and enjoyed the relative safety behind rocks shielding them from the Americans.

The village of terrorists was losing manpower every time they came into a Marine's sights. The enemy had to reconsider their options for a counterattack, but none of them had the military knowledge required to mount anything effective. The village, beaten inward, was on the verge of surrender. Yet they fired inter-mittent, poorly aimed shots in the general direction of Iman's team. They harassed the Marines through the night with sudden rifle cracks. Then they disappeared fast enough to avoid engage-ment. The brave showed in the open and were killed accordingly. The cowardly lived until morning light once again forced away the eerie darkness.

Rays of sunlight beamed over the rocky hills to the east. There was no audible call to prayer. The insurgents skipped early obligations to Allah for the sake of a fight. The Force Recon team knew some attack of some proportion was in the works. Yet no gunfire echoed the trail. The air was quiet and still. The Marines were exhausted and fought to stay awake. They had not slept for an eternity.

Iman, worse for wear, could no longer stand over his rifle at the edge of the fighting hole. He turned around and sat down with his back against the shallow grave. The muzzle of his weapon went vertical, and he rested his forehead against the hand grips to pray.

Fatigued and hurting, he called to Allah. However, the dying man could not feel the words he was trying to say. He stared into Rasa's face, seeing her only for the first time in the full light. Sunlight glistened against her black hair. Her face was soft but sad. Rasa's eyes were closed tight in death. Her lower jaw rested awkwardly and left her mouth agape in a shattered frown. Iman cried at the sight of the woman. He tried to stave off a sob, but he was beaten. He had no energy left to give for bravery. He was in an unspeakable amount of pain.

With tears in his eyes, he looked out to the southern sky over the open desert. Day brightened with each passing second. Iman wondered if the increasing light meant he was lucky enough to experience another day or if he was leaving the world of man. He looked out to the desert from the rocky hillside. *Paradise.* Iman stared into the distant gates of a promised land through blinding light. He squinted at a wonderful mirage. Iman saw two specs against the open blue. The winter air warmed under a clear sky. The sun was lifting ever higher as the day progressed. Then he squinted to confirm his hallucination. *Two?* Iman questioned the vision.

Iman reached over and tapped Sergeant Ingle's shoulder. The Marine turned to give his attention and saw Iman pointing in the air to their rear. The sergeant's eyes burned in a sleepy haze against the sunlight. Even still, Ingle was able to confirm that Iman was not imagining the vision.

"Inbound!" Ingle shouted with relief and excitement. "Inbound," he called out again for the team to hear. "Pull them off the hill and everyone get in the hole!" Ingle's heart raced at what was about to happen. He was distracted only for a second by his feverish want for the mission to end. Suddenly, bits of rock and sand bounced off the earth around his spot in the fighting hole. He was quickly refocused on the fight. Ingle turned his rifle back on the enemy and fired a single shot. Ingle's bullet tore a hole through another terrorist's neck, and the world went quiet once again.

"Clear out!" someone at the end of the line called to the corporals holding the hillside flank. Then the Marine turned and sprinted toward the fighting hole to join his team. Iman looked outward trying to identify who it was, but he failed to make out the man's face for his blurring vision. The flank-defending corporals acknowledged with a faint response and withdrew from their position atop the exposed area. The men sprinted down the hill in an attempt to outrun incoming air support, but they were not fast enough.

The world erupted. The air shattered around them. Concussions of massive explosions along the north knocked both of them tumbling to the ground. The corporals, out of blast range from any fire or shrapnel, were still shaken into nausea by the blasts. Their lungs became void of any air. Their intestines nearly rattled loose inside them. Every nerve ending in their bodies felt exposed to the cold air. Their teeth felt hollow and their brains seemed to swell against their skulls.

*One. Two. Three.* The enormous bombs left even larger signatures on the ground. Day became brighter with the flashes of light just before the sky turned black with smoke. All the Marines hunkered down as tightly as they could inside the fighting hole. They compressed their bodies to combat the bowel-shaking blasts. A Marine at the end of the fighting hole reached out and dragged the corporals into the mix of blended bodies. Each of the men was dragged in headfirst and tried to keep from landing awkwardly on his neck. Then they balled up like the rest, hoping not to catch any blasts in the confusion of the attack.

*Four. Five. Six.* Gigantic blasts ensued. The earth rumbled. Rocks shook loose from the soil. The shape of the hill seemed to implode into a cave at the north. The main body of camp was a blackened crater empty of life. No structure remained. No bush was left unburned. No man, woman, or child captured any breathable air from the clouds of fire and smoke. The camp was laid to waste. Nothing remained but giant holes of ashen soil. *Until there be no enemy, but peace. Amen.* Iman cited the Rifleman's Creed coyly as a slant against the dead.

The explosions stopped after the sixth bomb dropped. Remnant rolling thunder carried over the mountains and into the valley. The Marines stood in their hole and cheered. Victoriously, they roared at the forsaken. The enemy was destroyed. The mission was complete. *Jericho* was gone from the world, and all its inhabitants were permanently separated from any ability to kill Americans.

Steadfast as a leader, Sergeant Ingle checked the laser designator. The signal was gone. The battery had died at some unknown point in the conflict. He realized how lucky they were not to be caught in the raid. Then he recounted. He did not care to discredit the pilots' skills and the Lord's diviåne intervention for *luck*. "Thank you," he said aloud to amazingly accurate pilots and to God himself. "Thank you," he repeated through a whispered sigh of relief.

Ingle turned to Iman with a smile on his face. "Hey, Staff Sergeant," he called out. Iman did not respond. The wounded man simply sat next to Rasa and stared at an infinite distance. Iman's arms were draped around Rasa's body as if he were making a desperate effort to save her from the blasts. "Staff Sergeant?" Ingle questioned as he poked at Iman's foot.

Iman looked up at Ingle. The staff sergeant was still alive. Ingle was once again amazed and gave his praises. "We need to pull back, Staff Sergeant. Maybe if we pop smoke, the pilots can call in an extract," Ingle coached the dying staff sergeant. Iman just nodded. He could not gather enough air to verbalize any orders, but he agreed vehemently with Ingle's thoughts for extract.

Ingle took charge in the staff sergeant's stead. He stood up and out of the hole. Barking and pointing, Ingle pulled the pin on a smoke grenade and threw it out from them. Then he gathered his men and conducted a quick head count. Billows of green powder burned into the air from the grenade canister's open end.

The sergeant continued to look skyward. He knew the pilots would conduct a flyby to complete a Battle Damage Assessment. In doing so, they would see green smoke and make the call to headquarters. The Force Recon team was still alive and in need of a ride home.

True to protocol, the pilots looped back around to confirm the damages done. Ingle was right in his assumption. The flyby gave the ground-based Marines a second opportunity to communicate with someone beyond the fighting hole. The lead pilot passed and reported the smoke signal back to Command. The follow-on pilot rocked his wings to let the ground troops know the message was received and relayed.

The Marines were elated. Every ounce of relief they previously reserved came out of them with victorious cheers and bellowed hollers. Each of the men smiled uncontrollably at the thought of leaving hell behind them.

"Don't get too happy, boys. We're still in it," Ingle barked at the Marines for celebrating before getting onto an extract helicopter. "Let's get down the hill and establish an LZ. And let's not forget that we have other camps in zone that may or may not come looking for a fight. We need to move most ricky-tick, and we are still very much in the fight." The sergeant's leadership burned a path for the rest of his team to follow.

The team would have no trouble completing their new objective. The bottom of the hill was an open clearing. Widespread desert that seemed too narrow in the darkness of night patrols was vast in the daylight. The open area provided plenty of accessible space for a helicopter to land. Very little work would have to be completed in establishing a safe landing zone. The team might find an area where a bush had to be hacked down, but they would be readily available for pickup by the time the extraction bird arrived.

Iman struggled to his feet. He coughed a thick wad of blood that hung from his lower lip as he stood to leave. Ingle watched as Iman fought to lift Rasa's limp body from the hole. "Staff Sergeant..." Ingle stopped himself before making the claim that Rasa could not come with them. "Let me...let me help you with her," he corrected his line of thinking before speaking.

Iman lifted Rasa as high as he could to Ingle. The sergeant dragged the dead woman and her suitor out of the earth. Then Ingle stood amazed as Iman gathered enough strength to lift Rasa. She was light in her small frame and would have been easy to carry under normal circumstances. However, her lifeless body hung in dead weight over Iman's forearms.

"Let me carry her, Staff Sergeant," Ingle requested. Iman was too exhausted, too out of breath, and too near death to argue. He shook his head, unable to answer aloud for his lack of air.

"Them," Iman rasped and nodded to the Marines. Ingle understood the order. Iman wanted to make sure that the team had a leader in position to carry out the helicopter extraction. Ingle knew how to set up an effective landing zone. The capable and experienced sergeant was the head warrior of the herd. Iman was in no condition to lead, so he put Ingle in full charge.

Able-bodied Marines ran down the hill and established forward positions. They stayed alert to any enemy that might be found in the open desert. The rest of the Marines, wounded in the helicopter crash, limped together in exodus down the slope. Their primary objective was complete. Their new objective was to descend the hill without breaking any ankles over loose rocks and steep grades.

They finally had time for pain. Sitting in place through the night did not help their search for comfort. They simply ached their way down the hill as quickly as they could. Each man remembered a basic training cliché. *Pain is your best friend because if you feel pain, it means you are still alive.*

Iman was the last of the troop. He silently begged his legs for every step until gravity gave him some assistance. He fought to stay upright as he walked with Rasa in his arms. *This is my sacrifice.* He coaxed himself to keep moving. *This is my love.*

His gaze was once again distant. The physical exertion of clearing the hill nearly destroyed what remained of his spirit. Yet he was resolved to take Rasa from that place.

Broken and weary, Iman stumbled and struggled to the foot of the hill. He looked around at dispersed Marines ready to continue in combat. Each man pointed outward from a tactical circle. Their weapons were aimed at invisible foes. They had succeeded in destroying *Jericho,* but they were still deep in Afghanistan, deep in enemy-held lands.

Iman arrived just in time to hear several men yell out, "Inbound! Bird inbound!" He looked up and saw that a CH-46 Sea Knight helicopter was sent to pull the team out of the field. The corners of his mouth turned upward with half of a relieved grin.

"Pop smoke," Ingle ordered to the flanks. The Marines did as ordered and sent brilliant pillars of orange and purple into the sky. They signaled the designated area for the pilot to land. The team waited while two Cobra gunship escorts cleared the area. Then the dual-propeller Sea Knight finally set down.

Sand kicked into the air around the Marines under chopping twin helicopter blades. Each man lowered his head and tried to look away from the dirt being thrown about by whirling machine-made winds. The reality remained that Marines were not allowed comfort, not even in the relief of being pulled from a combat zone.

The helicopter landed and immediately lowered its rear ramp to freshly tilled topsoil. Every man smiled at the sight. An open hatch was the most inviting thing the Marines had seen in a very long time. Lightly injured Marines helped the wounded. The wounded continued on, trying not to die.

Iman made sure that all Marines, junior to his rank, were loaded onto the extract bird before he considered walking on. He was exhausted from his loaded travel down the hill and wanted nothing more than to sit down. He was spent.

The last Marine boarded the helicopter, so Iman decided his time had come to join them. He was so tired that he did not have the energy to resist when a lance corporal raised his hand at the aircraft entrance. The junior Marine screamed over the noise of the helicopter, "She can't come with us, Staff Sergeant."

Iman just stared back at him. He would have killed the man with his eyes if he was able. A new string of blood dribbled from Iman's lower lip. Iman was about to fall to his knees if he was not granted immediate access to a seat. Then Sergeant Ingle intervened.

Ingle placed his open palm to the middle of the lance corporal's chest and shoved the younger man rearward. "She's coming with us. Now get out of the way." Ingle was inaudible under the propellers, but his message was clear.

The lance corporal looked to his crew chief and was answered with a nod. Iman was allowed passage. He moved to the first open seat and plopped into place. Rasa remained rested in his arms. He hunched over to hug her as the helicopter lifted into the sky. He did his best to protect her from harsh and sandy winds swirling into the back hatch.

The helicopter climbed. Air temperatures became even colder as the machine ascended. The staff sergeant wrapped his arms tightly around Rasa to keep her warm against the unforgiving winter. He slumped over her and kissed her forehead. Then Iman finally rested.

# RED

Y es, sir," Special Agent McKenzee spoke into a satellite phone headset at the edge of the command center communications tent. He was attempting to answer all the questions being posed by the secretary of defense. However, the agent did not hold his usual air of confidence. He didn't have all the answers to questions posed, but he tried to appease the Secretary nonetheless. "Yes, sir," he repeated through the static-filled telephone.

A Marine standing next to the agent waited patiently. He was only privy to McKenzee's half of the conversation and had no idea that the secretary of defense was on the other end of the line. "Yes, sir," McKenzee repeated. From the Marine's perspective, it appeared that McKenzee was being lectured or reprehended by whomever. Yet McKenzee was calm. The agent didn't stir or seem uneasy to the call. "Yes, sir. I'll let you know as soon as I know. The last report I had was that the bomb run was effective..." McKenzee paused again. "Yes, sir. I'll go talk to them right now. I'll let you know as soon as I know."

McKenzee's answers became completely redundant. The eavesdropping Marine discerned that McKenzee simply wanted off the

207

phone. The agent needed more information before presenting any conclusions. The civilian commander had pertinent matters to accomplish before sending a report to higher-echelon parties. However, the person on the other end of the call was important enough to keep McKenzee stirring.

Time spent without communication between the Force Recon team and Command left a great deal of unanswered questions for the Central Intelligence Agency. Special Agent McKenzee was chomping at the bit to debrief Iman and Hasim. He was eager to gain as much information as possible from the men he sent on an impossible endeavor.

"Sir..." McKenzee faked a broken signal. "I can't...you're... breaking..." Then he handed the headset back to the communications Marine. The agent slid his flattened hand across his neck signaling the Marine to disconnect the call. A shared chuckle ended the line.

The Marine did as he was ordered. He hung up without proper verbal termination of the call and looked back to the agent for further guidance. McKenzee grinned at the smooth-faced kid handling the long-distance communications network. "Congratulations, Marine," McKenzee said, smiling boldly. "You might be the first lance corporal to ever hang up on the secretary of defense and get away with it."

McKenzee slapped the Marine hard on the back. He chuckled to the sight of the kid in uniform. The Marine's eyes widened with concern just before he questioned if the agent was being serious. McKenzee kept smiling and walked away having not answered the kid's question. He left the young Jarhead grinning confusedly with concern.

The front flap of the communications tent whipped open to a light breeze. The air was thick with a humid and sandy haze.

Winds were stirring up a sandstorm but had not gained enough momentum to create an atmosphere of complete misery for Marines on the ground.

Suddenly, the Division Command Center's landing zone came to life. Inbound helicopter blades chopped into the sky just above the gritty earth. Logistics Marines attempted to shield their eyes from dirt and tiny shards of rocks as they surrounded the open area. Downward pressure from the propellers pitched sand and stone into a dust-filled hatred that stung the skin of every man on site. Yet it was nothing new for the Marines, who had to load and shuttle cargo or troops aboard several helicopters per day.

Logistics Marines were responsible for the allocation of everything from bullets, to Band-Aids, to toilet paper. Field Marines loved and hated the men in charge of usable assets, contingent upon the lapse of time between necessity and delivery. Logistics Marines were good friends to have in garrison. They were close loved ones in the field. However, close-knit friendships were not needed when bribes and favors could be exchanged. That was the general rule of thumb when Marines dealt with one another. Every relationship, from one Marine to the next, was based on mutual benefit beyond brotherhood.

McKenzee, having never been a Marine, did not understand the politics within the Corps. Nor did he care to understand. He simply went to the logistics team and explained what he needed for mission success. It was no secret who he was or who shared the agent's interests in any given situation. McKenzee used heavy-handed influence around camp to make his stay more comfortable. He flaunted his status without being brazen. Yet he was not overly arrogant in presence. The agent was nothing more than disconnected from the reality Marines had to endure day to day. He illustrated such disconnected direction with the first helicopter he ordered for the Force Recon team along with two gunship escorts.

The Logistics Marine on duty tried to push back that using a Super Stallion for a single team drop-off was a misallocation of available resources. McKenzee nearly had the Marine busted down in rank on the spot. The younger man may have been accurate in his assessment, but he overreached his bounds by arguing with the CIA agent about any aspect of any mission. Logistics might have been a crucial aspect to mission success, but it was McKenzee's mission to direct. He was not going to be stopped by the under-use of a major aerial asset.

The agent would later regret the selected aircraft. As soon as news came through camp that the bird was down in the field, McKenzee's heart sank into nothingness. He felt like years of assessment and working his way to the right hand of the secretary of defense were brought down with a single shot. He felt the loss of his operatives and the Marines who supported them. He felt every bit of glory fade from the potential of mission accomplishment. Those feelings ate at his heart for an eternity until the laser designator signal showed on the net.

A little more than a day later, McKenzee stepped away from the communications tent once again. The buzz of the radios and the rumble of voices in the static-filled canvas room were quickly drowned out. The agent watched as a gray Sea Knight helicopter set down in the camp's wide-open landing zone. Then he smiled.

McKenzee could not wait to speak with Hasim and Iman. He wanted the details of their mission laid out before him. He wanted a tale of glory. He wanted the Marines to give the intimates of every shot fired, every enemy killed, and every hero-legend brought to life.

Slowly, the rear ramp of the helicopter opened. Sunlight gleamed off the gray bird. The black propellers still spun too fast to be seen. No one outside of the helicopter was able to view who sat on the inside of the hull.

McKenzee shielded his eyes from the brightness of the desert's day. Word around camp quickly spread that the helicopter was inbound with dead and wounded. The special agent placed his right hand over his brow and veiled his eyes from the harsh sun. He tried to peek into the back of the helicopter as it landed but was unsuccessful. His attempt to recover a sight of Iman or Hasim from the aircraft's black pit was made in vain.

"Who's wounded?" a nearby Marine asked toward the open helicopter as he came face-to-face with the enlisted crew chief. Those tasked to offload the bird were to tend to the wounded first. Doc Troy was expected to point out the most critical as priority. The Marines that were hurt, but would survive without doubt, took a proverbial backseat to those with life-threatening wounds. The Marine asked questions at the back of the helicopter, trying to establish a better means of early triage. He and the corpsmen on site attempted to minimize casualties once the Marines reentered base. The crew chief answered in a low voice, "Everybody."

All of base camp watched as the Force Recon team landed. Everyone watched as injured Marines filed out of the back of the helicopter. Most of them limped, or held their arms, or grabbed at their sides. They were alive, but looked as if they were on the verge of dying. They were victorious, but sulked in defeat. Each man had a broken bone or some very visible laceration announcing their ailments in brilliant red turned filthy brown.

McKenzee watched attentively. Not able to recognize specific faces among the living, he counted the Marines coming off the back of the helicopter. Then he added the dead that had been recovered from the initial crash site. The special agent's body count was still short.

Reality set in hard. McKenzee didn't see Iman or Hasim anywhere in the group of Marines leaving the back of the helicopter.

They were not among the men receiving immediate medical attention. They were ultimately unaccounted for in his view, absent from the team, and removed from the war.

The company man became perturbed enough to step away from his tent at the edge of the landing zone. He ran out to the open area. The helicopter engine whined and whirred as its propellers slowed. The blades chopped thick thuds against thicker desert air. McKenzee approached the Sea Knight and could see clearly into the bird for the first time. His heart sank. Once again, he felt the pounding sadness, the reality of war. He tried not to allow his emotions to show at the powerful sight.

Sergeant Ingle, the most senior living man on the team, sat across from Iman at the back of the helicopter's cargo space. Ingle simply stared at the staff sergeant with complete amazement. He was flabbergasted, at a loss for words, and awestruck with grief and respect.

Ingle looked up at McKenzee as the civilian agent approached. There were tears in both of their eyes. Neither man could find words appropriate enough for the moment. The victory was Pyrrhic. The loss was agonizing.

"He's gone, sir," Ingle advised. The sergeant didn't take his eyes off Iman. He stared, dumbfounded by one man's willingness to die for another. Then he corrected himself, "They're gone, sir." Ingle simply sat and stared at two dead bodies twisted into living love.

Iman had his arms wrapped around Rasa. His left arm cradled her fallen shoulders. His right arm wrapped loosely over her chest. His fingers barely remained interlaced. The staff sergeant's ability to hold Rasa tight faded when his breath did the same. Despite the loose grip, he held her with a closeness that might not ever be matched.

Rasa's legs draped over Iman's right thigh. Her hair was brushed back, out of her face, as if Iman had been talking to her on their way back. She looked peaceful and safe in his embrace. Yet the man's previously tight hold had softened in death. He died holding onto Rasa, his love. He died for her.

The staff sergeant was slumped forward as if he were set to ease Rasa to sleep. However, he did not rock back and forth. Instead, his limp body jiggled and vibrated with the helicopter's propellers. His lifeless form encompassed Rasa, ever protective of her safety even in death.

The helicopter's engines wound down. The propellers slowly circled the top of the aircraft and made no noise. McKenzee could finally hear Ingle with clarity. "He loved her, sir." Ingle remained on the bench seat across from Iman and Rasa. The sergeant took the helmet off his head and rubbed at a deep red line etched into his scalp. The Marine seemed to search for some phrase of wisdom. He prayed for something inspirational to say. Ingle invoked his emotions and begged for some deeply rooted relief. He simply could not gather the words.

McKenzee's eyes were fixed to Iman. He could not see the man's face, only the top of a black and dusty helmet. Iman remained wrapped around Rasa as McKenzee considered what to do with the bodies. Then the special agent considered the missing number in his body count. McKenzee asked, "Where's Hasim?"

Ingle gave very little detail in his report. "He didn't make it out, sir." The CIA agent looked to the wounded sergeant. McKenzee hoped to make the young Marine realize that some pertinent information was needed about the mission. "What do you mean he didn't make it, Sergeant?" McKenzee asked matter-of-factly.

The agent was clearly upset at the loss of two well-trained operatives. Iman and Hasim were the only men truly capable of conducting a Battle Damage Assessment about the enemies in place. The brothers had knowledge of the enemy's inner workings around camp. They knew who led and who followed. They knew what weapons were used in the fight and what might remain in the field. They knew the names and faces of the dead. They knew the intimate details of the village. Left living, the brothers could have told McKenzee of mission success personally.

McKenzee considered the bomber pilots' accounts and the Force Recon teams' ability to confirm the dead. Once the notion set in, McKenzee realized the business end of *Jericho* was handled. He had nothing left in the mission other than paperwork and mindless reporting to his higher echelon. McKenzee knew that he had nothing left to deal with but the emotional aspect of losing his friends.

"Where's Hasim's body?" McKenzee asked as he walked up the helicopter's ramp. He reached the open top of the cargo bay and sat heavily next to Ingle. Both men continued to stare at the entangled lovers. Iman and Rasa were statues sculpted in two pieces but obviously meant to exist as one.

Ingle sighed. Then he explained, "It was the bravest thing I've ever seen, sir. Iman decided to go into the village for her." The Marine pointed to the dead woman, not knowing her name. "Hasim went with him...because you back your brother's move. I get that. I just don't get..." He caught himself before he continued. He did get it. He understood completely. Iman so clearly loved the woman in his arms that he was willing to trade his life for hers.

McKenzee patted Ingle on the knee and explained, "Iman and Hasim spent a long time in that camp...the very place you guys just tore apart." A long and suffocating pause filled the air between the men. "They might have been Marines, but above all they were human...great men. It is not hard to believe that Iman would have found affection among the trouble." McKenzee swallowed hard.

Ingle interrupted. "It was a hell of a lot more than affection, sir. I've never seen anything like it. The look on his face...I mean, I offered to help carry her. He wouldn't have anything to do with it. Both of them were shot in the chest...dead." Ingle kept his eyes on Rasa as tears rolled down his cheeks. "She died quick, sir. I think she checked out as soon as she was hit. Doc couldn't do anything for her... We should have left her, but the staff sergeant... We just knew that she was coming with us...and he made it happen."

Sergeant Ingle reset his line of sight on Iman. He pointed, exhausted and broken. He continued, "He should have been dead just as quick. Doc told me that the good staff sergeant was hit square in the back and through his lung. There's just no way he could have." Ingle choked back a sob. The Marine was touched deeply once again by Iman's warrior spirit as he recounted the events. "He couldn't breathe, but he stayed in the fight. It was like watching a man try to breathe underwater. He was in charge and giving one-word commands until he couldn't stand up anymore. Then we were pulling out and he carried her down that hill and into the LZ. I can't imagine how much inner strength that took to fight off dying just long enough to get her out of that place." Ingle's eyes were flooded.

The Marine's chin wrinkled with sadness. Adrenaline from the fight was wearing off. Exhaustion was setting in. Muscle fatigue and hunger were beating him into a corner. All of which were things he had to deal with over and over in various combat zones. Yet nothing got to him like the sight of Iman wrapped around Rasa.

McKenzee had not seen what Iman accomplished on the battlefield. He had nothing more than a secondhand account from the information being passed. He was affected, but less moved than Ingle. The special agent then stepped back into his role. He asserted his need for information beyond his desire for compassion. McKenzee asked, "And what happened to Hasim exactly?"

Ingle broke his stare from Iman and Rasa to look at the civilian. The lapse in Ingle's hatred was short-lived. He wanted to remove

McKenzee's tongue in payment for the question that removed Ingle's emotions from the scene. Instead, the Marine answered, "Both of the staff sergeants went after her in the village. They were out of our line of sight for a while. Iman told us just to keep the target area painted no matter what happened next. Then they took off. The next we saw of them, they were being chased out of the village under heavy fire. They were pulling back, one after the other, just like we are supposed to. They would set and fire, then run and do it again. Except Hasim got shot in the back and knocked out of the race for a bit. Iman sent *her*"—Ingle pointed to Rasa again— "up the trail and went back for Hasim. He got Hasim to his feet, and they took off toward us again. We still couldn't see the enemy, but I saw Hasim's head come apart. He was dead on the spot, sir."

Ingle choked the memory down with a lump in his throat. "Then the zoomies showed up and dropped a fat one on his lap." Ingle's rhetorical jargon removed reality from a bomb landing directly on Hasim's lifeless body. Such language helped the Marine remove the stain of humanity from his beautiful war.

McKenzee nodded. "Do you think there is anything to recover?"

Ingle looked at the agent quizzically. He tried to gauge if the CIA commander was raising a serious question. He answered, "There's nothing to recover from that entire area, sir. You're looking at what remains of that place." Ingle pointed to Rasa once again.

"A pilot, copilot, crew chief, Gibson, Jackson, Hasim, and Iman." McKenzee held out all the fingers on his left hand and two on his right. "Seven people lost," he announced as he counted the casualties in the mission to destroy *Jericho*.

"Eight," Ingle corrected. He wagged his finger sadly to Rasa's body. "No doubt that she was one of us, sir. The staff sergeant didn't tell us why he went back for her...and I wouldn't expect you to understand without having seen it...sir." Ingle remembered to maintain respect among the disdain. "I mean, they told us there were no friendlies in that camp. We had a green light to end them all. To top it off, the radios were lost in the crash and all we had was that stupid laser. Even still, he went after her. He died for her...and I can't bring myself to believe that he went without a reason. No man would have gone into a firefight and opened the gates of hell without a good reason...sir."

McKenzee, less moved by the sentiment of the battle, was just happy to hear that *Jericho* was destroyed. He had his confirmation of a successfully completed mission. Seven lost Marines and one extracted civilian were more than he would have liked to explain. However, he was most thrilled to give the Secretary a report that his primary objective was complete. The self-proclaimed grand imam, Farhad, was gone. The village was left in a series of bloody, ash-filled craters. Through the resilience and perseverance of a few Marines, the enemy suffered a major blow. Then he hoped that all the other target sites were hit just as hard. He hoped that the loss of several was not in vain.

The agent had nothing left to offer Ingle. He patted the Marine on the knee once again and stood to disembark from the helicopter. McKenzee leaned over and softly patted his condolences to Iman and Rasa. He looked to the floor, whispered a quick word of praise, and left the back of the bird.

Ingle continued to sit in place. He stared. He was shaken, but not by the battle. Ingle had been through so many fights and killed so many people that he stopped counting bodies sometime prior to finding *Jericho*. He lived through firefights where he killed two or three men at a time with a single grenade. He cared nothing about the enemy, or the fight, or the ensuing atrocities that no man should ever see. He cared only for the humanity that Iman had shown.

"Sir!" Ingle called out to McKenzee. The agent turned around to face the new team leader before stepping away from the ramp. "What are we supposed to do with their bodies?" Ingle asked, genuinely concerned for the well-being and care of the dead.

McKenzee shrugged. He looked disappointed and lost. The agent simply answered, "They are without record." Then he turned away again and sadly stepped off the back of the helicopter.

Ingle watched from behind McKenzee. The agent cleared the rear of the bird, and Ingle could see the rest of his team standing at the back of the aircraft. Exhausted and wounded, they stood ready for orders, ready to prepare Iman and Rasa for passing from one world to the next. Ingle squeezed his lips together, trying hard not to cry at the sight of the bloodied and bruised men. They should have been seeking medical attention. They should have been looking for food and shelter. They should have been relieving their bodies from pain. Rather, they were seeking to help take care of Iman and Rasa.

Ingle looked out at his team with resounding pride. He was happy to have lost so few in such a devastating impact against the enemy. The sergeant knew they had won the day, but he still felt the depth of their loss.

# HOME

Sergeant Ingle stood from the bench in the back of the helicopter. He placed his hand on top of Iman's helmet. Ingle prayed, "God, keep them." Then he nodded. He bent down and gently slid his arms under Rasa's knees and shoulders. He took the lifeless woman's body from Iman's arms. Ingle tried to keep Iman from falling over. Iman's weight distributed unevenly beneath them and struggled to remain in place without toppling from the bench.

Suddenly, Corporal Perez was at Ingle's side. Perez reached out and held Iman by the shoulders. Then he nodded to the sergeant and tried to smile. Ingle returned the silent gesture and walked off the helicopter ramp. Rasa's body lay out in front of the broad Marine, her body limp over his tired arms.

Perez, exhausted and still bloodied from the crash in the open desert, did his best to pull Iman over his shoulder. He struggled with Iman's weight and unresponsive muscles. Hoisting the dead over wounded shoulders began to show its burden through Perez's fumbled movements. Then another Marine intervened to help the pain-filled corporal. The team worked together in escorting the deceased Marine and his love from the rear of the stationary aircraft. They exercised as much respect as possible, drawing grace from the cold wasteland.

The Marines were greeted by a series of corpsmen and officers at the bottom of the loading ramp. Medical attention, previously denied by returning warriors, was shoved aside once again. The war-torn and weary ignored the clean and well-fed. The Force Recon Marines pushed beyond the crowd, through the aching burn in their muscles, and past their shattered hearts.

*Without record?* Ingle quietly questioned McKenzee's notion of dismissal. The special agent seemed to wipe his hands of Hasim, Iman, and Rasa. He seemed to disavow them, as if to do so post-humously was a preferred method for the spook. Ingle gritted his teeth with bitter frustration and boiling discontent. *They were too great to have been pushed off for nothing, to be denied the recognition they so deserved.* Ingle stewed in his thoughts. His arms ached under Rasa's dead weight, but he carried her with care and concern. He tried to be as gentle as Iman had been. He tried to love her with the same depth as Iman, though he knew he never could. He carried her to the edge of base camp, to the edge of his strength, until he found the foot of a large Morus plant.

Ingle finally stopped and fell to his knees in the deep sand. He lay Rasa down on her back. Her eyes were still closed, but they were starting to sink into her skull. Her jaw involuntarily rested partly open and slightly to the side. Death consumed her, but even in death she was beautiful.

The sergeant brushed strands of hair out of her face as if the notion would bring her some form of comfort. He smiled at her beauty. He offered her respect that he knew Iman would have wanted for the slain woman.

The senior Marine was followed by Perez in the makeshift funeral precession. The corporal was as exhausted as any other man on the team, but he carried Iman with a sense of valor and purpose. He stomped through thick sand until he reached Ingle's side. Perez knelt next to the sergeant and placed Iman's body on the ground alongside Rasa's.

Limping and panting, the rest of the team joined around the bodies. Each of the men needed food and water. They needed medical attention and rest. However, their mission was not yet complete.

Ingle looked at the surrounding camp. He found no joy or solace in the city of brown canvas and strategically staged tactical vehicles. He felt ill at ease. All eyes seemed to be fixed on the Force Recon team. Every person at Command was watching with ripening curiosity. Warriors among many stood out as a compassionate few. They suddenly existed in contrast to the nature of their work, standing against the wind of their purpose to deal death. Instead, they showed a heightened reverence for their fallen brother and the woman he loved.

Sergeant Ingle looked back and watched McKenzee disappear into the communications tent. McKenzee finally had details to report and had a job to do. Ingle respected the need to get information to higher command, but he could not understand how the spook was able to dismiss the death of his men so easily.

The Force Recon team had only known Iman and Hasim for a few days, and they held more respect for the dead than the man that sent them to die. *To hell with him.* Ingle did not curse McKenzee aloud. He figured that the agent wasn't worth the extra effort. He simply went about his business of tending to the bloody and broken bodies. They became his distraction from turmoil, the center of his new mission in seeing Iman and Rasa to the very end.

"I saw this once," Ingle said over Iman and Rasa to no one in particular, "in a village outside of Kabul. They were preparing this old man to be buried." Ingle took a long pause, hoping not to offend the Islamic traditions of any tribe or people. He contemplated halting the effort so as not to falter in something meant to be sacred.

"I don't really know what to do here, but I know in my heart that these two belong together...here...at this tree. I can't tell you why, I just..." Ingle swallowed hard. He searched for the right thing to say. He begged God for wisdom, for a sudden ability to draw proper phrases and solid messages laden with the merits of heart and mind. Despite his prayers, nothing came to him. He swallowed hard again. He was lost.

Ingle's words of remembrance, thoughts thereafter, were interrupted by the sound of a field shovel being crammed into the loose and deep sand. One of the Force Recon Marines, Lance Corporal Williams, started chipping away at the top of the earth. The Marine's hands were crusted brown, bloodied and torn from the crash. His mind was tired from the fight. Yet Williams was filled with Esprit de Corps, and all he wanted to do was take care of his own.

The Marine's shovel was quickly followed by several others. They pierced the ground and sent heaps of dirt into a nearby pile. A large hole began to form around them. Little by little, the earth opened to their demanding shovels until the hole reminded them of the southern defensive position at *Jericho*.

"Doc," Ingle spoke to Troy. "Go see if you can get two white sheets from the Battalion Aid Station. You might not want to let them know that they won't be getting them back." Ingle grinned with a brokenhearted but friendly smile to the corpsman.

Doc Troy nodded. He sprinted from his team and went to carry out the orders. He was gone only for a few minutes before he returned with his hands full. Doc carried two sheets, one fitted and the other loose at the edges. The sheets were all that he was able to tactically acquire from the medical aid station, so they would have to serve whatever purpose Ingle had in mind.

The team continued to dig deep into the soft ground until the soil became hard against the points of their collapsible spades. They dug with even more fervor just to get beyond the packed ground. Hours dragged on before the Marines were finally successful in their blister-ripping endeavor.

Ingle did his best to remember the proper procedures and facets of Islamic interment. He knew that he would not likely execute all the details properly, but he would give his greatest efforts to show the appropriate respects earned by the dead. God, a just and loving deity, would surely understand the well-intended burial. Ingle accepted that the process would be clumsy. He expected to unintentionally mishandle the final burial niceties, which were foreign to him. He worried about his ability to conduct the ceremony, but he felt he should at least make an attempt to care for Iman and the woman rescued from hell.

Determined, the sergeant started with the woman. Ingle never had the opportunity to shake her hand, to see her smile, or to hear her voice. She was long gone from the world by the time Iman withdrew her from *Jericho*. However, Ingle was so moved by Iman's dedication to her that he felt a residual connection between Rasa and her Marine.

Ingle had two of his Marines lay out the fitted sheet. Then he surprised the onlooking camp when he slid his knife into the top of her gown. He cut the fabric upward and exposed her bloodied bosom to the afternoon air.

A lieutenant, standing outside of the command center, barked, "What is that Marine doing?" He was upset by the sight of the cleansing process and stepped out to intervene. However, General Gutzwiller was standing in the same place and within reach of the overzealous lieutenant. The general put out his arm and held the younger officer back. "But, General," the lieutenant tried to argue against the senior's silent command.

Gutzwiller glared at the young man and proclaimed, "If you go over there, I'll shoot you myself." The lieutenant withdrew his objections then walked back inside the command tent. He showed his contempt for the proceedings and wanted nothing to do with whatever was to come next.

Ingle carefully cut Rasa's clothes from her body. She was dead, but he made sure not to inflict her with more wounds. Then he sliced a strip of fabric from her blouse. He doused the cloth with water from his canteen. He poured a considerable amount of water over Rasa's body and washed away the dried blood covering her torso and legs. She was so bloody that Ingle wondered how much of Iman's soul had mixed with hers on the flight back to base. Ingle tried not to cry as the dark-brown mess covering the woman lightened to a trickling red. He scrubbed until the blood was gone from her skin. He washed her until nothing remained other than a charred hole in her side where an enemy bullet seared its way through her lungs.

Rasa was finally cleansed. She was rinsed free from the filth of the world, so Ingle and Perez lifted her body. They moved her from the open clothing onto the sheet that Doc flattened next to her. Her olive skin contrasted with the white cloth brilliantly.

Sergeant Ingle held Rasa under her shoulders. Perez wrapped his arms around her legs. They carefully laid her in the middle of the sheet with her hands crossed over her heart and her legs straight together. Ingle wrapped the first side of the sheet over Rasa's complete physical form. She was covered from her face to her feet. Ingle made sure that he tucked the bed sheet's edge beneath her as tightly as he could, as tightly as he remembered the villagers do near Kabul. Then Perez repeated the motion from the opposite direction. Her body was once again shrouded from the world's eyes. The impurities of her clothes would not follow her into the next life.

Ingle then turned to Iman's body. The staff sergeant's face was heavy and sad. The corners of Iman's mouth turned downward as if he had used his last breath to sob for Rasa. His eyes were slightly open and showed the absent gray of death. Perez tried to look into Iman's eyes. The feeling was eerie in death, to see the physical being evaded by the spirit, eyes empty and soulless.

The Marines peeled Iman's body armor from his shoulders and chest. Then they unbuttoned and cut away his uniform in the same fashion Ingle had done with Rasa's clothing. Their blades were sharp enough to allow gentle and reverent movements as dried blood failed to further adhere to Iman's skin.

The cloth of Iman's uniform rested open and shielded him from lying directly in the sand. Ingle had run out of water from rinsing Rasa, so the other team members used whatever they had remaining in their canteens to clean their fellow Marine. They pulled Doc Troy's bandages from the dead man's back and chest. Only then, the Marines realized how bad Iman's wounds really were on the battlefield. There was no logical explanation for how the warrior could have survived as long as he did. His body was covered with crusted flakes and coagulating pools of blood. His flesh was pierced and torn apart by the bullet that splintered inside him. His chest was hollow in a way that could have only been created with the loss of a lung. Iman defied death to rescue Rasa and dared not fade away until his mission, his higher calling, was accomplished. Eyes closed and heart still, the staff sergeant remained a source of awe for the Marines who fought alongside him.

Iman, scrubbed free of blood and filth, was finally clean. No trails of death or dirt remained anywhere on his body. Ingle and Perez then moved Iman from his open clothes to the sheet Doc

Troy previously stretched out next to the dead. They wrapped Iman as they had done Rasa. Ingle covered Iman and tucked the sheet's edge under the resting head, torso, and legs. Perez answered with the other side of the white cloth and pushed the edges in tight beneath Iman.

Together, the team helped move Iman and Rasa into the large hole, pallbearers without a casket. They edged along in a memorial parade with as much dignity as possible. Their respect commanded their arms and legs. Their reverence demanded their every motion to be steady and calm. The team was silent as they pulled the horizontal but separate lovers from the desert floor.

Marines outside of the hole lowered the bodies down to their teammates inside the hole. The living laid Iman into the deep grave first. Then they laid Rasa at his side. The lovers' shoulders and hips pressed together with a sense of permanence. They lay in narrow form despite the width of the grave, eternally connected, each belonging to the other until the white sheets appeared as one.

Once the dead were rested in a point of finality, the surviving occupants were hoisted out of the hole. The grave was clear of the living. The Marines could finally say goodbye.

Ingle grabbed the nearest field shovel and started pitching loose chunks of earth onto the tightly wrapped sheets lying at the bottom of the grave. The rest of the team followed his lead. They worked in unison until nothing remained other than a freshly turned dirt pile. The team's unified efforts carried on until nothing was left of Iman and Rasa—nothing more than a memory forever etched into the minds of every man they touched.

Out of breath and exhausted, Ingle choked down the dry lump in his throat. Then he spoke loud enough to be heard by the entire team as if to give a final sermon at a hometown funeral. "I don't know if we did that right...but it seems right," Ingle said, coaxing assurance from his thoughts. He looked around at his Marines. He stood up straight and rolled his shoulders back. His chest beamed outward with pride. It was not a boastful pride but a newfound affinity for his brother-in-arms. He had a new respect for the men around him and a deeply cut love for the man they just buried, the man *without record*.

"I'm not Muslim," Ingle said to the sweating and panting group of Marines as they tossed their field shovels aside. The sergeant knew that the remainder of base camp was watching, but he spoke only loud enough to share his thoughts with his team. He continued, "Before coming here, I really didn't know much about the culture, the people, or the religion. I just thought they were all strapped with bombs and didn't care about anyone or anything..." Ingle paused to look at each of his Marines. "I cannot begin to tell you how wrong I was."

Ingle pointed at the ground. "That man carried out one of the greatest feats of humanity I have ever seen. I will never forget the day the staff sergeant carried the woman he loved...in life and in death. I will never forget the day that we were all spared by a miracle. I will never forget the day that we did the right thing. They," he said, still pointing to the loose soil of the fresh grave, "might be *without record*, but they will never be without each other again." His eyes filled with tears.

"I'm going to say a prayer, so bow your heads if you want," Ingle said. Each of the men bowed their heads and listened. No one objected to the gesture of open faith.

"Dear Lord, we come to you today thankful that you spared us. I'm sorry that we couldn't all make it home, God...but we are subject to your plan...we all know that. Please God, accept our fallen brothers into your kingdom...and I know that we might come to you a little differently, but I ask you to accept this man and this woman into your kingdom as well, Lord. I might not be the smartest man in the world, God...but I have no doubts it is your plan for them to spend eternity in Paradise together. This man carried out the most decent thing I've ever seen, Lord." Ingle's words echoed into the hearts of every man around him. "And if we aren't here to do the decent thing, Lord...then why are we here at all?"

# ABOUT THE AUTHOR

J onathan Ball grew up in Dallas, Texas, before graduating high school early to join the United States Marine Corps. He served his time proudly as a sergeant with the 1st Marine Division at Camp Pendleton, California. His time in service as a Marine, experiences in the Middle East and Southeast Asia, and love for his brothers-in-arms are the driving forces behind his war-fiction genre writing style.

Jonathan Ball is a devoted father with a great passion for the protections of individual liberties and national sovereignty, all of which inspired the novel *Operation: Jericho.*

CPSIA information can be obtained
at www.ICGtesting.com
Printed in the USA
LVOW03s2058260717
542507LV00007B/7/P